Second String to a Tennis Racket

Second String to a Tennis Racket

Stuart Charles Neil

Second String to a Tennis Racket

Copyright © 2018 Stuart Neil

The proceeds from all these books will be donated to Stuart's two charities:-

Star Action (Reg. Charity No. 1111137)
www.staraction.org

The Quiet Mind Centre (Reg. Charity No. 1029636)
www.quiet-mind.org

For Bobby
(I borrowed an Angel)

Many thanks to Jenny Dent and Wendy McInnes
for their advice and constant 'listening ears'

PRINCIPAL CHARACTERS

NOW

BRONWEN
RACHEL
POPPY

DEIRDRE   CORALIE

PETER = **HELEN**   (**ERIK**)

LUCY   **CALLUM**

GEORGE LEE

THEN

LINDSAY

OLIVER

GREG

SALLY = CHRIS

MAGGIE   ALAN

SAMMY
(Samuraja)

PART ONE

ONE

NOW

"Play a let" called the Umpire

The ball girl bounced another ball to Joel. He stepped back to serve again to the 'advantage court'. The linesman's error had increased the tension. Absolute silence.

"Fault"

The ball missed the service line by six inches.

15,000 spectators held their breath………then expelled a huge, united cheer as the rare second service ace flew past his male opponent.

Joel and Monika had won the last event of the Wimbledon Fortnight – the Mixed Doubles of 1997.

"Game, Set and Match to Eriksson and Miss Kristensen 6-4 6-7 7-5"

Joel let his tall partner step first into the Royal Box to be presented with the silver plate when………whoosh……..a large articulated lorry accelerated by, rocking the white Porsche parked in the layby. Joel awoke immediately. He shook his head of curly blond hair and climbed out of the car. He badly needed a pee. Not here though, out in the open, in England.

He was on the A35, ten miles East of Dorchester.

Climbing gingerly back into the low sports car he continued his journey West. Only about forty miles to go.

There would be a public loo somewhere soon. He passed the sign for Poole, then Puddletown, and then Tolpuddle. The association of ideas was beginning to become painful. Another road sign: Piddlehinton and Piddletrenthide. It was just not possible to cross his legs whilst driving. The last straw was the sign for Tincleton. Joel braked to the side of the road, jumped out and leapt over a field gate. His relief was so immense that he thanked the tree and hoped he hadn't killed it.

* * *

Doha had changed beyond all recognition from the small town Peter Walker found when he had first arrived in 1994. From an uninteresting port on the coast of a desert with hardly a building over two stories high, it had become a major commercial centre in the Arabian Gulf in just twenty years. Peter worked for a shipping company which owned tankers that took liquified gas from Qatar to the world. The geologists and quantity assessors in the industry are not sure of the extent of the gas reserves in Qatar, but they are acclaimed as the second largest on earth. Having persuaded his fiancée, Helen, to join him as an `expat` wife, (expatriate), and then later together after producing a son, Callum, and daughter, Lucy, the Walkers decided to come back to England.

Peter and Helen saw an advantage for the children in an education in Britain, together with the extra creature comforts of a cool climate and access to sports venues and theatres around London. They had not, however, calculated the vast increase in income tax that Peter would have to pay from his salary as an International Gas Shipping

Consultant. Life had treated them well in Doha. They lived in an air-conditioned, detached house on a residential compound near the Pearl. The Pearl is a well-designed complex of apartments, shops and restaurants, built on land reclaimed from the sea, with a surround of sandy coves and marinas, walkways and views to rival Venice. The Emir and his son, the current Emir, had set out to put Qatar`s name in front of the world by creating a five star city of original and beautiful buildings and mosques along a skyline framed beneath the desert sun. Admittedly, the cost of living is close to the highest on earth, but this is more than matched by salaries and the tax-free haven in which they are paid. Airfares for all the family were provided by Peter`s company twice a year on the latest passenger jets flown by Qatar Airways, which was now one of the world`s top airlines.

Helen enjoyed the luxury of a maid to do the heavy housework twice a week and a gardener to daily tend the frangipani and bougainvillea that overflowed the walls of her garden. She spent most afternoons sitting in the club and watching her children swimming like fish in the large crescent-shaped blue pool. The prospect of moving back to Surrey became more and more attractive as she imagined shopping in Guildford and London`s West End, and being able to bring her children and their grandparents closer together. Peter would commute to Waterloo and work in an office in the City. The children would attend well respected schools close by.

It was a cold, misty day when the family landed at Heathrow Airport and collected their luggage that had been packed to weigh up to the last kilo of their allowance. A drop in temperature of thirty degrees did not improve their mood as they wearily made their way to stay temporarily with Peter`s parents in Haslemere. Although they had lived an enviable few years in, what many would regard as the lap of luxury, saving was not one of Peter`s prominent qualities.

Prices were much higher than he had realised. Whilst searching the internet for a suitable house to purchase he realised that a large mortgage would be required. Since the world banking crisis the Banks now demanded a minimum of a twenty per cent deposit which he realised he did not have. Houses to let in this area, which would have satisfied Helen's inflated taste, were few indeed; most being owned by the occupants. Peter decided and Helen agreed, having fallen out with Peter's mother over Callum's table manners, that a move to a more affordable part of the country would be better. They had read in the Guardian, whilst in Qatar, that a very good county to educate children was Devon. Apparently the best teachers often decided to make their last move or promotion to a school in an area they planned to enjoy later for their retirement, and there were sixty applicants for most teaching posts in the county.

Peter began to look towards Devon for the best house to rent until he was in a better position to purchase. He and Helen set off clutching a file of brochures and downloaded details of four or five bedroomed houses in West Dorset, Central and East Devon. After a long weekend of driving from one village to another and finding nothing to compare with the pristine, new and spacious houses of the Gulf, they returned in the car dejected, to Peter's harassed parents, who had had the delight of caring for their grandchildren for forty eight hours. Next weekend, armed with another clutch of papers, they drove once again down the A303, leaving Ernestine (Peter's mother) babysitting again and muttering something like `those kids better behave less like animals this time, or I'll swing for them.` The smiles of the rental agents were beginning to wear thin for Helen when they arrived outside a worn- looking detached house in its own extensive grounds just outside a village near the East Devon coast. The property was vacant and needed a good coat of paint. In the light drizzle, and being tired at the end of Saturday, they decided not to inspect the barn or the one bedroomed cottage that were part of the rental arrangement. The main house looked substantial and the log-burning fire looked capable of heating both house and water to their `tropical` needs. The price was average for this part of the West Country, but seemed a bargain to a couple who had been searching in the commuter belt around London.

They signed a rental contract for a year, having agreed that the house would be repainted inside and out before they moved in. Kirkhaven house sounded quite imposing and would satisfy Helen`s desire to impress friends and relatives about their new abode. Peace just about held between the families at Haslemere, but relief could be written in the air around grandparents and parents, as they left early in March to meet their furniture arriving at Kirkhaven House. The Maersk container arrived via Felixstowe harbour half an hour after the family did, and each piece of furniture was hastily given a home in one of the rooms of the newly painted house.

Peter set off at an early hour to drive to Axminster and catch the first train to Waterloo with a small suitcase of clothes. He would work in the City, stay at his parents' home in Haslemere on weekday evenings and come back to his new home on Fridays. Helen, however, suddenly realised that she would be alone in the evenings after the children had gone to bed, for five days of the week. At the moment she thought this a small price to pay for retaining her sanity and some sort of relationship with her mother-in-law. How did families in the Developing World all live together harmoniously? Or perhaps they didn`t. She had never ventured close enough to find out.

Her first job was to settle the children into local schools. Helen took Lucy down to the local village primary school and met the school secretary and then briefly the head teacher, who welcomed Lucy and put her into Class 4 with the other eight and nine year olds. Then, after making an appointment by phone, she caught the bus to the nearest comprehensive school, six miles away in Lyme Regis, to enrol Callum. This time, the Head of Year Nine was waiting to welcome a sour-faced thirteen year old and try to find out the kind of education he had enjoyed in the Gulf. Callum decided to be as unhelpful as possible as he didn`t like the school or the uniform.

"We`ll do our best Mrs Walker" said the teacher. "Perhaps you could trim his hair before he comes tomorrow."

"Tomorrow! I`m not going tomorrow" announced Callum.

"Don`t worry about uniform until you have the chance to get it at the weekend. We need to get your lad up to speed as quickly as possible as we are already over halfway through this school year. See you at 8.45am in the morning, Callum. Goodbye Mrs Walker."

The journey home was conducted in silence. They later went to fetch Lucy from her school in the village. She skipped across the playground seemingly very happy.

"I`ve made a new friend. She`s called Saskia and is still seven. Her Mum runs the sweet shop in Seaton and she has told me all about the sweets there.

"Can I go home with her tomorrow?"

"Maybe, darling. But not if you are going to eat sweets all the evening."

It was very hard work moving furniture around and putting away books, toys, ornaments and a hundred things in the kitchen, especially with no adult to help and the children more of a hindrance.

Callum reluctantly caught the bus to school the next morning. After arranging with Mary, Henrietta's mum for Lucy`s transport, Helen decided to explore the nearby village. Initially the prospect had not attracted her. When she was about to come back from Qatar she envisaged shopping in London`s West End and lunching in the smarter restaurants of Guildford, or in the Yvonne Arnaud Theatre. As with many villages in Devon, the small street was dominated by an oversized church. Helen imagined labourers` families putting much of their meagre salaries towards the building in the fifteenth and sixteenth centuries, under pressure from the parson, the third son of the local Lord and owner of the land.

Opposite the church was the inevitable antique shop with chairs, a table and brasses displayed on the pavement. Beside it was the Post Office, which sold stationery and doubled as a newsagent. Helen caught the eye of a lady behind the counter and received a pleasant smile. She moved on quickly. Smiling at strangers was not how she had behaved in the Gulf, nor even in her earlier years in the family home in Hampshire.

On the other side of the road was a pair of shops, one a branch of Spar the small supermarket and the other an intriguing small, almost boutique cafe with a mouth-watering display of home-made chocolates in trays in the window. A small curved bright yellow and white awning screened the chocolates in the window from the sun. This was more Helen`s scene and she increased her pace, crossing the road towards the door. The name `Poppy, Chocolatiere` seemed out of place in this small country village. Inside were three ladies sitting around the table nearest the counter. They each had steaming cups or mugs of coffee in front of them and were engrossed in deep conversation about something, or probably someone. The talk ceased as Helen came in, the doorbell ringing pleasantly above her. They all looked at each other and made `don`t know her` gestures as Helen sat down at a small round table near the window.

It was hard to tell which one was Poppy. None looked like a `Poppy`, but what would a `Poppy` look like? One was obviously tall and thin, wearing rimless glasses and looked like a librarian. The second was about five foot four inches tall, Helen estimated, wearing quite loose clothes like someone conscious of being overweight. She appeared to have a happy disposition and was grinning at one of the others` gestures. The third was a standard size ten with short bobbed blonde hair, about forty and her glasses were hanging on a black string in front of her and clattering against the table. This third woman stood up and Helen immediately saw the dog collar above a navy blue knitted top.

"Hello" she said, "I`m Poppy, the vicar. Are you here for the day?"

Somewhat surprised, Helen answered:

"Yes, er. No. I live here.....now....well, just. We moved in two or three days ago."

"Welcome to the village. This is Rachel, who runs the shop for me," introducing the tall, thin one and not the other one who looked more like the product of a chocolate shop. "And this is Bronwen from the Library."

`So much for my judgement of character....or career, ` thought Helen. This time she smiled briefly.

"You must have our special `Chocolate Disaster`" to celebrate your arrival. "Dreadful name, I know, but irresistible. It took us weeks to get it right after dozens of disasters and when you drink it, it is disastrous for your waistline!"

"OK. I`m game" said Helen, deciding to be sociable.

"So, where are you living?"

"Kirkhaven House."

"At last someone has taken it" said Rachel from behind a silver boiler which was huffing and puffing. "It has been empty for so long that we wondered whether it was becoming uninhabitable".

"We like it" said Helen. "Although it will be hard work keeping it clean with the demands of a small family. Incidentally, do you know of anyone who would like to cook and clean for three or four days a week?" The three looked at each other and shook their heads.

"We'll ask around" said Poppy. "There is bound to be someone looking for a job."

Helen didn't tell them much more about herself because she wasn't enjoying the prospect of becoming the centre of the village's gossip for the next few weeks, but also because a blustering character with a moustache and wearing a sports coat and a bow tie clattered into the cafe. He demanded a cherry flapjack because he had missed his cooked breakfast today.

"That was the Brigadier" said Bronwen to Helen. "Watch him. His hands are usually everywhere you don't need them to be when he's near you."

"But I am a respectably married woman" said Helen primly.

"That won't stop him. He thinks Brigadiers are bullet proof and have nothing to lose."

"Is he really a Brigadier?"

"Retired, dear. Probably made Major before retiring disgracefully" replied Rachel. "Brigadier Roper. We call him `Roper the Groper! Runs the antique shop over the road."

"I had better go" Helen said. "Thanks for the welcome `Disaster'. It really is delicious and very naughty. How much do I owe you?"

"Nothing. Consider it a `welcome drink'" said the Rev Poppy.

"No wonder we run this shop at a loss" muttered Rachel.

Helen reached home in time to hear the phone ringing in the hall. She reached it in time, having found that it only rang seven times before cutting into the answerphone.

"Mrs Walker, this is Callum's school nurse."

"Oh, has he hurt himself?"

"Not much. But he has broken another boy's arm and I have just sent him off to 'A and E' in Exeter. The Head of Year Nine would like you to come to see him today or tomorrow.

Helen sat down feeling alone at having to deal with this when she felt it was more her husband's department.

Callum arrived home with a cut on his cheek and stormed upstairs to his room. Later at tea he was coaxed to tell his side of the story. Apparently two boys were goading him about being a terrorist from the Gulf and he had grabbed one and twisted his arm behind his back, breaking it. The other hit him in the face at the same time with a piece of wood.

"We`ll hear the other side of the story tomorrow, when I come with you to school" said Helen.

"I`m not going there anymore" was the response.

That evening, Helen called Peter. "I need some help here, in the house and with Callum who is in trouble at school. Also I need a small car to be able to get around."

"Car as soon as I can afford it, my love" he answered. "Surely you can cook a few meals and tell the teachers to sort Callum out. I am busy here and I have to go to Moscow next week."

"I am trying and I have put out some feelers for a cook. It will be better when you are home at the weekend."

TWO

NOW

"Hallo, hallo. Anyone at home?" said a voice at the back door.

"Good morning, who are you?" replied Helen from the kitchen.

"I`m Deirdre. I`ve come to cook your lunch. Didn`t Rachel tell you I was coming? She said you were on your knees and desperate for some help."

"Hi. I`m Helen. Yes. Great. Come in. Everything is still in a muddle. We only arrived three days ago."

"Where is everyone?"

"Gone to school. Well my daughter has, but my son has gone missing.

Playing truant. I`ve just come back on the bus from trying to sort out the problems he caused at school yesterday."

"Only two kids? I though you'd have at least five and probably a babe in arms too! Anyway I can do Thursdays and Mondays, cooking and light cleaning. Can`t bend down for the heavy stuff no more. Back not so good these last two years. Ten pounds an hour - cash in hand. Saves you that PAYE nonsense."

"Yes. Well, lovely. OK. Can you start now?"

"That's why I'm here, Mrs Walters."

"Mrs Walker. Could you make lunch for you and me and a cooked tea for the three of us? There are some things in the fridge and the larder. I must get out and look for my wayward son." "I'll do my best" said Deirdre.

Helen put a light jacket around her shoulders and headed into the village, down the Kirkhaven driveway and along the narrow country road down the hill towards the main road through the village. Callum was quite self-sufficient for a thirteen year old but she was not happy about his state of mind. The meeting at school had revealed that he was the aggressor and it was made clear to her by a firm but pleasant teacher that this attitude is not acceptable in their school.

Helen was looking for Callum, and also for someone to talk to and offload her problems. So she headed for the only place likely to be mildly sympathetic - Poppy's boutique cafe. The door opened to the light tinkling bell and there they were, sitting at the window table this time, her three new acquaintances. Helen briefly acknowledged the trio because ensconced at one of the other tables was Callum, hiding behind an enormous coke with a scoop of ice-cream floating on the surface. With him was a quite devastatingly handsome man with long, curly blond hair, about forty years old. Realising that this must be Callum's mother the man politely stood up and introduced himself.

"Good morning. I am Erik from Sweden." Joel had decided to use a false name.

Helen was far more concerned that she had not repaired her make-up after the journey to and from school than she should have been at finding her young son in the company of a strange man.

"Hallo. You have probably guessed that I am Callum's mother. Callum, what are you doing exactly? You are being missed at school."

"Drinking a coke, Mum."

"Perhaps you can explain, Mr Erik, how you came to be together?" She was acutely aware of three silent occupants of the window table with imaginary ears the size of African elephants.

"It must look odd to you Mrs Callum......"

"Walker."

"Mrs Walker, but we have both found ourselves keen to purchase the same boat, so decided to negotiate over a cup of coffee......and a coke." "There is a boat for sale in the harbour."

"I want it and so does Erik. The owner told us to go away and come back when we had decided who should have first choice," chipped in Callum.

"How much is it?" Helen asked the wrong question and immediately regretted it.

"One thousand eight hundred pounds with all the sails and a towing trolley" said Callum nonchalantly.

The expressions of the trio needed to be seen. One was incredulous - a boy buying a boat at that price! One was thoughtful - his parents must be stinking rich! The third was laughing inside - OK, some people can spend that much on leisure, but how does a thirteen year old manage to sail it.

"Erik says he can pay for it by Bank transfer tomorrow. I have four pounds eighty now and can pay the rest over the next few years," said Callum.

Erik was looking slightly guilty but not at all amused.

"Didn't you wonder why a thirteen year old was buying a boat and not at school?" said Helen to her new bronzed acquaintance.

"Yes. We were talking about that when you came in. It seemed better to discuss it in here in a place where he is safe and with me, who is a safe companion," said Erik.

"I don`t know you are not a child molester."

"Well I do, and I was the only adult around when that decision was being made."

Much nodding and shaking of heads in the window.

Helen stayed standing and noticed how casual Erik was and how he was treating Callum like an adult. She had once read that that was the main secret of dealing with teenagers.

"I am told Qatar schools are brilliant and English schools are the pits," said Erik. Tell me about Qatar. I went there once, but only for two weeks and without much chance of sightseeing" asked Erik.

Erik wore a lighter blue denim shirt and jeans of the colour she had seen on Scandinavian tourists before, and a worn brown leather jacket was thrown over the fourth chair at the table. His sleeves were rolled up revealing brown, muscular arms. Helen told him a little of their colonial life style in the Gulf. The children had opportunities to mix with wealthy friends who had well rewarded jobs in the gas and construction industries and to oversee the employment of migrant workers under contract from India, Nepal, Pakistan, the Philippines and Sri Lanka. Their children's` expectations were very high and their patience too limited she added.

"Is that the problem at school, Callum, classes bigger and the others not ready to be friendly yet?" asked Erik.

"They`re just a load of prats who know nothing. They thought Qatar was in Australia and my tan came from a bottle."

"I`ll do a deal with you. Go to school without missing a single day. Apologise for anything you have done wrong. We`ll buy the boat together and the better sailor can teach the worse one how to sail. I am here for the summer. At the end of July we will sail across the channel and along the coast of France.

"You have four pounds and eighty pence' I have about one thousand six hundred pounds. We`ll try to knock the price down if we go back in a minute. Deal?" Erik held out his hand.

"Deal" said Callum grabbing the hand in a high five shake."

Helen looked on speechless. She nodded her head not knowing what else to say or do.

"We`ll be back in forty minutes.", said Erik and off he and Callum went.

A moderately concerned vicar turned to Helen and said "Coffee?"

"Strong. Double thing, please. Do you think I was right to let him go off with Erik like that?" Helen said to the window table.

"Don`t ask them" said Poppy. "They are in love."

"What? With Erik? He`s too smooth and confident for me. I just hope Callum really is safe."

"If you don`t let Callum go with him, I will" said Rachel. "I`ll leave Jim tomorrow and sail into the sunset with Mr Swedish God."

"Oh Rachel! Jim would be heartbroken" said Poppy.

"No he wouldn`t. He only said yesterday that he fancied a long weekend with Meryl Streep."

"Mama Mia" said Bronwen, and collapsed in laughter.

"Meryl Streep wouldn`t want rough carpenter`s hands all over her" said Poppy, "Although, I suppose she may. Now, enough of this.I am back to work." She left with a flourish of long skirt.

Two strong coffees later, Callum and Erik returned.

"We bought the boat, Mum. One thousand six hundred and fifty pounds, and we can have it on Saturday. Erik put the registration in my name too and I owe him four pounds eighty."

"Callum mentioned that he has no school uniform yet" said Erik "And that you have no car. If I run you into Exeter in mine to buy the main components he won`t feel so different on the bus in the morning."

"Well, yes please. I was going to wait until my husband came back on Saturday to get it," said Helen.

"I`ll collect you at 2pm then." Erik smiled at the ladies whose knees began to collapse, and left the cafe again.

At 2 pm sharp a Porsche Carrera, white and quite old, came along Kirkhaven driveway at about twenty miles per hour faster than any other car probably since the postman came to collect his Christmas box from the previous owners.

"Wow!" said a small boy looking out of his bedroom window and then charging down the stairs two at a time. Helen had smartened herself up and put on a white turtle necked shirt and tight black slacks tucked into calf length black leather boots with a ribbed pattern up the side. All this was set off with a wide black belt with the clip the shape of two wings of a butterfly in cloisonné. Callum climbed into the back of the sports car and Helen sort of lay in the front, feeling as if she was midway through a seduction routine. I am not being seduced by this man, even if he may want it. He is a confident predator who dresses and drives the image,` she thought to herself.

The bus driver whose vehicle was overtaken on the road to Exeter, spent his spare money following motor racing and appreciated the patience of the Porsche driver and then the calm acceleration past him. This was no kid with a new toy that Daddy had bought for his birthday.

"The Qataris often have cars like this" said Callum "but I have never had a ride in one."

"This is an old friend" said Erik. "I leave it with someone in London when I am away from England."

"What do you do.....I mean what you are doing here in Devon?" asked Helen, holding on to the side of her seat!

"I like to do some painting and the light here and in Cornwall is good in the mornings and evenings."

"What do you paint?"

"Naked females whenever I can" he replied.

18

"Really, why?" asked Callum as Helen felt the embarrass-ment rise from her neck to the edge of her hairline. `That confirms my suspicions` she thought, pressing her knees tightly together.

They went into the St. Mary Arches car park in Exeter, and drove into the very first marked space after the barrier. Helen thought `Typical. If it had been me, I would have driven around the whole car park twice before I found a gap! ` Not knowing the city they had to ask directions to the school outfitters. Helen was fortunate that this was mid-term and she was not swept into the scrum of the last few days before the beginning of the school year. That can become more exasperating than the January sales, when many of your child's size garments are already out of stock. Today, however, there was something of everything for Callum and Erik watched as the total bill came to almost five hundred and fifty pounds....and this was for a govern-ment comprehensive! Thank God there are no boaters and tuck boxes like the school her mother in law would have chosen.

They left before the rush hour, such as it is in Exeter, and Helen began to enjoy being driven in a car that everyone looked at. On arrival at home Lucy had made friends with Deirdre and had found that she was only a year below Deir-dre's granddaughter in her school. Lucy was official `taster` of the batch of butterfly cakes that had been made by the new cook.

"Where are you staying, Erik?" asked Helen.

"In a room over the pub at the moment, but in a few days I may move to the boat. It has a small cabin and I like to hear the water and feel the gentle movement of the boat at night. Come down to the harbour on Saturday, Callum, and we shall officially take ownership of our purchase. And you owe me four pounds eighty pence."

Callum rushed upstairs and emptied the change left

from the ten pound note his grandfather had given him last weekend. He handed it over to Erik with a serious face.

"Thanks partner. Goodbye. Oh! Can I call you Helen?"

"Of course, and thanks so much for the ride to Exeter." Erik accelerated fast down the driveway for Callum`s sake, leaving a small shower of stone chippings further behind him than they were earlier.

Deirdre served a cooked meal for Helen and the children, cleared away and washed up.

"I`ll be off then. I have left a shopping list for some of the things you need and I can prepare when I comes on Monday. `Spect you`ll be up the supermarket when you have the car and your husband can carry the spuds."

'Thanks, Deirdre. Can I pay you weekly? I need to go to the bank first."

"There`s a `hole in the wall` cash machine in Tesco's. Get some there when you do the shopping." Deirdre put on her coat and left her apron behind. "I`ll run along afore it gets dark."

"I am her official `food taster`" said Lucy. "I taste every-thing, and if it`s no good, she has to make it again."

"Bet she never makes it again. Anyway, what do you know? Are you some sort of a food expert?" asked Callum

"Yes. I am the family expert on food and I decide," said Lucy finishing the conversation and going upstairs to her room.

Callum went to school the next morning and apparently even muttered an apology to David with his arm in plaster. He was aware of each teacher watching him for much of the lesson and even accommodated the French mistress by sitting at the front. Although sitting alone on the bus, he finished the week in a better mood. Unintentionally he had established a presence in the school and a springboard from which to choose his own friends when he felt ready.

Peter arrived home late on Friday evening. He drove home from the station and reached the house looking tired and somewhat dishevelled at nine thirty pm. Revived by a glass of Chablis he related his week to Helen. The first weeks in a new office were never going to be easy, so she listened to a day by day, blow by blow account of the incompetence of colleagues, the inefficiency of his p.a. and the tastelessness of the beef sandwiches at lunchtime.

"Perhaps Moscow should be better next week" she suggested. After a roast chicken dinner, profiteroles and the rest of the wine he retired to bed and was gently snoring in less than five minutes. Helen wondered why she had worn her most flattering nightie, and settled down to read the rest of the library book she had borrowed from Bronwen. It was all about infidelity. She put the book down and thought about Rachel sailing away with Erik and Jim chasing Meryl Streep around a film set. Her eyes began to close and sleep took over. Her last thoughts were of how their lives had moved on in just a few weeks

THREE

NOW

Saturday began with Callum dragging Peter away from his paper to talk about his boat.

"Don`t be ridiculous. You can`t own a boat. You can`t sail and would have to have someone to hold your hand anytime you went near water" said Peter.

"I do own a boat now and I will learn how to sail it this summer" retorted Callum

"Huh. Not with my money you won`t" and Peter brushed aside the irritation and picked up his paper again.

"You would learn more if you went to school and did some homework instead of messing about like some country bumpkin."

Callum had tried unsuccessfully to interest his father in his activities since his first Lego birthday present. Peter had failed to praise any of his efforts at building toys, drawings or reading about boats. He had pleaded `pressure of work` for missing school plays and exhibitions and the junior cricket match in which Callum scored twenty two runs and took three wickets. It was part of the cause of Callum`s withdrawn nature and it was unlikely to change because they had moved to another country.

Callum put on a pair of old trainers and made his way in the sunshine down to the small town harbour at the mouth of the river. Erik was leaning on an open fence separating the footpath from the water.

"This is one of the river estuaries that attract the widest range of seabirds to feed and breed anywhere in the British Isles. Bird watchers come from all over Europe to see the different types." Said Erik.

"I was good at Geography at school in Qatar" Callum said.

"This is more `natural fact` or `nature study`. It was a subject we learnt in early school in Sweden."

"Sweden is next to Norway and has a lot of lakes. Most people have blond hair and are rich."

"Correct, except for the rich idea. It depends how you compare rich and poor. It is not always about the money in your pocket. You can have no money and be very wealthy with friends and knowledge and love".

"How can you be rich with love?"

"Many children in this world are alone. Their parents have died or are in prison or have to work years away from home. They are often poor in love and need to be surrounded with loving friends and people who care. You have loving parents and I expect grandparents who will always be there for you."

"My Dad is only there for himself. He never wants to talk about anything except his damn gas ships and his football team or when his dinner is going to be ready."

"He is probably busy all day at work and comes home tired and hungry. It is not easy being a dad and having to pay all the bills!"

"Are you a dad?"

"No. Not yet. Maybe one day."

"You are very old."

"I am forty years old. Pretty old to you but not to most grownups."

"Are you married?"

"No. I have had a few girlfriends and married for a short time. I travel around too much to be a good husband. Now. Let`s go and see if our new purchase is ready."

They walked together across the road bridge to the harbour side, where they could see the little cabin boat up on blocks on the quayside and someone rubbing the keel with a sanding tool. The owner greeted them and said the boat was all theirs now. He had been just tidying it up a little. The transfer had come through from the bank in Sweden and the sale was complete.

"Did you get your contribution from your partner?" the owner asked with a smile on his face.

"Oh yes. Paid in full" said Erik, patting Callum on the back. "What is the boat`s name?"

"No name now" replied the owner. "I named it after my wife, but she died last month, so now it needs a new name."

"I am sorry to hear about your wife. We shall take good care of your boat."

The former owner drove away in his van.

"Think of a good name, Callum."

"Viti Levu" said Callum. "It is an island in Fiji and I want to go there one day."

"You did like Geography, didn`t you? OK. We shall call her Viti Levu, and every day you see her you can dream of your visit one day to Fiji."

They walked around the boat standing high on the blocks.

"You said her. Maybe it is a male boat."

"All boats and ships are female. It is a tradition around the world," said Erik. "Before we can sail her there is a lot of work to be done. She was so cheap because of the things that need repairing or renewing. And we shall need to buy an outboard motor to use in case the wind drops and we cannot sail along. At least, until we can get the inboard engine repaired"

They began by making a list of all the things they had to buy. There were ropes, anti-fouling, some wires and chain, special yacht varnish and, of course, the motors. The nearest yacht chandlers was in Exmouth, so they drove to Exmouth after Erik had called Helen to tell her their plans and ask whether Callum could stay out all day. After managing to accumulate most of the items on the list they ate a pub lunch in Exmouth. Erik then asked the Harbour Master whether he knew of anyone wanting to sell a good outboard engine.

"I haven`t any more money yet" said Callum. "We can`t buy it today."

"Ok. We will have to wait until one becomes available and you can get a job."

"I get pocket money usually on a Saturday, but Dad was in a bad mood this morning" said Callum.

They decided to do all the repair jobs before buying the outboard.

Callum and Erik were unaware of the angry exchanges going on at Kirkhaven House once Peter had found out about his son`s new interest. He and Helen disagreed about Callum wishing to sail and his interest in having his own boat. They disagreed about Erik - his likely influence on Callum and his likely attraction to Helen. They disagreed about the trip in the Porsche and that the school uniform had already been purchased.

"I hope you are not going to come back every weekend in a foul mood" said Helen.

"I just cannot understand how, in a few days, you have teamed up with a Scandinavian playboy and allowed our son to run riot at school and at home."

Helen took a folding chair out onto the overgrown lawn and read more of her book about infidelity without allowing her own thoughts to overlap the story. Peter listened to football on the radio, enjoying one of the luxuries he had been unable to have in Qatar. His concerns for Callum did not extend to making the effort to get in the car and investigate the boat situation.

Saskia`s Mum called Helen to ask whether Lucy would come for tea and Helen decided to walk to Seaton and take a look at the intrepid sailors on the way. The sunny afternoon showed off the last of the primroses and bluebells in the roadside banks perfectly and Lucy skipped along beside her, holding a DVD in one hand. Saskia and her mother also walked, but from the other direction, the centre of Seaton. They all stood on the road bridge and looked at Callum sandpapering the hull of a boat that was out of the water and on a stand. Standing beside it was a long limbed, bronzed, muscular man with long curly blond hair, painting a black thick glue onto the hull.

"Who is that" asked Saskia`s Mum with more than passing interest.

"That is a good reason to show an interest in sailing. He is called Erik and is Swedish and, for some reason, enjoys the company of my son."

"Have you checked him out? Sometimes these guys come from abroad and they have been up to no good in their country."

"Well, for a start I wouldn`t know how to check with the Swedish authorities and anyway, he is quite plausible and helpful" said Helen.

"Beware. They all are. We`ll bring Lucy home by bedtime. Next week may be a sleepover if they are still talking to each other."

The DVD had become the main topic of conversation with the two girls as they headed back to Seaton. Helen walked down the slope to the boat, which was obviously getting a good makeover. Callum had never been known to lift a finger to help with anything at home, yet was beavering away vigorously with his piece of sandpaper. Erik greeted her with a bow and pointed to the boat without saying anything. He was creating a name board as well and this was drying on a table set up nearby. A rectangular piece of wood had been painted blue and was drying before letters could be added. Erik returned to the hull painting whilst Callum continued rubbing down the other side.

"She will look good when we have finished. We are working hard because I will live on board," said Erik, "And I plan to move in soon."

"Have you lived on board a boat before?" asked Helen.

"Yes. Once for parts of each year. It was a special time of my life. Helped me to calm down."

Helen climbed the ladder fixed to the side of the hull and stood in the steering well. It was a jumble of tools and pieces of sailing gear. Inside the cabin were rolled up sails, some documents, fenders and a couple of old blankets. She tried to imagine the finished article. Varnish was peeling from the woodwork inside and out. The `For Sale` sign was still attached to the mast.

Erik had cleaned his hands and stopped applying anti-fouling paint. He joined her up above.

"What is she called?" asked Helen.

"Viti Levu. It is an island in the Fiji group. A South Seas island. Palm trees, surf and warm breezes and all that. Ask Callum. It was his suggestion."

"Is he being useful?"

"The best partner. I`ll run him home for his tea at dusk. We had a pub lunch."

"What? A pint and a pasty?"

"No. A coke and a steak and kidney pie, chips, peas and cheesecake. Hungry work this boat repair!"

Now that two of her three charges seemed happy Helen walked back home wondering if something, as yet unspoken, was troubling Peter. She would cook his favourite steak meal that evening and try to get through to the once cheerful character she had married. On the way through the village she passed the Brigadier, who stopped, and seemed to recognise her.

"You`re the stunning brunette who was in Poppy's the other day" he said, doffing his Bavarian style hat with a feather in the side. "They tell me you are living up at Kirkhaven House."

"Yes. We moved in last weekend."

"You`ll be needing my advice on some decent antique furniture to blend in with the house then. I`ll pop along and see you sometime next week. Good day."

He was several paces down the road before she could think of a suitable rejection, so decided to leave it. Although the prospect of Roper the Groper visiting when she was alone was a little daunting.

After enjoying his meal Peter was more sociable. Callum, however, just walked into the house and went upstairs to shower and wash flakes of paint out of his hair. He joined the family and a chattering Lucy for dinner, but said nothing. Ignoring Peter he said

"Mum, I will need my pocket money to help buy an outboard motor. Goodnight" and went straight up to bed.

"You are going to have to work to get back any respect from your son" said Helen to her husband, who said nothing and left the table to pour himself a whisky from the decanter on the sideboard.

Sunday was happier. Callum disappeared at eight am, having eaten breakfast alone and the other three took the car to Tesco in Axminster to buy a week`s stock of groceries. Having forgotten about Sunday`s limited opening hours they had to drive around for half an hour before the store opened at ten am. Peter left just after lunch saying that he had to catch an earlier train because of his flight to Moscow leaving before lunch on Monday."

"Can I run you to the station and keep the car?" suggested Helen.

"No, I need it to be in situ for my return."

"But I can meet you on Friday with it."

"No. That would mean leaving the children alone as it will be after their bedtime. We`ll get you a small car in a few weeks." He kissed her and drove off as Lucy ran down the stairs, too late for her hug.

"Don`t worry, darling. Daddy has a lot to think about and a long journey to London this afternoon.

Erik brought Callum back home at seven pm. Paint was evident in her son`s arms and face. Callum shook hands in the `partner` way and ran upstairs for another shower.

"Come in and have a glass of wine" said Helen.

"Yes please, just for a few minutes. I am too scruffy to stay longer."

Erik too had paint evidencing extensive use of blue and white on `Viti Levu` today. Helen thought he was too good looking to be allowed out on his own. And noticed how slim he looked in his well fitted jeans and brown leather loafers.

"Cheers. Here`s to your new home" said Helen. "Do you have a home anywhere else?"

"My secret if you will keep it." Without reply he added "Four actually. In Sweden and in Monaco and......well just those two will do."

"Wow. You must have been successful in something" said Helen through an open mouth. "What was it?"

"I told you I paint" said Erik.

"Yes. Naked women!"

"Something like that. I want to ask you. Are you using your barn?"

"No. Not yet. Probably not at all. I haven`t even opened the doors since I have been here."

"It will be impossible to paint in the cramped space on my boat, and rocking up and down on the water. If I try on the quayside I will be plagued by people looking over my shoulder."

`And the models may not like being so public` thought Helen.

"Please could I come up here without imposing on you, and paint in your barn or in the garden?"

"The garden is a mess. Probably the barn is a mess too."

"I`ll clean it up as my rent and tidy the garden."

"OK. That would be good. But I can`t have naked women lying all around the garden with the children coming and going. Also, the postman looks on his last legs and that could finish him off."

"I promise I will not drape any women around your property, naked or clothed. Deal?"

"Deal! I can`t do that funny handshake that you do with Callum."

They practised and finally got the shake right to much laughter.

"I must go and take a bath. Can I come and inspect the barn tomorrow?"

"Yes. The cook is here again. There may even be lunch available" said Helen letting him out of the front door.

Helen went to bed thinking more about Erik than she should have. There was something deliciously mysterious about him. Handsome forty year old bachelors don`t appear in the countryside for no reason. Or perhaps they did in Devon. Maybe there was more to this country living than the city dwellers even suspected.

After dropping Lucy at school she wandered towards the library and arrived as Bronwen was opening the door. A young girl, about seventeen years old, went in first carrying a heavy bag of books'.'

"Jenny. A/S levels in a month`s time" said Bronwen, as

she got the girl settled at one of the reading tables. Helen started to look for a new book to read. She glanced through the recently returned books. They were often the best ones and other people had already recognised this. Nothing appealing there. Then the shelves of romantic novels. They had become more and more sexually descriptive in recent years and she didn`t really enjoy the intimate details of peoples` private encounters. Only one book jumped off the shelf. The cover was fairly bland but it was published by Harper Collins. The title` Playing Second String to a Tennis Racquet` sounded quite interesting. Like many women she enjoyed watching the Wimbledon fortnight on TV, but had not seen it for years, being in the Gulf every June. She had never heard of Sally Shaunessy, the author, before.

"Are you coming over to Poppy`s for a coffee this morning?" asked Bronwen.

"I must get back. Someone is coming to inspect the barn next to the house. I haven`t even opened the door yet. It may be full of farm machinery. Maybe tomorrow" said Helen.

She was back home by nine forty five am to find Deirdre sitting on the garden wall near the back door.

"Sorry Deirdre. I wasn`t expecting you quite so early" apologised Helen.

"The work isn`t going to get done by itself" said Deirdre. "I thought you had forgotten I was coming. I told Arthur when he brought the letters, that I`d give you another fifteen minutes and then I`d be off."

There was no sign of Erik all morning as Helen left Deirdre to the dusting and ironing, and cooking the lunch for three, and sat on the garden bench with her book. In the blurb it stated that this was Sally`s own story. It started with her description of a happy childhood in Gloucester and meeting her future husband, a Royal Marine Commando, on a weekend visit to Taunton where he was based. Just after twelve noon Erik`s white Porsche came sedately down the drive, and Erik, wearing a ridiculous sailing cap perched on the top of his thick curly hair, found his way around to the garden seat. Helen put down the book and went to the barn door. There was no lock on it. The door opened on a cloud of dust, and there was dust laying thickly on everything. The barn was virtually empty except a heap of things leaning against the wall at the far end and shielded behind a protection of cardboard sheets. They walked towards this and gently pulled the cardboard away from part of it. Behind were paintings, all original and no prints, some were on canvas and some framed. The paintings were of animals, birds and boats.

"What a shame to have left them here to deteriorate" said Helen.

"There is a limit to the space most people have to display large canvasses" said Erik looking at the art in a strangely interested way, Helen thought.

FOUR

THEN

The roadside bomb detonated as the small convoy was almost past the culvert. It was a hot, dusty road in Bosnia. Chris Shaunessy, a career and dedicated Royal Marine, was sergeant in charge of the last vehicle through. The blast threw their partially armoured truck onto its side leaving a gaping hole in the side and Corporal Shiner and Marine Garside dead and Chris and Dave Hearn injured. The two others set about using their cursory paramedic training to patch Chris and Dave ready for the helicopter ride back to the base hospital. The Surgeon Captain explained to Chris that they had had no option but to amputate his right leg and it was likely he would lose his right arm as well. During a further spell in a Birmingham hospital back in the UK, it was agreed to remove his shattered right arm and to provide him with a hearing aid to help the bone conduction, which was all he had left of his hearing in the right ear.

Royal Marine Commandos don`t give up easily, and in two years Chris was walking and able to write slowly with his left hand. The mental challenge of it all was more debilitating than the physical and he began to drink to save imposing his problems on Sally and their son Greg. His savings and Sally`s income, together with the compensation from the Corps, enabled them to buy Kirkhaven House in East Devon at a time when the mortgage officer at the bank was not too observant about the Shaunessy`s continuing income.

Greg was just thirteen and arrived at a good time to join secondary school when all his fellow pupils had only a year ago been promoted from a dozen primary schools in the district. He settled quickly and befriended Michael, a farmer`s son in the same class. Because of the high number of applicants for teaching jobs in the same county, Sally could only get relief status with the Education Committee and became a supply teacher waiting for a gap in the English complement of the local schools. A few weeks at a time, or a term covering maternity leave was the best she could expect. Chris would have adapted to an office job in the Corps but he was right-handed and the learning process to write with his left took too long for the Forces. He left his chosen career at the age of thirty four with much sadness.

Eighteen months after they had moved to Kirkhaven the school bus skidded on black ice and slid into the group of waiting teenagers outside Michael`s farm. Michael died of his head injuries in the ambulance, halfway to Exeter. The effect on Class 9H at school was profound and difficult for the teachers to cope with. The effect on Greg was life changing, coming as it did not long after coming to terms with his Dad`s injuries and later tendency to withdraw from the family unit. Nobody saw Greg smile for the next six months. He spoke little, sat alone on the bus and dropped out of every school club he had joined. He began to take a packed lunch every day to avoid sitting in the school canteen with others in his year. Greg had begun to play golf on the cliff top course overlooking Seaton. He had had one lesson to show him how to hold a club and borrowed a set of clubs from the Secretary each time he played. There were seven boys and one girl junior members, and a tournament was arranged every Saturday to keep their interest and so they didn`t get swamped by the adults.

Greg no longer joined the Saturday group but now played on his own, not wishing to see or talk to anyone. His Head of Year was already monitoring this and expressed his concerns to Sally when she came to a meeting at the school with her and her deputy. They debated consulting an educational psychologist but decided to wait and try other methods of rehabilitation first.

Sally was also worrying about Chris, who was staying in the house all day and becoming more withdrawn and morose. She was sure he was drinking more than he admitted. It was the beginning of July and Greg had gone to play golf after school. The evenings were light for long enough for him to play all eighteen holes. She decided to wait at the bottom of the long drive leading to the Golf Club, enjoying the evening sun as it reflected from the Devon red cliffs in the distance and the white limestone around Seaton. It usually took Greg three hours to walk to the club and play a full round. Sally was early so she wandered along the hundred metres to the bridge that took the road over the river and into Seaton. Leaning on the bridge she watched the local boat repair men pack up in their small yard, and two sailing dinghies returning into the harbour after racing each other along the seafront. Almost under the bridge she watched a fit looking young man in his mid-twenties seemingly preparing a white ketch for sailing. The clothes drying on a line across the deck showed that he was living on board. The flag fluttering on a short pole at the stern she thought was Finnish or maybe Swedish, and vowed to confirm this when she got back to her reference books at home. The sailor looked up and greeted her, his blond curly hair blowing in the light breeze that was keeping them both pleasantly cool in the setting sun.

"What brings you here?" Sally called. "This is not a popular international harbour."

"I have only just arrived. I keep the boat moored here. The yard looks after it when I am away."

"Are you planning to sail away tonight?"

"No. Just tidying the jumble I left last time and catching up with my laundry" he replied in impeccable English.

"Are you from Finland?"

"No. Yellow and blue flag. I am from Goteborg in Sweden." Come down. This way around the bridge and we can talk without my getting a frozen neck looking up at you." Sally walked around the buttress of the bridge and down to the edge of the harbour. Her contact was paddling an inflatable tender towards her and looking already the most desirable man she had seen since Chris was in his prime. She watched him climb out of the tender and then pull the craft out of the water, lifting it effortlessly with bronzed, muscular forearms. He wore a white T shirt with yellow piping around the collar and the edge of the short sleeves, blue shorts and had bare feet that were both taped across the toes. His blond hair almost reached his shoulder, the curls keeping it in place as he moved. Sally began to wish she had worn more flattering clothes, and then remembered that she had come to meet her son not meet a handsome man in a most unlikely corner of the town!

"I am Erik" he said holding out his hand.

"And I am Sally. Nice to meet you. Do you sail this big boat alone or is there a crew member around?" `Stop it Sally', she thought, 'You are already fishing to find whether he has a wife or partner! `

"I am a lonely bachelor, who wanders around the world alone, trying to earn a meagre living" said Erik.

"What do you do when you are not sailing?"

"I play a little sport, which pays for the groceries and a few other things."

One of the other things was an apparently brand new white Porsche that he now opened to put a package inside that he had brought across in the tender. As he did this Sally looked to see whether Greg had begun to walk down the long slope from the Golf club, and saw him heading along the road beside the river, oblivious of her presence. She called as loud as she could. "Greg, Greg, come back, wait for me." No response. Erik joined in. adding strength to the call.

"Greg. Greg, we are here!"

Greg heard this and looked back. He trudged slowly back towards the harbour.

"Good evening, Greg. I am Erik. Have you been playing golf?"

"Hello. Yes."

"Did you play well today and keep score?"

"It was OK. I played two balls. Eighty one and Eighty four."

"What is your handicap?"

"Fifteen but they don`t accept it in the Club because I don`t play in the juniors or with anyone else. Is this your car?"

"Yes. It is only four weeks old. I earnt a little extra money in May and ordered it from Germany."

Sally decided that she had better return home and feed her son before it was bedtime.

"I hope you will come by again," said Erik.

Whilst waiting for the call to attend a supply English job Sally has been trying to write short stories to sell and to boost their income. The bills were greater than their earnings and the lump sum compensation paid to Chris was rapidly diminishing. She and Chris shared a Skoda Octavia and were surprised at how well it went and how economical it was, in view of the reputation of Skoda cars in recent years.

When she ran out of inspiration for her writing Sally would drive down to the Harbour Cafe, close to the bridge where she had first spoken with Erik. The Cafe was owned by an extraverted gay man, Oliver, who pranced around being outrageous to everyone. Customers were sometimes embarrassed or offended, but mostly amused. Today he was wearing purple and red patterned braces holding up something that looked like a mixture of hot pants and lederhosen. His white shirt had a frilly collar and he wore a panama trilby with a yellow and blue headband.

Oliver bounced out from behind the counter to greet Sally and kissed her hand to the rather shocked expressions of the two pensioners drinking tea in the window.

"You look - well - ravishing today Oliver" said Sally

"I have to make an effort, dear. Now that Bruce has left I am quite depressed and in need of stimulating company."

"I like the hat."

"Oh, yes. The headband is an addition today. I bought it in the Swedish colours because of the return of Bjorn or Adonis, or whatever he is called, with the Porsche.

"Erik".

"Yes, Erik. Isn`t he delicious? And he's single. If he is gay too it would make my summer bearable."

"When did Bruce leave?"

"On Thursday. I only asked him to help with the dishes. We had had a coachload in from a Women`s Institute somewhere in Dorset and they had used all my best crockery. Next thing I saw was Bruce walking out of the front door carrying a suitcase. I chased after of course, pleading love and apologies. I tripped over that long apron with the Boobs design and fell `a` over `t` into the refuse bins left by the dustmen. By the time I had pulled myself together he was waving to me from the top deck of the Jurassic Coast bus and on the way to Bournemouth. He has always fancied one of the young lifeguards on the beach near Sandbanks and I`ll bet that is where he is headed. Well, good riddance!"

"You can do much better than that."

"Yes, I should, but I am nearly thirty five now - oh, all right, nearly forty. I don`t want to miss the boat. Talking of which here comes the boat owner."

He rushed back behind the counter to look at his reflection in the hot water boiler`s shiny stainless steel exterior.

Erik walked casually down the pavement and in through the cafe door, this time wearing jeans and slip on rope-soled shoes. "Hello, Oliver. My usual, please."

"Hello Bjorn, er Erik. Be there in two mins."

"Hi Sally." `He remembered my name`, she thought. "I didn`t see you walk past the harbour."

"I came by car this morning."

"Is that your Octavia outside?" Sally nodded.

"Aren`t they good now that VW have taken over the factory. I heard last week that their engineers have been so well trained that VW are taking them back into the main factory to run a refresher course for their own mechanics!"

Sally smiled.

"Can I buy you a naughty cake to go with your latte? I am going to have a Danish pastry."

"I`ll bet you have had a few Danish pastries in your time" said Oliver from the counter.

More po-faced expressions from the window seats.

"Only beautiful ones, with very long legs."

Erik obviously had no problem with sexuality, any more than did Oliver, and Sally, found it increasingly refreshing. The couple in the window quickly paid and escaped down the street.

"Your Greg is very reserved. Sorry, I am a painter and I tend to notice things. Is he always like that, or was he having a bad day?"

Sally told Erik of the tough challenges Greg had had to face in the last few years. His school work had gone steeply downhill and he had no friends. She hoped his reclusive behaviour was just his way of grieving for his friend and the lost, lively part of his father.

"I play a little golf" said Erik. "Perhaps I could accidentally on purpose meet up with him on the course and try to coax him to play with me, as I have time on my hands"

"You`re not some continental paedophile, are you?" said Outrageous Oliver from behind the counter. Erik gave him one of his cold blue-eyed stares in reply. "Well, Sally will be wondering what your interest in a young boy is out there in the bunkers and the bogeys. I think I had better come along as your caddy to referee this match!"

"You stay here making the sandwiches. We`ll come back and eat them if my plan works," said Erik.

Sally was quite amused by this exchange and some of its implications.

"Look, there goes the Brigadier" said Oliver, pointing out a military looking character in cavalry twill trousers, brogues and sports jacket, striding towards Seaton town centre. He runs the antique shop near you, Sally, and is probably off to the auction sale room to buy some stock."

"Is he really a Brigadier?" asked Erik.

"I know you don`t get too many of those to the pound dear, but he tells everyone he is. Probably a corporal in the Sappers in Malaya or somewhere. He won`t come in here to save his life. Thinks I am depraved and tells everyone so. And then goes into the Co-op and feels his way along the queue of young mothers at the checkout. `Roper the Groper` they call him. There is a switched-on policewoman here now and she is after him. If he tries groping her he could find himself in one of the positions he hasn`t been reading about."

"You are a bad man, Oliver"

"Yes, ducky, but you still love me, don`t you?"

Sally laughed, thanked Erik for the coffee and the suggestion about Greg, and left to drive home.

Two days later, in the evening, Greg was surprised to find Erik walking out of the bushes on the sixth fairway holding a ball and carrying a bag of clubs.

"Hello Greg. Are you playing this hole? You have caught me up. I hooked my drive into the clump of trees. As we are both singles, shall we play on together?"

"I am playing two balls."

"OK. Carry on with the two. Or maybe, pick up the one not doing so well and play the better one."

Greg reluctantly agreed "I`ll play this one. It`s only two over."

"Good. I am two over as well. Let`s see how we get on. I don`t play much these days and you can point out the direction of each hole and give me some local knowledge."

"Play to the left of this green. Flag is on the right but it slopes from the left."

Erik hit a five iron into the heart of the green inside Greg`s but, when they got there, Greg sank a birdie putt from twenty yards. They continued all the way around without saying much to each other as Erik thought it better to wait until Greg felt like talking. They finished with both getting par threes on the eighteenth.

"I make you eighty" said Erik. "That is fourteen against the low standard scratch of sixty six. Tomorrow we could mark a card and, with three of those, you will have an official handicap by the weekend.

Sally had assumed that Erik must be a footballer because she knew that this was the time of year that there were no league matches and the players were on leave. Also she heard from Greg that Erik used to play with a handicap of three, she felt this confirmed the footballer status, because she knew they were always playing golf in the spare time after training.

The next visit of Sally`s to the harbour found Erik on the quayside with palette, paints and as easel and faced with a life-size painting of a herring gull that was almost complete. Two people were walking away looking very pleased with themselves.

"That is very good" said Sally. "Hallo Sally. Actually, I've just sold it."

"How much?" "A hundred pounds. It all goes into a pot. I support a little charity in India and they get my painting purse."

"Why India particularly?"

"One of my sports colleagues comes from an orphanage in South India. It was started by a young girl for picking up and educating abandoned babies. He was her very first baby - left at a bus stop apparently. They gave him a great education and the school realised his skill at sport. Now he is a wealthy man, but he has never forgotten his origins and has just financed a new home for boys in the Charity. I just help a little too. Is Greg at home catching up with his schoolwork?"

"Reluctantly, but he is there, and he brought the books home with him this time. I wanted to talk with you. You seem to be able to get through to him. His school report arrived this morning. It is awful. Chris has lost patience with him and so he just ignores his Dad and goes down to the old gardener's cottage at the bottom of our lawn. Greg was always given A`s and B`s at Primary School and, before Michael died, his Christmas term report had only one C in it, for music, which he doesn`t like anyway. Have you any suggestions about what we could do?"

"Maybe. I'll think more about it. By the way do you ride horses?"

"I did once as a teenager. I was horse mad in Gloucester when I was thirteen and fourteen. Not recently."

"Is there a nearby stable?"

"Yes. Run by my friend Maggie. It`s attached to her father`s farm on the Colyton road."

"Will Chris mind if we hire a couple of horses tomorrow morning and go for a ride? I may have some suggestions for Greg then. Maybe Chris could come too.

"I`ll ask him and call you. Give me your mobile number." Sally went on to describe Chris" injuries.

Chris didn`t seem to worry if Sally went off with another man if Greg's welfare was the reason. . He and Erik had not met yet and Greg had said nothing about the golf encounters. Sally and Erik rented two horses from Maggie, who was all `big eyes` and `suggestive gestures` around Erik and full of advice about not stopping and resting for too many hours in the long grass etc. etc.

"Thank you Maggie. I am a big girl now."

"Yes and you can be sure he has noticed where you have more than your share of endowment!" Maggie replied conspiratorially.

"Bye Maggie." Sally kicked her gentle mare into a walk alongside Erik out of the farm gate and onto the moor where beacons were lit during the time of the Spanish Armada. After twenty minutes of cantering and trotting on open heathland, they dismounted in the shade of a twin pair of oaks overlooking Lyme Bay. Erik produced a flask of iced tea which they shared in silence.

"I want to come here one day and paint one of the does in the herd of that magnificent stag, whose photograph was in the local paper last week" said Erik.

"When do you start training again" asked Sally.

"The end of the third week of August. But now I am relaxing and catching up on a private life in a part of England where I am not plagued by the public. Greg breaks up from school in another week. Would you trust me with him for a few days in the school vacation ?Perhaps to teach him a few of the values that I learnt the hard way."

"I would be delighted. I love him dearly and can`t bear to see him so deeply inside himself. It has been frightening not being able to get through to him. I am sure Chris would value your help too."

"Can I meet Chris and tell him what I plan before I approach Greg?"

"Of course, we can`t really afford to pay you much."

"I had a mentor in my teens. At fourteen in Goteborg - I must start to call it Gothenburg as you do in England. At fourteen I used to storm out of my sports club, slam doors, and break equipment if anything went wrong or I played badly. The Club President had enough of this spoilt brat and he banned me from the Club for six months. I missed the game, my friends and the atmosphere very badly. I watched others improve to be much better than I was and knew I would lose out if I could not get back to practise. The President made me promise to behave before he renewed my membership. I never did anything like that again and I am now known as one of the calmest players for temperament. I am very grateful to that good man, so perhaps it is now that I have a chance to help a teenager with a little guidance."

They re-mounted the horses and began to trot down a hill. Suddenly Sally dropped her rein and her mare began to gallop. Sally held on to her as best she could. They were heading for a small coppice.

"Steer her with your legs, Sally" called Erik. He was some way behind and beginning to catch up. The mare began to head to the left side of the wood but still went in under the trees, which were above her head level.

"Duck, duck" cried Erik.

Too late, a branch caught Sally full on the shoulder and she stopped as her horse ran on, falling to the ground with a thump. She lay groaning as Erik pulled up beside her. He kneeled down, and helped unclip her riding hat after checking she had no pain around her head.

"Where does it hurt?" he asked.

Sally was so winded she couldn't yet speak a word, but

with her right hand, pointed to her left shoulder. The two broken parts of her left collar bone could be seen through her shirt, clearly separated. She recovered her speech as Erik began to check the rest of her limb by limb.

"You could make a good paramedic" she said through clenched teeth as the pain began to make itself felt. "No, not there. Who do you think you are - the Brigadier?"

"No other damage except a few bruises." He replied.

Erik took off his shirt and tore it right up the seam at the back. He gently folded Sally`s left arm up towards her chin and turned his expensive looking shirt into a perfect sling.

"Can you walk?"

"Oh yes. It`s only this silly arm."

Erik walked over to where Sally`s mount has stopped and was chewing at a tuft of grass, took hold of both horses and together they all walked slowly back to the farm.

The first person Maggie saw as they rounded one of the stables was Erik, shirtless.

"You might have dressed properly after enjoying your little exercise.........Oh! Sorry." She caught sight of her invalid friend approaching beside one of the horses. "Are you all right? I mean, do you need an ambulance?"

"She will be fine. Just a freak accident. The horses are fine. I`ll take Sally off to a Casualty Dept. for a check up on the collar bone."

The Porsche was not the easiest vehicle to enter with a useless arm. Maggie helped as Erik climbed into the driver`s seat.

"Come again when it is healed. It has been lovely to see you, and to meet you Erik."

"We will. It was great whilst it lasted. Lots of love. Call me soon" answered Sally.

Sally was patched up at Axminster Hospital by a Practice Nurse and with only a passing check from the Doctor on duty. `Simple fractures heal quickly if you follow the rules` were the words ringing in her ears as Erik took Sally home. He sat her in an easy chair in the sitting room with the TV Times and the remote and told her to watch something. Twenty minutes later there were omelettes and chips for four, a bowl of mixed salad, a dish of tinned peaches and a sliced up Viennetta ice cream, all followed by a pot of coffee.

FIVE

NOW

The phone call was very odd and rang all sorts of alarm bells after she had picked up the landline receiver. Did Mr Walker live here? Does he live alone? Are you his housekeeper? It was a man`s voice. Helen would have had more bells ringing if it had been a female. She thought, `Moscow. Moscow. I hope the KGB are not after him! ` But then she was not sure if the KGB still existed now that the cold war had finished. She planned to ask Peter what this was all about on his return on Friday evening.

"You will need a strimmer and a grass mower" said Erik over coffee and his first visit to the Barn. He borrowed a broom and then set about sweeping up a pile of dust and leaves that had blown in last autumn under the door. He decided that the wooden struts of the barn needed brightening up and chose an Oxford Blue gloss paint to cover these and the large brown doors. It took all afternoon to put on the first coat over the faded maroon that he himself had painted eighteen years before.

"If I give you the money, will you go and buy some garden tools ?" said Helen to Erik.

"I can get a strimmer into the Porsche, but not a mower. They will have to deliver it later in the week."

He bought them both at a hardware shop in Seaton and strimmed the edge of the lawn and the overgrown garden paths by evening.

The next day he brought along all his art materials and placed them in the centre of the barn floor. The rest of the morning was spent cleaning up the canvasses that had been leaning, unloved against the walls. He arranged these on floor and walls to act as decoration. By the end of the second day the barn was looking like a real artist`s studio.

Erik had brought three lemon soles with him for Deirdre to cook for their lunch and she served these with a cauliflower and cheese mornay.

"Did you mean one for me, or for the children`s tea?" she said, and as Erik nodded, she added "I`ve never had lemon sole before. My Bill will be proper envious."

"How are you going to paint all those nude pictures if you don`t bring the models here?" asked Helen. There was a noticeable straightening of Deirdre`s body as she left the room.

"I set them up, have a really good look and then paint from memory. Sometimes I need to have a second look to get it right."

"I suppose it will be some innocent young thing on your boat after half a bottle of wine, and then a practised seduction routine before she can get her knickers back on."

"Not exactly, but something like that" said an amused Erik. Have you had the routine tried on you in the past? You seem to speak with some knowledge."

"Good Lord, no! Well, not exactly. When I was a student there was a greasy guy who took a lot of photographs. He promised me a modelling contract with one of the fashion magazines. I only half believed him but I went along to boost my ego. I had nice skin and a passable figure then."

"So you understand that nakedness can be beautiful and attractive to see?"

"I wasn`t naked! When we got down to the basics I stopped. Though I am not sure whether that was prudishness or because I had such tatty underwear trying to live on a `nothing` grant. Erik could imagine this conversation leading only one way. He thanked Deirdre who was giving him a wilting look, and went to try the new mower on the lawn.

Erik was not sure he wanted to sell his work. Money was not a problem and he liked to keep his paintings to enjoy, at least for a few weeks. Only this evening, with the sky barely dry, he had sold his latest. It was a yacht, a Silhouette, sitting gracefully on her twin bilge keels on the mud at low tide. Another hundred pounds for the children though. He knew he was leading Helen out of her comfort zone, leading her up a pathway, neither of them knew how far. It was tempting to continue the fun. He placed a bet with himself that the train would not stop. Helen, meanwhile, has spent half an hour looking at herself in the mirror and deciding that she was not slim enough and that her skin was too white to be seen by anyone other than fully clothed. She fed the children and left them pottering in the garden. Opening her library book at the marked page she read on about Sally`s unlikely encounter with a sailor in the distant corner of England where she lived. She read that Sally was born of a single mother, who was pressurised by society in the sixties to give the little girl away. She had fought to keep her and married Kirk, the father, two years later.

Peter phoned. He was in Moscow and was catching the Friday morning flight to Heathrow, going briefly into the office and then train home. He arrived at the same time as last week with a suitcase of washing and only desiring a relationship with a bottle of whisky. Helen thought she looked pretty good in one of her most flattering dresses, heels and the necklace Peter had given her last Christmas. She had put her hair up in what she imagined was her most sophisticated style. Peter did not seem to notice she was even in the house.

"I am going to bed early" he said, "Not much sleep this week. Have been sending Rose piles of work all week."

"Don` t you mean your new secretary, dear. Rose was in Qatar."

"Oh. Didn`t I tell you. Rose came back at the same time as us. Decided to split form that useless husband and come back to Blighty."

"That is a surprise. Where is she living now?"

"Somewhere in Wiltshire, I think. Must ask her next week. Forgive me if I am asleep when you come up."

Peter spent a second weekend in isolation and left again early on Sunday. This time Lucy received a hug and kiss from Daddy before he left. He called from Axminster station.

"I have just seen an old Ford Focus in the station garage. They were working Sundays so I put a deposit on it. Go and collect it tomorrow and I`ll settle up on my credit card from the office. Have a good week."

Helen was pleased that he had remembered her transport difficulty and had done something about it. She asked Erik to take her to the garage next morning to look at the Ford. All the cars in Qatar were huge, like many in the U.S.A. No one worried about the cost of fuel, it being a fraction of that in England. There Helen had driven a Nissan Patrol, the size of vehicle that seems compulsory for mothers to drive to school in West London, though she didn`t carry skis on the roof rack! The Ford Focus seemed small, but was just right for her needs and for driving the tall hedged Devon lanes, with its high driving position. Helen was petite and needed the seat set as high as possible. Erik concurred with the purchase and thought it was reasonable value for the money. They completed the paperwork and he followed Helen home. She stopped outside Poppy's and called him in for a `thank you` coffee. Rachel was there and the bus driver was seated next to the counter. They both ordered cappuccinos and listened to the continuous rumble of a hard-done-by bus employee.

"It`s all right for them teachers today. Start work at nine, two hour lunch, home by four thirty, ten weeks holiday and a pension. I left school at fifteen and start my shift at six, five days a week and now I am getting piles from forty years sitting on them hard driving seats."

"Stop moaning for a minute, Keith, while I make up drinks for my regular customers," said Rachel.

"I`m a regular customer. Two or three times a day I come in here."

"You are a regular depression, Keith. Always happy to be grumbling and making everyone else depressed."

"I shall consider taking my trade elsewhere."

"Who else is going to give you discount on a cup of coffee within walking distance of the bus stop?"

"Might try the Groping Brigadier. He could even have a bottle of scotch there to put a kick in the coffee."

Keith left to begin the bus route back to Exeter. It was lonelier these days than when he had a conductor as a companion.

"I think my husband is cheating on me, or has plans to," said Helen.

"Do you still love him? asked Erik.

"He has a lot of good qualities and he is the children`s father and our breadwinner."

"But, do you still love him?"

"I don`t really know. I think so."

"Do you still sleep together?"

"Yes. In the same room, in the same bed, but that is about

all. I have a sixth sense that there is a lot going on that I don`t know about."

"A good policy is to do nothing and see what transpires" said Erik. Don`t lose sight that you are an attractive woman and he would be a fool to give you up."

They drove back to the house and Erik disappeared into his studio. Ten minutes later the doorbell rang and it was the Brigadier. Helen was relieved that he had come when she had Deirdre in the kitchen and Erik on the premises.

"I`ve come as I promised to advise you on what furniture to buy" said the Brigadier.

"To be honest, we don`t need any. We brought all ours by container from abroad. Come in anyway."

"Hello again, dear lady," he said gripping Helen`s hand and holding on for far too long. He strode into the house as if he was an estate agent valuing it for the owner. "You`ll need an occasional table here and two or three brass vases in this room to make a strong statement."

"I think my husband may make a strong statement if I start filling the house with valuable antiques" interrupted Helen. Undaunted, Brigadier Roper continued.

"That suite of furniture may have been acceptable in Vietnam or wherever you were, but it is far too dominating for this delicate sitting area. I have two perfect Georgian chairs and a chaise longue that I am constantly refusing to sell to people living in the Regency towns. Now, what about the dining area? Oh, hello Mrs.......you are here too."

"Good morning, Brigadier Roper. Yes. I am here and before you go, I`d like to have a word about you and our Maisie in the bus queue yesterday morning."

"Well Mrs...Er....young Maisie has grown into a big girl these days and it was unfortunate that we both tried to get onto the bus at the same time."

"Bit of a squeeze was it? Well, Maisie isn`t ready for that kind of squeezing yet and, when she is, it isn`t going to be some randy old man doing it!"

"Quite so, quite so. You will need some horse brasses around the fireplace to add a period and country feel, Mrs Walker."

Deirdre left the room muttering something about `too much feeling going on in the country already.'

He continued around the house placing pieces of furniture and ornaments in a number of places, and suggesting the addition of a four-poster bed in the Master Bedroom that once had been slept on by Marchioness Antoinette d`Alsace, whoever she was.

"Let`s have a look at your needs for the garden." Exiting through the back door the Brigadier put his arm around Helen`s waist and guided her across the patio. "I have an exquisite set of table and four chairs in ironwork, with a delightful Victorian filigree design, that will go perfectly here, to replace those plastic horrors."

He guided her towards the garden bench, on which she had been doing much of her reading. Sitting down she found that her waist was still slim enough for the long arm of the intrepid Brigadier to have crept remarkably close to her left breast.

"I expect your husband tells you frequently what an attractive and curvaceous woman you are" he said, his moustache twitching in anticipation of an encouraging reply.

"Not very often these days, actually" she said.

"He doesn't, but I do" said a voice from immediately behind the bench. The Brigadier shot to his feet and spluttered.

"Ah! Goodness. Is that the time. I must be off. I`ll make a list of your needs and the prices and pop it through the door later. Good day." And off he strode. Helen and Erik were convulsed in laughter as they headed back into the house for coffee.

As they passed Deirdre she said, "This was in one of Mr Peter`s shirt pockets. I took it out or it will go through the wash. Don`t know if he still needs it?" It was a rail ticket for a journey from Paddington to Swindon on Thursday last.

"He was in Moscow last Thursday" said Helen.

"Maybe not his" said Erik.

Callum`s school had broken up for the Easter holidays. He rushed into the house, ran upstairs, changed into jeans and T shirt, and Helen heard his trainers running down the gravelled driveway towards the harbour. She was getting ready to receive Lucy when the phone rang.

"Hello Mrs Walker, this is Ray Benetti, Rosemary Wood`s brother. Would it be convenient to drive down to meet you this evening? Rosemary is very keen to discuss something of importance with you."

"Is that Rose, my husband Peter`s secretary?"

"Could we arrive at about 7 pm if that`s convenient?"

"OK. Come for dinner. My cook has left a tray of cold meats which we can share."

"We`ll try not to take up too much of your evening. See you at 7pm then. I have your postcode and the SatNav should direct us to you without problems.'

`How odd`, thought Helen. `Perhaps this will unravel some of the mystery around Peter.'

"Hello Mrs Walker" said Rose as she walked through the front door. "This is Ray. He has come to give me Dutch courage this evening."

Helen ushered them inside and wondered why Rose would need extra courage, although she was beginning to have an idea. She had asked Lucy to stay upstairs and play in her bedroom as she was not observing strict term time `lights out` on the first day of the Easter holidays

"Do you want to eat first, and talk later or vice versa?" asked Helen.

"Let`s talk first. I have been psyching myself up to this

the last few days. May I call you Helen? That is how I think of you because Peter calls you by your first name all the time. Helen, Peter and I have been having a relationship for some time. There, I`ve said it. I don`t know whether to apologise or what. It just sort of happened. My husband turned out to be a brute, violent and horrible and I was planning to leave him and come back home. I confided in Peter and I am afraid it led to him falling for me. Once it had got so we both loved each other I felt we couldn`t mislead you, or not tell you."

Helen was recovering from the blunt revelation and beginning to be glad of the full knowledge of the story.

"My God! I knew something was wrong. He has not been affectionate for months, and the decision to return to the UK was sudden and without a strong reason. The company was doing well and the children were happy at school. Have you come to ask me to divorce him or just to get the guilt off your chest?"

"He was supposed to tell you the whole thing and ask for a divorce last weekend, but I gather he said nothing. I can`t go on deceiving you any longer, so I took the step to deal with it myself - with a lot of help and advice from Ray."

Ray then spoke. "Two years ago my wife left me and I have only just found out why and what attracted her away, so I was not keen for Rose to leave you wondering and agonising any longer."

"I hate what you have done to our marriage and I hate what you have done to our children. However, I appreciate your honesty and openness and how difficult it must have been to come this evening. What I really abhor is the part my creep of a husband has played in this and I will deal with him in my own way. Are you sure you want this unfaithful snake in your house? He will do the same to you one day."

"He probably won`t want anything to do with me when he finds out I have been to see you" said Rose.

"I need to think all this mess out and talk with him when he gets home. Leave me your phone number before you go. Do you live in Swindon by any chance?"

Rose nodded.

"We found the rail ticket in his dirty washing."

Rose and Ray declined the offer of dinner but drank a cup of tea before heading back to Wiltshire. Helen remained in her chair trying to come to terms with the news and the events of the last few months. 'What a rat Peter was. She still offered him everything, every ounce of herself and support of all his activities, did everything for the children. He hardly acknowledged Callum`s existence and never took Lucy to any of her little girl fun outings. If he carried on like he had in the last two weekends she wouldn`t miss him at all. He had become too much like his mother! However it seemed wrong to throw away her marriage without a fight.'

Callum arrived back, washed his hands and sat at the table. Helen stood up and went behind his chair to give him the biggest hug she had in years. She then served his dinner with a double portion of almost everything. Lucy had put herself to bed. Helen kissed her lightly on her cheek and prayed that she would have a loving and faithful husband one day. Callum sought her out to return the hug, burping hugely in the middle of it after consuming so much food.

Then Helen put on her best nightie again and looked out of her bedroom window at the stars and the moon peering above the clouds on the horizon. An Astrologer had once told her that things were moving so fast in this Aquarian age that we probably lived two or three lives in one incarnation. Perhaps she was coming to the end of her first life. She looked herself up and down in the long bedroom mirror. 'I really still am pretty good. No wrinkles, shape OK, good legs - maybe my best asset, hair still thick with no grey. Wish I was taller and wish my waist was slimmer, but nobody is perfect at thirty five. Helen climbed into bed and hugged a pillow, thinking that there may never be anyone again sleeping on the other side of the Queen Size bed. When she awoke in the morning the pillow was still wet from her tears and streaked with mascara.

SIX

THEN

"Are you into girls yet?" asked Erik.

Greg had completed his first year at school. They were sitting on the deck of Erik`s boat with their legs hanging over the side.

"Not like the Year 10 boys. I think Sophie Turner has great legs. She said she would kiss me behind the Biology lab as my next birthday present. Trouble is my birthday is in the holidays and I won`t see her until September."

"Next week isn`t it?"

"Yep. First August."

"Why not ask her over and show her your new friend`s boat" said Erik patting the side of the ketch.

"She lives miles away in Dorset."

"There are buses you know" said Erik.

"Has Dad told you anything about the differences between girls and boys and how things change in your teens?"

"No. Mum told me about periods and things, and how girls are grumpy for a week every month."

"Ha. Ha. Right. Depends on the girl. What about sex? Did you cover reproduction in Biology at school?"

"Not yet. Is that the banana and condom lesson they all talk about?"

"That`s the one. Pay attention when it is being taught, but remember it is all about love or else just forget it. I used to think every part of a friendship with a girl was the physical and when you could get it together. It isn`t. Love is the key to a beautiful friendship and the physical is the bonus."

Greg had never heard anyone talking so casually about sex. It was usually a taboo subject with adults, and they gave the impression there was something not very nice about it. Even on television it was usually only hinted at or laughed about.

"This morning, boat tidying. This afternoon, golf. First game in the World Series. Greg versus Erik. I play off three, you are now officially fourteen. I give you eleven shots. In a full competition it would be only four fifths of the difference. What would that be - let me see....."

"Eight" said Greg

"Yes. Eight shots. But we stay with eleven at the moment."

"Where was your last tournament?"

"My last match was played in the London area. Do you think I earn my living as a golfer?"

"Mum does. She thinks you have been earning a lot of money on the golf circuit."

"I am a professional sportsman, but not at golf. Who would possibly be free in July and August and not in daily training? Give me a list of possibles."

"Footballer, Rugby Union, not Cricket, Basketball, not Hockey they are still amateur. My sports teacher was a hockey international. He said there was no money in that sport. Can`t think of any others."

"If I was a golfer, and good enough, I would have played in the Open this month. No, none of those. I played at Wimbledon and am now taking a rest before getting in shape for the U.S. Open in September."

"I didn't think of tennis" said Greg.

"For a top golfer, playing off three is nowhere near good enough. I would have to be in the plus category - at least plus two."

"I think you are the lowest handicap at our Club. There are two playing off four but no one lower than that."

They jumped into the little tender and went to the Harbour Cafe for lunch. Erik explained that around ten per cent of people were gay and enjoyed same-sex relationships and that Oliver was a very outgoing gay man.

"Tell me what you think as we go back."

"Hello Gorgeous" Oliver greeted Erik as they came through the door. "Have you got a spare berth for me on your boat yet?"

"Not yet. Oliver this is my new friend and partner Greg. Greg, meet Outrageous Oliver, who owns and runs this five star eating house."

Oliver genuflected and offered a limp hand to be shaken. Greg responded looking unsure.

"Menu please, Mr Proprietor."

"Yes sir."

They ordered Tuna fish bake and a side salad, apple crumble and ice cream. ` It was good.

"You are an excellent cook, Oliver" said Erik

"Chef please, dear. A cook is just a mediocre kitchen employee. I`ll come and chef for you permanently as soon as you give me the nod."

"I think you should change the boring name of this fine emporium to "Outrageous Oliver's" said Erik.

"Now Boring Bruce has gone, I may well do that. Now Greg that will be twelve fifty five please.

"I only have a fiver at the moment."

"Then you will have to do the washing up, dear."

Erik paid up and then they left. Oliver blew them a kiss. They walked part way back to the harbour before Erik said

"Well?"

"He is strange. Like a woman in a man`s body. His clothes were half men`s and half women`s."

"Oliver is much more outrageous than most gay people. He is very effeminate - like a woman - and doesn`t care what people think. He will always be attracted to other men as partners and regard women only as friends."

"Why is he being like that?"

"At some time during his childhood he will have realised he was more attracted to male friends than female ones. No one really knows why. There are some social scientists that believe we are born to prefer one or the other. It is only recently that most of the people in the Western World accept gay men and women as equals and normal is their own way. Years ago it was difficult for them and it is still a crime in some countries."

"It doesn`t do any harm does it?"

"None at all. And there is a fallacy that gay people are more likely to abuse children, so don`t believe that if you hear it" finished Erik as they climbed back on board the boat.

"Did you win anything at Wimbledon? Asked Greg.

"Lost to Tim Henman in the quarter finals. His forehand was too accurate for me on the day. But Monika and I won the mixed doubles and a nice plate."

"Do you get paid for losing?"

"Yes. Far too much for doing what we love. It is a privilege to play sport for a living and I guess I am one of the lucky ones. With my winnings this year I bought the Porsche and put some aside for the future and for the Children`s home in India."

"Is Monika your girlfriend?"

"She would like to be. Monika is very tall and very blonde and she has nice legs like your Sophie. She is six feet tall but always tells everyone she is five foot twelve inches because she thinks six foot is too much for a female. I play with her because she has very good ground strokes, whereas my advantage is serve and volley. Also because she is Danish and we can swear at each other in our own languages and the crowd don`t understand!" They walked up the straight slope towards the car park and the hilltop Golf Club. There was no queue for the first tee so they drove off immediately with Erik driving the first green and just missing the putt, finishing with a par.

"I will have to start trying if I want to beat you, giving away eleven shots," he said.

Sally decided that worrying about their income and their misfortunes had no future, so she began to do some creative writing. She preferred to write in long hand, rather than type, and this was just as well because her left hand would be useless for a while. She wrote a short story about a pro-fessional golfer living in a remote part of the South West of England, falling in love with the owner of a stable and thereby thwarting the efforts of a best friend to snare him.

Upon hearing of Sally`s accident and realising that the two men in her house were unlikely to know one end of a saucepan from the other, Sally`s mother, Dawn and father Kirk, decided to come to stay and produce the family`s meals until Sally recovered. The prospect was daunting although welcome. Their two Shiatzu dogs would enjoy the garden but would probably yap incessantly at everyone. They arrived in a flurry of hampers and canvas bags and dog bowls and pooper scoopers late one afternoon in the middle of the week.

"Thanks Mum," said Sally. "Chris is spending his time re-living his marine days by watching videos of marine action since 1940 and films involving sea and land conflict. He is drinking too much and getting no exercise."

"You deal with him and I`ll feed you all up as I used to. Just tell them meal times and not to be late."

"I`ll get Greg to give me a chart of the times he will be in for food. He has a new friend who is helping us bring Greg back to our planet. It`s good so far," said Sally.

Greg phoned Sophie and she came over on the bus for his birthday on Erik`s ketch `Nasty`. There were two other boys and two girls from Greg`s year at school. Erik had offered to provide boat and steering skills and lunch if the friends helped crew the ketch. One of the boys, Billy, was already a quite capable sailor and took charge of the job. Greg and Erik coped with the other sails from the cockpit whilst the three girls and Tom lay out on the deck. They slipped out of the little harbour and through the sandbar sailing in a gentle breeze along the coast to Beer before dropping anchor at the eastern end of Branscombe pebble beach and transferring to the beach in pairs by tender. After collecting some drift wood and kindling they built a barbecue and cooked steak, burgers and jacket potatoes to add to the plastic bucket of mixed salad that Erik produced from his trip in the tender. Erik then built an awning on `Nasty` so they could doze in the hot afternoon sun that reflected from the surface of the blazing blue green sea. Arriving back on the incoming tide they were greeted by a `welcome party` of `transport` parents including Sophie`s Dad holding a birthday package that Erik thought closely resembled a box of a dozen golf balls.

"Did you get your birthday kiss?"

"Not yet, but I am still on a promise. Only it wasn't private enough on the boat or the beach, and they were all my school mates and the worst gossips" answered Greg.

"She is nice, your Sophie, worth pursuing I would have thought" said Erik.

"She is rather old. Eight months older than me" offered Greg. "Dad once said to beware of older women."

Erik didn`t answer and cast his thoughts back to some memorable evenings spent with older women in recent years. Greg reached home in the new Porsche to a special birthday tea laid out in the traditional way by Gran, and added to with a chocolate birthday cake and candles. As he blew them out with one puff he volunteered that he was almost the youngest in his class. All the others on the boat had birthdays already. The school year finishes on 31st August.

"What is the boat called, lad ?" asked his Grandpa.

"Nasty."

"What a stupid name" said Gran

"It is after his tennis hero and the player he tried to copy - Ilie Nastase. That was what all the Australians used to call him - usually after he had beaten them."

"I thought Erik was a golfer," said Kirk.

"No Grandpa. He is down here on his break between the two grand slams - Wimbledon and the US Open."

"I think he is telling you a tall story, dear," said his Gran. "I watched Wimbledon throughout the fortnight this year and I don`t remember an Erik." And collecting some dishes she went out to the kitchen.

Greg ran out to the barn with a slice of cake for Erik and went to watch him beginning to paint the feet of a bird half in water.

"It`s going to be a cormorant" said Erik.

"Gran said there weren`t any Erik's playing at Wimbledon this year and she watched the TV all through the fortnight."

"There weren`t" he replied. "One of the downsides of being good at sport is that people are very kind. They want to be with you and ask all about you. If they recognise you they want autographs and pieces of your clothes. So, when

I come down here I change my name and hope I am not recognised. Your Gran will have watched Tim Henman win his quarter final playing a chap wearing a headband called Joel Eriksson. Tell her, if you like, but make her promise to keep our secret."

Gran, of course, promised and then vowed to get his autograph and one of his shirts, if possible, for the Women`s Institute first prize in the raffle.

The next day Erik had offered Greg a chance to go horse riding. He had never been before, but overslept and was late meeting Erik, who passed the time in the barn with his paints trying to get a mix right for the water around the cormorant.

"Sorry Erik. It must have been the sun yesterday. I`ve overslept."

"I have a friend who helps me wherever I go. I have to wake up at odd times of the day and night to catch planes and play matches at peculiar hours, day or evening. With the help of my friend I can catnap and catch up with short bursts of sleep. He is a trainee angel called Wilfred. One of his tasks is to wake me up whenever I tell him the time to do it. So, just before I go to sleep I say `five thirty am please Wilfred` or 'ten pm please Wilfred.' He has not let me down in five years and the extra sleep gives me an advantage over my opponents.

"How does he wake you?"

"I am not sure, except that I always wake up between ten minutes before and the time I asked. I always try to remember to thank him. Try it. Just ask for a new trainee angel to become your own personal alarm clock."

"My friends will think I am mad."

"Don`t tell them. Don`t tell anyone. It is between you and the angel. I have tried to get friends to do it, but they think I am joking and continue their battles with alarm clocks and alarm watches, often waking up two hours early to check that they have remembered to set the alarm."

They zoomed off to Maggie`s stable in the Porsche. Maggie was ready for them, wearing a figure-hugging shirt and jodhpurs and flirting obviously with Erik. Together they showed Greg the basic rules of riding and went through the uses of each piece of tack. After ten minutes Erik and Greg set off along the same track that Erik and Sally had two days ago, walking the horse and pony across the bumpy ground. Greg learnt how to stop and start and turn to left or right. Then they tried a trot along the flat ground at the highest part of the heath.

"Where did Mum fall off?" asked Greg.

"Right down there in that coppice. It was no fault of hers. We discovered the rein actually severed and she only had one part left in her hand. She tried to steer the horse to the left but had to abandon it and hold the mane to stop falling off in the gallop. It was a tree that caught her and broke her shoulder."

"Can I try galloping?"

"Not yet. We`ll advance in stages. You have learned a lot today. Next is to practise the knowledge."

Maggie was awaiting their return, having unpinned her hair and unbuttoned a good depth of shirt.

"Sally says you are a painter, Mr Swedish Man. When are you going to come and paint me?"

"I will paint you with a red haze in front because I think you are a scarlet woman."

"Me? You`ve got quite the wrong idea. I am as pure as the driven snow. Always faithful. Or I would be to you" she whispered out of Greg`s hearing.

"Sally warned me that I was not safe up here. And that your horse box has seen a lot of action in recent years."

"Beastly woman. I thought she was my friend."

Sally tried all afternoon to write. She had decided to write about her life in chapters representing each experience. This afternoon, however, was a blank and she could not get going. Arthur delivered the mail. Amongst the bills was a letter from the Education Committee offering her a term`s work as an English teacher at Sidmouth Comprehensive covering maternity leave. She jumped for joy, setting off the dogs in a frenzy of barking.

"Hurray. Work at last. And time to prepare."

During the next weeks Erik taught Greg to sail, to ride and to improve his golf technique. Greg became an excellent putter, which all golfers know represents forty per cent of the game. His handicap went down to eleven and the best amongst the juniors in the Club. Maggie turned up on the quayside twice in August and invited herself aboard `Nasty`. The second time it was after Greg had left to walk home and she produced a bottle of burgundy.

"Are you still painting, Mr Swedish Man?" she asked.

"Only innocent, unsuspecting subjects, Miss Oversexed Horseperson."

"Well, I am innocent and unsuspecting of how you would want me to pose for my portrait."

"You are about as innocent as Nell Gwynne and, judging by the fact that you are wearing no bra, you probably have already worked out how to pose for your portrait."

Mock shock passed fleetingly across Maggie`s face.

"If I painted you topless it would be so good that the nation would see it in their newspapers and art magazines and your life would change overnight."

"How would it change ?"

"Every garage from here to Plymouth would have a colour copy pinned up in the canteen. No woman in this town, or any other around here, would talk to you. Every randy male would be propositioning you and a visit to the pub would have a crush of bodies around Maggie, each one trying to touch the merchandise."

"Mm Mm. Can you start tonight?"

"Carry on like this and I may have to give you a good spanking and send you home before we open the wine."

"Oooh! Goody" grinned Maggie.

They drank the wine and ate a large bag of crisps made in Dubai that Erik had found lurking in his bag earlier in the day. He drove her home in the Porsche and kissed her goodnight briefly before he opened her car door. Maggie rang Sally with a grossly exaggerated version of events the previous night. Sally believed every word because she knew Maggie`s intentions well, having been at university together. 'So Erik had fallen for Maggie`s charms.' She didn`t know why that made her sad.

Erik invited himself into Kirkhaven House for an afternoon cup of tea the next day and announced that he was leaving to spend a week at the orphanage in South India. Then he was flying to Florida to train hard for his next events. If he left his painting equipment in the barn, please could he return in the late autumn? Erik and Greg put `Nasty` in the hands of George Mercer in the quayside yard and asked him to take her out of the water to store her in his boat park. Erik wrote out a cheque and left it on George`s apology for an office table.

Without a fuss Erik said `Goodbye` and drove off to London.

SEVEN

NOW

"It`s Bronwen, isn`t it?"

"Er. Yes. Do I know you?"

"Andre. Andre Perkins from school."

"Andre, yes, of course. I should have recognised those deep brown eyes. But, you were short and...... fat then. What happened?"

"I do a few triathlons now to keep the weight down and I grew another five inches when I was seventeen."

In between the customers Andre caught up the years and they recalled some funny experiences at school. Bronwen heard that he now owned a small campsite and made an income from letting space to touring caravans as well as having ten static eight berth caravans to let through the summer season. She related her time at college and now nearly eight years as Librarian for Devon County Council. The inevitable marriage enquiry revealed Bronwen as single and Andre divorced for two years with weekend access to his four year old son, Craig. In Bronwyn's break they moved on to Poppy`s to continue the reminiscence. There they met Helen, sitting in the corner in front of a half consumed `Chocolate Disaster.`

"She's having a bad time" said Rachel in a low voice, "Poppy has been talking to her for half an hour. Husband problems."

"Helen, would you like to meet an old classmate of mine? Andre. I haven't seen him since we left school." Bronwen said, as an attempt at cheering Helen up.

"Yes, yes. Hello Andre. Come and sit over here."

Helen rather red-eyed, told him about the Chocolate Disaster and how it came to be and that she must buy him one to celebrate his reunion with Bronwen. They talked, of course, about everything except the cause of Helen's suffering until Andre left. promising to call Bronwen soon and leaving his mobile number. Rachel joined them. "You have been keeping him close to your chest" she said.

"No, not that close. I only met him again a couple of hours ago. He has changed so much from the fat boy who always had highly polished school shoes."

"Well, don't lose his phone number is all I can say."

Helen told them her story. They advised her to retaliate with everything from cutting his clothes into shreds to full castration. She drove the Focus home more depressed than before. On the doormat was a letter from the Brigadier listing all her `needs` and his prices, and a message expecting her to phone him today because he could deliver on his `early closing day` tomorrow. `I'll be lucky` she thought `if I can afford to continue to rent the house when all this fiasco is over, without contemplating new furniture.`

There was a message on the answerphone from Peter. Work was lighter this week and he was coming home tonight instead of waiting until the end of the week. He would arrive around five pm. Helen sat on the bench in the garden and thought aloud about what to do. Erik joined her and suggested they go for a drive. The golf driving range at Lyme Regis Golf Club was away from the Club on the other side of the road. They sat in the car in the car park and

Erik listened to Helen`s outpouring of Rose`s disclosure last night as they watched one golfer hitting balls down the driving range.

"I have decided I don`t want him around here anymore, but I am damned if I will give him a divorce so he can shirk his responsibilities and go and sire children with someone else" she said.

"It is important that these decisions are yours. Listen to advice - Rachel, Poppy, even me, but make a decision that you can live with. They say moving house is the most stressful time, followed by a death in the family, but I think marriage and divorce must be up with the worst," said Erik.

"I want him out of here and away from the children as soon as possible. Also I want to show him how hurt I am that his lover had to be the one to break the news."

"Suggestion. Pack a bag for him and leave it with a note by the front door. Take the children off for an outing in your new car for the afternoon. He may realise what he is missing if you are positive about what is not acceptable to you, and return in a few weeks time.

"How will I know whether he has gone or is waiting back in the house for us?"

"I`ll be working in the barn and I`ll call you when he has left" said Erik.

So Helen left a note beside a suitcase of Peter`s clothes and a few personal things she thought he could not do without. She knew he was returning early because Rose had told him that she had visited Helen and done his dirty work for him.

`Go now. Don't contact me or the children for at least a month. You can come then and I will have boxed up the rest of your belongings to take. I expect you to pay all the bills promptly and I will send them to Rose`s house. Transfer one hundred pounds every week to my bank account for us to live on. You don`t deserve a loving family and you don`t deserve Rose, who

has more courage that you will ever have. Just get lost. `

Her anger was subsiding already and she knew that if she didn`t seal the envelope now, she may go back on her conviction. Fourteen years of marriage was ending too abruptly.

Erik drove Callum back home after putting the first coat of varnish on Viti Levu's sliding cabin roof. Lucy ran in from the garden at the same time and they prepared for lunch.

"I`m taking you to Crealy for lunch and for the whole afternoon. We are collecting Saskia in twenty minutes and we can all have lunch at Crealy Park" announced Helen.

"Wow, Mum, you`re the best," said Lucy.

"Erik is expecting me to do more varnishing this afternoon" said Callum. Erik was still hovering in the doorway and explained that he wanted to get on with a painting this afternoon in the garden and would welcome a quiet time. Callum agreed to go too, anxious to see what Crealy had to offer his age group as he had heard a lot about it at school.

Peter drove up at four thirty and sat in the car for five minutes as if wondering quite what to say when he went indoors. Erik had positioned his easel in the shade of a chestnut tree and was painting the tall cherry tree growing a few yards in front of him. The shade obscured his form from most casual lookers. Peter went inside using his door key. The first thing he saw was the open suitcase, then the envelope with no writing on it. (Helen could not even write his name as she was so keyed up writing the note). He read the note twice, then started to call her name, thinking she was still in the house - then Lucy and last Callum. It was not even one of Deirdre`s days. He sat down and stared out of the window without noticing the view. `Was this what he really wanted?` With his business mind engaged, Peter thought in terms of pluses and minuses. The pluses of the situation included Rose, younger than Helen, more attentive and wholly in love with her `boss`. No more family pressures of finding schools, buying children's clothes,

Saturday afternoons away from the sport, bloody Christmas for the kids, and Callum`s wingeing about leaving Qatar. He perked up. Then he thought of the bad things. What would his friends think? The men would understand when they met and saw Rose. What about Lucy, his little princess? Surely he would still see her a lot. Rose would let her come to stay. Oh God. I will still have their expenses to pay for years and years. At least it was only rented and he wouldn`t lose half the house value. Anyway, Helen would probably marry again soon and he could get a court to change the divorce settlement.

Without the concept of `love` getting the slightest consideration, Peter decided, on balance, he would go. He went upstairs and added a number of things to the quota of clothes going with him, putting them in an Adidas grip. He put both pieces of luggage in the car and then walked around to the Barn and went inside. Erik watched from his painting. Peter seemed to be inside for a long time. Peter looked at the paintings and couldn`t help admiring the detail and bold use of colour. He walked around the barn looking at each in turn on floor and on wall. Even the pile of four canvasses left in the corner didn`t escape his scrutiny. He pulled them out one by one. Until now every painting had been of animals, birds, trees or boats. Here was a considerable work in almost Rembrandt style of a beautiful woman lying naked in the grass beside a stream. The curve and shadow of the female form and the detail of the hands and feet were very accomplished. Perhaps later he could buy some of them and sell them at a good profit to the galleries in London. He doubted the beach bum who did the painting knew their potential.

Erik watched Peter drive slowly away in his BMW and waited before phoning Helen. He went into the Barn through the open door left by Peter. He had wondered if Peter may have decided to vent anger on his work. The only change was that his hidden canvasses had been left on the floor. He carefully secreted the painting of the woman back between two others in the far corner of his new studio. Helen returned, dropping Saskia at her `sweet shop` home on the way back. They had enjoyed a lovely afternoon. Callum had tried all the older rides and games and then spent ages helping the two girls on swings and slides and sharing a train ride. They ate all the `wrong` things, and a lot of curly wurly ice cream with flakes on the top.

The trio arrived home to find that Erik had cooked them a pizza dinner and opened a bottle of Helen`s favourite Chardonnay that was chilled to bring out the maximum flavour. Neither of the children had realised that Peter had been and gone and Helen decided to tell them in the morning, rather than spoil their happy day. She kissed Erik her thanks on his unshaven cheek and he drove back to the harbour to spend his first night on `Viti Levu`.

Erik left much of his stuff in the car. He was an experienced traveller and good at only taking the minimum of belongings around with him, preferring to wash his clothes almost daily to keep the quantity down. Luxuries like aerosol shaving cream and a choice of deodorant were substituted by soap and one roll on. The Yard had lowered the boat into the water with the help of the ancient crane and cradle fixed to the quayside. `Viti Levu` now veered with the tide on the short length of chain secured to a round buoy, which in turn was attached to a lump of concrete at the bottom of the mainstream of the river. The river passed backwards and forwards through the harbour with the changing tides.

One of the peaceful luxuries that Erik now enjoyed was being rocked to sleep in his bunk by the gentle movement of a boat underneath him and the slap and clink of the rigging in the light breeze. There seldom was no breeze on the East Coast of Devon, in contrast to Erik`s younger years spent inland in Sweden, when still days were commonplace. Erik had bought a tiny skiff or wooden rowing boat to get from quayside to boat and back. He collected Callum from the side a little later than usual and noticed he was quiet. They sat together in the well behind the cabin door.

"Dad`s left home" Callum said. "He buggered off yesterday. Mum just told us."

"You are now the head of the family."

"Yeah. Great. Just like in the Gulf. When the man dies, the eldest son takes over. Even if he is only a kid."

"Mum will be looking to you to be strong for her and for Lucy, but Dad will still have to pay for most things. That is the law in England."

"Well, so he should. He took us away from our friends just so he could continue bonking his secretary."

"He may have fallen in love with her and realised he had fallen out of love with your Mother."

"Dad is only in love with himself and couldn`t care about anyone else."

"Will you miss him ?"

"No. I hope I never see him again. If I do I will get a door key and scratch it all around his car."

"You may feel different in a few weeks. But, for now, being extra kind to Mum will make life better for her. I know you are big enough to do that" said Erik, moving forward to look up the mast.

"I think it is time we sea tested this fine craft and, to do that, we need to check all the rigging today and stretch out the sails to look for tears or weak spots."

They worked all morning and, with a couple of new cleats and one new sheet for the jib were ready to go for a careful run along the Seaton seafront. Before setting off, however, Erik opened a half bottle of sparkling wine and poured a glass for each of them. He raised his glass and clinked it together with Callum's.

"To Viti Levu. May she always be a safe and happy ship?"

They drank and Callum spat his over the side. "Ugh. It`s horrible."

"I`m glad we didn`t waste expensive champagne then" said Erik.

A Ford Focus drove into the harbour car park and Helen and Lucy climbed out and waved. Erik cupped his hands and called as though they were a loudspeaker.

"Come and join us for our first trial sail along the seafront."

"I`m not dressed for sailing."

"Come anyway. We will do all the work."

Erik collected them from the quayside and noticed a large red cool box coming too."

"I`ve brought a kind of lunch" said Helen.

"Then you are doubly welcome" said the rower. They set the jib and slowly steered out of the harbour using the wind that blew straight down the river valley. Callum beetled up and down the deck setting the jib sheets in their clews and heaving the mainsail up to the top of the mast.

"Duck your head, Mum, when we change tack so the boom can pass without hitting you" he called.

"He is the Bosun and does all the hard sail work" said Erik. "I just sit here beside you, steer and give orders."

Helen noticed that he still hadn`t shaved and also that he had an attractive lop-sided grin.

`I`ll bet he has been really naughty in his youth. I`ve read some tales of `footballers` wives` she thought. They sailed leisurely along the sea front and exchanged waves with some of the families braving the spring weather to sit on the pebbles and enjoy that `very British` pastime of looking out to sea. On instructions from the stern, Callum dropped anchor fifty yards off the Chine at the western end of Seaton beach. Helen opened the cool box to reveal cans of iced tea and a chicken salad followed by honey flapjacks that she had made early in the morning, whilst calculating how to break the news to Callum and Lucy. As Helen bit into her chicken leg Lucy said to Erik very earnestly:

"Daddy`s run away with another lady and so you will have to help arrange my birthday party."

"Of course I must, Lucy. When is it to be?" replied Erik.

"My birthday is on the fourteenth but that is a Thursday, so how about the sixteenth on the Saturday?"

"Sounds sensible. How many people shall we invite?"

"You and Mummy. Not Daddy. Callum because he took me on the big slide yesterday and all my class at school."

"How many in the class?" asked Erik?

"Twelve girls and sixteen boys" said Lucy nonchalantly. Helen caught Erik`s eye and shrugged. He winked back at her.

Back in the harbour they took off the life jackets that Erik had insisted they wear throughout the journey.

"That was a lovely afternoon. Thanks" said Helen.

"Thanks, Uncle Erik. Do you want to come back and make birthday plans now?" added Lucy.

"Perhaps tomorrow, darling" said Helen. "Uncle Erik will be tired after the long day on the boat."

Erik looked sideways at Helen and offered to follow later with Callum after they had put the boat to bed. The Ford Focus moved away along the road beside the river towards Kirkhaven House.

Callum, coiling a rope then casually said "They were at it in Qatar too, you know." Erik looked at him across the deck.

"Dad and Rose. I caught them at the Compound Christmas Party, kissing behind a big bougainvillea bush! They didn`t see me. I was looking over a wall, searching for next door`s cat, which had been spooked by the loud music. That`s why I wasn`t too friendly with Dad and tried to spite him by messing up at school when we got here."

On the following morning Henrietta`s mother phoned and asked whether Lucy could go over and play short tennis with a group of girls in the Sports Centre at Ottery St Mary. She would look after the transport as it was her idea. Helen was conscious that her car had brought Lucy home every day from school and that she had not yet played a part in taking Etta (as Lucy called her) anywhere.

"It`s OK. We drive past your house on the way home so it is no hardship" said Etta`s mum.

"Lucy only played for the first time today but the coach of their girl`s group says she thinks I have a natural racket player in the family" Helen told Erik as she cooked him a meal later that evening.

"Let me take her to the game next time" said Erik. "You come too and we`ll see how good her hand/eye co-ordination is."

"Do you know anything about tennis?" asked Helen.

"A little. If you play one sport a lot you either play some of the others or are interested in the finer points of technique."

Two days later they took Lucy in the Porsche and collected Etta en route to the Ottery Sports Centre. They drove along an almost straight road from the top of Branscombe to the cross roads above Ottery St Mary. Erik told Helen that he had a theory that the Romans built the road to transport goods from his little harbour to their garrison at Exeter. He explained that there was a historical theory that once there was a two hundred yard wharf alongside the harbour. It was no co-incidence that the Fosse Way began there and followed an almost straight route across the country as far as Lincoln. Helen committed the cardinal sin of yawning right in the middle of his monologue.

"OK, OK. We`ll concentrate on the girls and their tennis," he said.

"Sorry, sorry, I really am. It`s just that we had the most boring history teacher at school."

They peeled out of the Porsche like dried figs in one of

those packets you only see at Christmas and headed into the Sports Hall. The Coach greeted them and was already changed in tennis gear. She constantly was looking past Helen at Erik and, as Helen moved towards the changing room with the girls she came towards him. She opened her mouth to speak, and Erik playfully put his hands around her throat.

"Say one word and I`ll throttle you" he said.

"They think I am a footballer." She grinned and stayed quiet.

"Can I tell my friends later?"

"Maybe a trusted few." He gave her his lopsided smile and they walked into the Sports Hall.

"Are you still playing?" she asked.

"Just occasionally in the senior tournaments. When they remember to ask me," he replied.

"I got your sweatband about fifteen years ago when you threw it into the crowd at Queens. It's still in my bedroom looped around my bedside lamp!"

"God, how revolting! I hope you washed it first."

She organised the little girls in pairs for the short tennis games. With his practised eye Erik could see that Lucy moved well and with exceptional anticipation. Her co-ordination was good considering this was probably only the second time she had tried to hit a ball with an implement as an extension of her arm. He had not expected her to be left-handed as her right hand was dominant in everything else, but was an advocate of the `left-hander advantage` often discussed in tennis circles. He respected the coach for not having forced her to play right-handed and leaving the decision to Lucy.

Helen had promised to meet Poppy in her cafe the next morning and it gave her the opportunity to thank the vicar for her calm guidance through the Peter crisis. Poppy was single but had an experience of assisting with domestic problems that her parishioners and friends had become involved in over several years.

"Would you get married if you met the right man, or are you deliberately celibate?" asked Helen.

"I would be delighted to be married one day, but the trouble is men tend to shy away from the dog collar. They think they are in danger of losing their souls as well as their trousers. I did think I had it made at Durham University. He and I both were studying theology. But he went off to Borneo or Papua New Guinea to convert the unsuspecting and we lost contact."

"Do many people come to your services?"

"Not so many these days. All sorts of reasons. Other activities on Sundays, sport and family commitments. No pressure now from the community if you are not seen at church. Also we have not been very good at selling our spiritual truths in recent years or for setting a good example by our own behaviour. A few child molesters and the ongoing fiasco over women bishops has not attracted new followers. Our role is changing. We care for the devout as before, but we have a new role as casual counsellors to everyone needing impartial advice."

"And as chocolatiers to chocoholics everywhere." added Helen

"Absolutely. Another coffee ?"

The letting agent had written to Peter and Helen pointing out that the rent for April had not yet been paid, and reminding them of the terms of the lease in a pleasant but slightly threatening letter. Helen put the letter back in its envelope and re-addressed it to Peter in Swindon. As she wrote Rose`s address she wondered if he still wore his socks in bed! She had never got him to change this habit, which he blamed on years of walking on cold dormitory floors at Public School. She remembered the first time her foot had come into contact with a sock. She shot out of bed thinking that an animal had somehow crept under the covers. Poor Rose may still have these horrors to come to terms with. What would they do if he flatly refused to pay the bills? They would be evicted and homeless before she persuaded a Court to grant her the rights of an estranged wife. Perhaps she should try to get a job now, before it was too late. But what could she do ? Since leaving university she had worked in a bank for eighteen months before following Peter to the Gulf, where she had been an expat wife and mother with more than a normal share of assistance from migrant workers who needed domestic jobs. Maybe a local bank needed a cashier with a 2/2 in Economics.

EIGHT

NOW

Helen sat on her garden bench and read more of Sally Shaunessy's book to take her mind off the mounting problem of unpaid bills. Sally had met her old University companion Maggie and together they had enjoyed a wild time at Bath. They stayed up often into the early hours debating topics that could change and improve the world, drunk too much and loved too much. They together had worked through nights to complete the essays and theses needed to guarantee a pass in psychology. Both finished with upper second class honours degrees, though Sally believed that Maggie`s attraction to a bearded and ferocious lecturer could have influenced the decision to lift Maggie above her predicted `Desmond` as they called a two/two in those days.

Helen reflected on her own three years at Bournemouth studying Economics. She was going to be an Investment Manager in the City and marry the CEO of a successful company, whose launch she would organise as a public quotation on the Stock Exchange. Moving to the Gulf was a long way outside her dream at that time. Passing with a lower second degree precluded any of her City applications for jobs moving to interview. Too much time spending boyfriends` grants in the Students` Bar and sunbathing on the Bournemouth beaches had not helped her cause.

Erik had left the area now and the children were back at school having moved up a class. Erik was involved with some charity in India and had gone there for a few weeks. He asked if he could leave his paintings and return towards the end of the year. Having lifted Callum and made him a useful sailor during the Spring and encouraged Lucy with her short tennis, Helen would be pleased to have him back - if she was still there and the landlord had not decided she was a dodgy tenant.

"Mummy, why is there a lid on our bidet?" asked Lucy.

"I really don`t know, darling."

"Etta says that only posh houses have bidets and they are for washing your pants in if you have an accident."

"We don`t always have bidets in houses in England, but on the Continent, they are in every bathroom. They are meant for washing your bottom."

"Oh! I use toilet paper" said Lucy indignantly.

"If you want to keep very clean, you can wash yourself as well. They use water too in Asia and it is much cleaner than toilet paper."

Helen realised she had now sentenced the bathroom to a Lucy flood as she tried to master the use of a bidet. Since then Lucy had gone to school. Helen decided to see what Erik had left in his studio. She took the Barn key from its hook in the front porch and walked around to the Studio door.

Inside the Barn was a typically tidy corner with folded easel and stools. Palettes and paints were either boxed or bagged up and piled neatly on his small table. Erik was very tidy for a man. Helen reckoned it must be from years of travelling around with his football team. As she looked around the wall, admiring his quality of art she wondered whether, at forty, he would go into management. She knew many players retired from the game and tried to be successful managers. It was precarious because, every week, one seemed to get the sack and all the attendant media coverage, but it probably paid well.

She realised that it would have been courteous to have asked Erik who he had played for. She thought it would have been one of the lower league teams, not the beloved Tottenham Hotspur of Peter`s. What a stupid name! Stupid man! If he doesn`t pay the rent this week, I am going to call Rose. At least he had transferred money every week to enable them to buy the necessary daily foodstuffs and cleaning materials.

"Mum. I`m not sure Erik was a footballer" said Callum after Helen had enquired about Erik`s team. "He doesn`t say and I was talking to Mr Johnson, our P.E. teacher, and he couldn`t think of an Erik who had played in recent years for a top team in England or Scotland. He thought he could be a Rugby player or even Squash or Tennis, but couldn`t remember an Erik in those either."

"What a delicious mystery' said Helen.

"It`s a mystery definitely, but not delicious. We only have to ask him, I suppose. But now he is in India I think with the orphanage that he helped build years ago," replied Callum.

Helen set off early the next morning to top up a few things in the fridge because Deirdre would be scolding her otherwise on Thursday. She collected a mixed bag of food at Spar and went next door into `Poppy Chocolatiere`. The Exeter bus was parked outside with two passengers already waiting for the time to tick over to ten o`clock.

Keith was seated in his usual place beside Rachel`s counter.

".......and it`s only two pounds above minimum wage after all the efforts of the Union" he was saying.

"However will you get by?" said Rachel looking skywards as Helen began to greet her.

"Just a coffee please Rachel. I am trying to keep a better figure by eating sensibly" said Helen.

"Cor. I wish I could keep a figure like yours" said Keith. "The one I keep at home looks like one of these bouncy castles the kids play on. And she eats like someone who has been stranded in the jungle for weeks."

"Off you go, Keith. Look, it`s ten o`clock. The church clock is ringing" said Rachel.

As Keith left, in came Poppy looking rather red in the face.

"Those damn choirboys. They have been sticking their used chewing gum under the shelf in the choir pew. Wait till I see the little sods at practice on Thursday evening!"

"I didn`t think vicars swore" said Helen.

"Oh How! We invented swearing" Poppy replied. "Most of the best swear words are good bible blasphemy."

"Actually, I have heard a member of the cloth using `oaths` before" added Helen. "I worked in a bank once and they send me to Gibraltar for the summer, to boost their staff in the busy time of the year. On the very first day, I was waiting at my cashier`s counter as the junior opened the doors to the public. No one seemed to come in for five minutes to this long line of eight cashier desks. Suddenly I heard a fist beating on the wooden counter at the top end of the room and a broad Irish accent saying:

"C`mon. C`mon. Let`s have a bit of bloody service around here!" Everyone laughed because it was the Irish priest from the big Catholic Church carrying the collection from Sunday`s services. They told me later at our coffee break that one of the other clerks had been given several `Hail Marys` and a couple of `Lords` Prayers` at Confession for admitting swearing to the same priest" Helen went on.

"I need your help with two dilemmas. You don`t mind hearing all my most private information do you?"

"We are souls of discretion" said Poppy.

"Well, discreet about who we tell, at least" added Rachel.

"First I need you to tell me why there is a lid on our bidet" said Helen.

"Ooh! She has a bidet. How very upper class!" said Rachel.

There was a pause; sipping of coffee and scratching of heads.

"They didn`t tell us the answer to this in theological school" said Poppy.

"Don`t know. Next question?"

"My husband is not paying the rent. Do I shout at him? Plead with his lover or begin Court proceedings ?"

"They both chorused, "Plead with his lover."

"She will be feeling guilty just about now, and will not want to jeopardise a divorce by Peter not being reasonable to you and the kids," said Poppy in her `counsellor` voice.

"Hello Rose. I found your number in the book" said Helen that evening after more advice from her friends.

"Is Peter there?"

"No. Still at work."

"Good. It`s you I wanted to talk to. Rose, you are keen to marry him if I agree to a divorce, aren`t you?"

"Yes. Yes."

"I am still making up my mind and obviously one of my considerations has to be the security of the children."

"Of course."

"I don`t know if he has told you, but the rent has not been paid on our house for two months and the latest electricity bill was red?"

"I didn`t know. He told me he transfers money to you every week."

"That is just the amount for food and day to day living" Helen went on.

"Anyway, I just wanted to confirm your intentions towards him before I make any long term decisions."

`I hope that works, girls` she thought after pressing the red button on her mobile.

When the children has gone to sleep, Helen took up the book again and read about Sally meeting this super-fit Marine Commando who had won a prize at the Commando Training Centre at Lympstone when awarded the green beret. During the next years he had been in the forefront of the action in which British Forces had been involved. His parents had advised Sally not to marry their son because his job was too dangerous and she could find herself becoming a widow after only a short marriage. Love won the day and they were married with Sally delivering Greg only eleven months later in the August.

Postman Arthur delivered a beautiful purple orchid the next morning with Helen answering the door at eight am fully dressed and preparing for Deirdre.

"You`re up early this morning, Mrs Walker" said Arthur.

"Did you expect to catch me in my nightie?"

Arthur`s face closely matched his red postbag.

"I.....I brought this up for the Parcel Force man, because he didn`t know where Kirkhaven House was.'

"Thanks. I don`t know who could have sent it."

"It was probably that curly blond chap who was here twenty years ago. `Spect he is the only one that could afford them flowers. Him and his sports car. Huh!"

Helen missed the reference to Erik's previous visit.

It was indeed Erik. The message said:

`Keep smiling and avoid all gropers and chocolate disasters` Erik.

Erik was actually at Flushing Meadow on the Eastern Seaboard of the United States watching Maria Sharapova play Kim Clijsters in the semi-final of the U.S. Open. He had been spending a contented fortnight meeting up with old friends and adversaries and making a daily half-hour summary video for Swedish Television. That morning he had read an e mail from his letting agent in Sidmouth telling him that his tenant at Kirkhaven House had now defaulted on two months' rent and asking whether they should give the Walkers a month`s notice to leave the premises. He had replied.

`No. Definitely no. Allow more time to pay. Domestic changes in process. Keep me advised.`

At the same time he emailed Callum to ask him to get George Mercer from Mercer`s Yard to take Viti Levu out of the water and put her back on blocks in the car park, which they used as a boat yard in the winter months. George was used to getting adult requests from or through Callum and knew Erik would have been consulted and would always pay.

"After this weekend though, please George" said Callum. I want to tidy up the cabin and dry out the sails properly before we put her away for the winter." George wished that his boy was as confident as Callum.

Helen was feeling good today. She had checked the Electricity Account on line and found the outstanding balance had been paid. A phone call to the letting agent revealed that one of the two outstanding month`s rental had also been settled. She found herself daydreaming in the playground of Lucy`s school. Lucy had run off with her friends a few minutes ago and Helen had been enjoying watching the small children arriving full of enthusiasm for the school day. She had to look up to reply to the greeting from a tall man standing beside her, he being around six foot two or three inches tall and she being a petite five foot four inches.

"Hello. It`s Helen I think?"

Helen nodded, vaguely recognising the man.

"George Lee. I own the farm next door to your home. I have been meaning to introduce myself before but the school run always seems to be a rush."

They shook hands and described their own children who were attending the little school. George had both his still at the primary level. His farm was `organic` and he admitted to blatantly jumping on the organic bandwagon after his earlier dairying business ceased to make any profit. The supermarkets had driven milk prices so low that they had lived only on EU subsidies for the final two years.

"It`s been hard work but we are just beginning to see the light at the end of the tunnel. Last week I signed a broccoli contract with Waitrose to supply their shops in Devon and Dorset. This could be our breakthrough."

Helen asked George back for coffee at Kirkhaven House but he had a meeting to attend later that morning. However he said he would call in for a cup of tea on the way back from Axminster. True to his word he turned up at four thirty in his Range Rover.

"I haven`t seen your husband`s car around recently" said George. "Is he working away somewhere?"

"Yes. Working away and moved away. Into the arms of his secretary" answered Helen from the kettle on the work surface.

"Good riddance too" added a voice from the Dining Room. "Leaving this poor girl to look after the kids, pay the bills and try to pretend everything was still all right."

"Thank you, Deirdre" said Helen. "Deirdre sticks up for me here and in the village" she added.

George apologised for having brought up a painful subject and vowed to mind his own business in future.

"You weren`t to know, so don`t feel bad" said Helen.

He then went on to explain his own circumstances. George's wife couldn`t cope with the long farming day and no holiday, and had gone back to North Somerset to live with her sister. Neither had wanted to be without the boys and the Court had asked each of them what he himself wanted. They both had said they wanted to stay with George. However, an Order was only made on condition George engaged a full-time housekeeper who lived on the premises and was able to be on hand for Luke and Robin when their Dad was out on the farm. With difficulty George had found Mary Yvonne to do the job, after trying modern day nannies and even an au pair from Italy. The boys liked Mary Yvonne who came from Torquay and had started life in Paris as Marivonne, daughter of the owners of a successful `Boulangerie.

"She`s a right little gold digger", the voice came again from out of sight.

"The locals don`t like her much" said George.

"She comes into Spar and demands the personal attention of young Matthew, asking him to order all they fancy French things that he`s never heard of.

Poor kid was nearly in tears other day trying to serve her and normal customers" said the voice.

"Sorry Deirdre. Is Matthew your son?" asked George.

"Ha, ha, ha. No. He isn`t mine, but I knows his mother and she doesn`t rate Mary Whatsername at all."

George began to speak more quietly.

"My problem now is that Mary Yonne has designs on me and I am having to play a careful game. I don`t want to lead her on, but I am conscious of the boys needing a mother figure and she is the most stable of the ones we have tried."

The dusting next door seemed to be moving closer to the kitchen where he and Helen were sitting.

"What a problem I have given myself. First I marry someone who did not know much about life on a farm. Then I try to be a single father. Now I am in danger of compromising everybody and everything."

"I appreciate you confiding in me. It will go no further" Helen said whilst making her head nod towards the slowly opening door to the dining room.

"Would you and Lucy like to come and see what we do in your next door fields one day? I have a trailer kitted out for school visits so the children can have a ride behind a tractor and a tour of the farm."

"Most definitely. I think Lucy and Luke are in the same class, so they will know each other already" replied Helen.

When she saw who was sitting in `Poppy Chocolatiere` Bronwen realised she had made a mistake and should have waited until later. She had dressed in her most flattering outfit which made her look taller than her five foot five inches and emphasised her quite ample curves. This was aimed at Andre, who had not yet arrived, but it was also able to instantly stimulate the imagination of Brigadier Roper, who was well into a Poppy`s Continental Breakfast. The Brigadier stood up and with his mouth full invited her to join him.

"Thank you Brigadier. I am waiting for a friend to join me for coffee."

"Not a male friend? You are not being unfaithful to me are you?"

Rachel caught her glance from behind the shop counter and ducked behind the cake display to avoid the Brigadier seeing the half-smile, half look of horror on her face.

"You are looking good today. Spilling over with rav-ishability" he continued, spitting pieces of croissant in two different directions at the same time. Rachel disappeared again behind the cakes making noises that could have been mistaken for a food processor.

"I was watching one of those French films last evening and the actress looked rather like you. She was particularly well endowed and offering favours all around the village.

`Thanks a bunch` thought Bronwen.

He rumbled on

"Actually I like Elizabeth Taylor - especially in Cleopatra when she was bathing in ass` s milk."

"Why on earth was she bathing in milk?" asked Bronwen, who was too young to have seen the film.

"It`s good for the complexion, dear" said Rachel and if it didn`t attract Anthony she could still have a cup of tea!" Rachel went out of sight again, laughing at her own remark as Andre burst into the shop.

"Sorry I`m late. The officials from the Caravan Club turned up unannounced, wanting to check my touring pitches."

"Ah. So this is your latest beau is it ? No wonder you tarted yourself up this morning" came the latest uttering from the corner. The Brigadier left his seat, paid for his food and headed across the road to open his antique shop.

"Who was that obnoxious character?" asked Andre. "There was no need to embarrass you in front of me. Anyway, you always look good these days, especially this morning."

"Thank you, kind gentleman" said Bronwen.

Rachel left them alone, only making drinks and serving the cakes they ordered. She hoped this would be a winning friendship for Bronwen. `Latest beau, indeed. ` It was her first one for quite a long time.

Whilst shopping in Sidmouth, Helen looked into the letting agent handling Kirkhaven House. She asked whether a standing order or direct debit had been set up to pay the rent into their `Clients Account`. The young man replied in the negative, but let slip that the owner had given instructions not to hassle the tenants or to take steps to evict them. Helen drove home with the birthday present she had bought for Lucy to give Saskia. She was puzzled by the decision of the absent landlord and wondered if it could be George.

NINE

THEN

Sally had been teaching English at Sidmouth Comprehensive for a month and loving it. The journey was about
twenty five minutes from her home and pleasant. The time
was long enough for her to rehearse her lesson plans for
the day but not too long to be a chore. The Octavia was
still a good friend having clocked up over one hundred and
forty thousand miles in its life. Sally`s salary was good as a
`supply teacher` but still the domestic finances seemed to be
going backwards. She budgeted carefully every month, but
something was working against her. Another evening spent
pouring over bills and housekeeping calculations convinced
Sally that it must be Chris` drinking which was draining the
funds. She tried to persuade him to stop drinking so much.
It was not spirit but barley wine which was his addiction.
Spar was now delivering a box of twenty four bottles with
alarming frequency. She was reluctant to be too heavy with
him because of the psychological burden he was carrying
and that the lump sum compensation from the Government
had been paid for him, for his injuries. However, she was also
determined he should realise that this was all the security

the three of them had and, at least some should be retained for any 'further education' that Greg was to pursue.

At half term, at the end of October, the crisis reached decision time. Chris felt he needed the prop of his drink and his reminiscing videos. Without worrying Greg, who was not only now attending school, but actually studying in advance of his lessons from his bedroom at home, Sally decided to place the house on the market and for them to move into something smaller and more financially manageable. She approached three estate agents during the week's break who valued Kirkhaven House, barn and unused cottage at similar amounts. She chose the one offering the lowest fee to market the property.

Advice from Oliver did not encourage her. He admitted he knew nothing about property; his previous job had been as a perfumier in mid-Wales, and Bruce had dealt with 'all that'. During the summer he had conducted an acrimonious and emotionally draining legal battle with Bruce over ownership of the cafe. Bruce seemed content now to remain in Bournemouth and investigate the future prospects of several temporary partners there.

"He's going through the change, ducky" said Oliver to Sally one half-term morning as she relaxed at his cafe window table. "He's changing from a loyal, jealous partner into a randy sod." Anyway, I now have full ownership of this magnificent eating house and a vast mortgage as a gift from my wayward ex-lover."

Sally had noticed the new signs 'Outrageous Oliver's' hanging sideways above the pavement and swinging in the breeze.

"It will attract the confident and amusing customers and the rest will walk past and visit lesser establishments," he said. "Look, I will let you sell your house but you are not allowed to move further away than Sidmouth or Lyme, dear."

"Thanks Oliver. I hope I am doing the best thing for Chris and Greg."

"Where is your Knight in shining armour? It`s about time he rode up on his trusty white Porsche. He will be gutted if you sell his barn, although you may get a better offer if you include the paintings."

When she returned to the house Chris was still asleep. The rain had stopped during the night and Greg was out in the garden with a five inch wedge, practising pitching and chipping on to the temporary putting green he had made in one corner around the cherry tree.

It was almost as though Oliver`s thought had been transported electronically across the ether because the very next day an e mail came from Erik in Florida asking whether he could return in two weeks for a month or so and resume painting. Also, as `Nasty` was in mothballs for the winter, please could he look at the possibility of staying in her worker`s cottage. He would pay rent and make an attempt at re-furbishing the little place.

Sally replied that she had been forced to sell Kirkhaven and that their next months were uncertain. In fact it was being marketed to a portfolio of retained purchasers that very day. The agent claimed that he had eighty or more contacts up country that were waiting to move or retire to East Devon when the perfect property became available. Later that day she received a phone call to say that a cash buyer had offered the full price and insisted upon first consideration whilst they investigated his status as a purchaser. The caller added that she should not get too confident at this stage. It was a poor time of year to be selling and there were many rogue purchasers who turned out to have no credibility. They were especially dubious because this person had not yet viewed the property.

"If he turns out to be genuine, Mrs Shaunessy, the chances are that he will need planning permission to do something dramatic, or he will commission a survey, point out a dozen defects and offer a considerably reduced price.

We shall continue to contact other potential buyers in the usual way."

From a height of ecstasy, Sally came down to reality by the time they finished the conversation. She went to tell Chris, who was blaming himself for putting them into the position of having to sell at all.

Sally emailed Erik again and explained they had already received an offer that, if genuine, would be acceptable. Therefore she felt it would be better if Erik found some accommodation elsewhere in the area. He must continue to paint in the barn studio for the period of this visit because it would be after Christmas before they would be able to move. She suggested that, because his relationship was going so well with Maggie, he should ask her if he could stay in one of her spare rooms at the Stables.

Greg kept himself in golf balls by searching all the hedge-rows and places around the course where players were most likely to hit bad shots. Fifty yards from the tee on either side of the fairway were good places, especially if there was a spread of vegetation. Over the backs of greens was often a curtain of grass and trees. That was another likely area. There was no water on his course, which would have been another `lost ball` magnet. He kept his birthday present from Sophie`s parents for competitions, and had used only four of the dozen balls from the box so far. Sally watched him chipping ball after ball towards the trunk of the cherry tree. She was immensely proud of the way he had come through the challenges of the last year. Chris and Sally had intended having at least two children. They had planned to wait for some time after Greg to add to the family but the trauma of Chris` injuries had curtailed his ability to help Sally conceive a second time. She didn`t know whether Greg's friendship with Sophie was still ongoing because

Greg seldom discussed his personal feelings with anyone.

Sally`s collarbone had healed nicely leaving only a small lump where the repair had calcified. By the Friday of the holiday week she fancied treating herself to a gentle hack up at Maggie`s stable yard. She needed to test her nerve riding again after the accident, and only partly admitted that she intended to enquire about Erik at the same time. Maggie lent her the same passive mare which she had ridden earlier. As a long-standing friend Maggie always only charged Sally half the usual fee. There were no other clients booked that day so later Maggie asked her inside and they caught up on what had been happening since the summer. Sally related a difficult day in class when one of the ninth year girls had an epileptic fit. It was the girl`s first and a shock for her and the class. Sally had managed to prevent her damaging herself by quickly pushing desks and chairs out of the way. Since then she has been on a daily tablet and seems fine. It was the ideal opportunity to explain to the class about epilepsy and its causes, and what to do if they came across someone experiencing a fit. She had always used her teaching as a vehicle to help children with their understanding of life skills and, in her time, had covered everything from sex to mortgages. Even though it meant more intense English for the next lesson to catch up, she thought it part of a teacher`s duty. Only teachers and parents have the unique opportunity to inform face to face.

Maggie told how well the stables were going. She was caring for five privately owned horses and ponies as well as her own. The Pony Club took up most of Saturdays and that too was thriving. One of her old boyfriends was being a pest, driving up from Bodmin on evenings and weekends, and wanting more oats than her black stallion in the field opposite.

"What about Erik? Is that relationship still steamy hot?" Sally asked in some trepidation of the reply.

"Oh yes. Pretty good. He will be back soon searching me out for more of the same. You know what Swedes are like. They keep warm in the winter with vigorous physical activity whilst the snow plies up outside. It`s all steamy saunas and beating with twigs over there."

"I have never been out with a Scandinavian" said Sally. "I have missed these finer points of debauchery in my innocent life."

"You. Innocent? I remember when you had two guys going at the same time and kept your room locked in Hall because you didn`t want one to come in while you were bonking the other. If I recall one was a medical student and Juan was studying languages. You had a chart inside your wardrobe door of their lectures so that your own private seminars with them didn`t clash."

"Mmmm. All right, but that was before Chris made an honest woman of me.

Mags, we are having to sell the house. Downsizing is what they call it. I call it being skint."

"Don't move out of the area, Sal. Stay local."

"We will if we can. We`ve had a good offer on Kirkhaven already so next is to start looking for something much cheaper. Erik emailed to say he is coming back soon. I expect you know the date. Can you lodge him here for a month ? He wanted our cottage but there is no point in spending out to do it up only to sell it for the same as now."

"You bet I can. The spare rooms are full of tack and office files but, if he doesn't like the clutter, I`ll try to find a space in my bed" said Maggie.

"That is if Bodmin is not already there!"

"You are a very bad woman, Maggie Soames, and a corrupting influence on a law-abiding and God-fearing community. You should be ashamed of yourself. Thanks for the tea and the ride. I feel quite happy back in the saddle. Bye."

Once Sally`s collar bone had healed she had packed her

parents and their dogs back to Gloucester, where she knew they were missing their twice weekly bridge four and Dawn`s involvement with the next production of the Operatic Society. She had a small part in HMS Pinafore and had loved her singing since being a little girl between the World Wars. They left in the same flustered flurry in which they had arrived and invited Sally, Chris and Greg for a family Christmas and a week at their home of forty years. Sally managed to keep her money problems to herself and Kirk`s enjoyment of a glass of Barley wine shielded Chris` developing addiction. No hint had been given of a likely move.

The phone rang. The estate agent wanted two appointments to show the house to interested buyers. They both have accepted offers on their homes in the Home Counties, although one has a long chain behind him. Sally thought it made him sound like a St Bernard, and when he arrived half expected there to be a flask of brandy in his hand. Both parties showed interest and the second one wanted to demolish the cottage and build a summer house to maximise the sea view. Greg had been home, changed and gone down to the harbour whilst the agent was giving the second visitors the full sales talk. Sally was not sure how much of this was to impress her and how much the buyers, who didn`t seem to be listening a great deal. The clocks were due to go back an hour that night and Greg had decided to make the best of the last light evening of the summer. He had borrowed a dinghy together with an Evinrude outboard from George Mercer and, on an unusually still sea, had gone outside the harbour entrance spinning for mackerel. It was late in the season but he struck lucky and picked up a shoal chasing whitebait in towards the deep water just off Seaton beach. He caught eleven using the tail of one of the first on a couple of hooks and his two spinners on the others.

As he handed the dinghy back to George with a carrying string of four mackerel for his family`s dinner he saw Oliver walking his wire-haired dachshund Giles, (named because he looked remarkably like the Seaton butcher!) and watching him come ashore. Greg passed Oliver as he rode his bike towards home and stopped to give him two for his tea.

"What an unexpected treat. Thank you, young man." Sometimes Oliver wished he could have had children. One would be just as nice as Greg, he was convinced.

Greg arrived home with five fresh fish for their evening meal just when Sally`s inspiration had deserted her. She gave her son a big lingering hug. He was at the age when he didn`t quite know how to respond and laid two hands and a good many mackerel scales on the back of her blouse.

That evening Sally began writing again. She found it a relaxation as if she was a water cylinder that filled up with ideas and then had to have its tap opened to release some of its contents and prevent an overflow. They always said in literary magazines for beginners that you may have only one story inside you and that is your own life story. Sally abandoned her attempts to write short, saleable tales and began to write her own experiences. She adapted the format with which she was familiar, and wrote each event or period of time as a `short story` chapter. Her childhood completed Sally moved into her University time at Bath and her meeting the popular Maggie. She rapidly discovered why Maggie was so popular, rarely finding her in her own bedroom at breakfast time! They both were studying `psychology` and it was only right that each needed a partner to study. Both were pretty girls and most of their physical assets were the acceptable and desirable shape and size. Their leisure time was spent with members of the Rugby Club and that often over-flowed into parties and events together with the well-established Bath Rugby Club at their ground `The Rec` and its bar.

Sally lost that status of innocence, much cherished historically by women and, for some reason, much sought after by insecure men, early in her first year at Uni. This was to an irresistibly tall and well-built lock forward, who used to play his CDs very loud to prevent other students in Hall sharing their expressions of enjoyment. The writing flowed easily and Sally vowed to try to write a few words each day or perhaps evening after Greg had gone to bed. She was not planning to have this published. It was merely a record of her life for her alone to read in her dotage, whatever that was.

The Estate Agent sounded quite amazed on the phone. Not only had the `St Bernard` now offered the full asking price on Kirkhaven House, but they had received a five-star credit rating for the cash purchaser and ten per cent of the value had been transferred to the Shaunessy`s solicitor as a deposit. In view of the chain trailing behind `St Bernard` he was recommending accepting the cash offer and hoping that surveys etc. may not lead to a later reduction in the price.

"Are you sure you have not undervalued my house? It is surprising that two full offers have come so quickly. You yourself said this was a bad time of year to sell in Devon."

"Good Heavens, Mrs Shaunessy! It is more than the reputation of my firm would allow. We have been established for over seventy five years in this profession and jealously defend our history of honest service to the client."

In view of two others having given similar valuations, Sally checked with Chris and agreed to accept the cash offer. Ten minutes later Charles, their often helpful solicitor from Ottery St Mary, phoned to check that they were comfortable with the sale and the price, and promised to send the usual form to complete, listing everything that was to be left behind and included in the sale. The purchaser apparently was a sportsman from Florida. Charles expected to hear from his lawyer soon regarding the purchase requirements.

"Chris. You must get up early today, and start to look for

somewhere for us to live. I have to go to work. I suggest you make a note of places to view and we can arrange visits for Saturday."

Chris phoned all the Estate Agents he could find in East Devon and asked them to send online details of all properties in their price range with three bedrooms and a parking space. By Friday afternoon Sally could see a pile growing on her dining table of agent's properties for sale or `to let`. Their pages and brochures of photos and details were all very attractively presented. Sally and Chris settled down to read each one together. They put them into three sections: `probables`, `possibles` and `no chance`.

Although it was a Saturday most of Devon`s Estate Agents realised that this was often the only day of the week that buyers could become free to view the properties they wished to consider. On that first Saturday they took Greg into their confidence and told him that he too must be happy about the house they chose to purchase. They looked at five during the day, taking a lunch break in Sidmouth. The two at the back of Sidmouth were good 1930s semi-detached houses with tidy gardens. They discounted the one which only offered parking in the road. Greg liked the only house they were seeing in Lyme Regis and they had viewed that one earlier in the morning. He was at school in Lyme and many of his friends lived there or in the immediate area, including Sophie who came to school from Charmouth, further into Dorset. In the afternoon, one of the two was in the village of Woodbury and had distant views over the River Exe and a new golf course behind it. The second was in Exmouth, a large town and close to the Commando Training Centre that had once been a happy place for Chris.

In the evening, sitting around an Indian Take-away, they went through the attractions of each house. Then, rather than influence each other they all wrote on a piece of paper the house of their personal choice. Not surprisingly, Chris went for Exmouth and Greg for Lyme Regis. They looked at Sally for a casting vote, but she had chosen Woodbury for herself, wanting to retain the village atmosphere, but also for Chris, it being still close enough to old friends and for Greg with golf in mind. They went to bed having decided to look at more places as soon as possible. Many of the `possibles`, four of the seven, would have meant stretching their budget to leave very little for re-decoration or new carpets and fittings. They arranged to see two of the others on the Monday evening after school hours. During the day the phone rang again and Chris took a call from Charles, the solicitor dealing with the conveyancing of Kirkhaven House.

"The prospective purchaser - the American - has expressed through his lawyer, that he has no intention of occupying your house for several years. It seems he owns houses in other countries including his own. He asks whether you would like to stay and rent your own house - his home - on an annually renewable lease. Now, in normal circumstances, I would not advise this, Chris, because you will lose the long-term advantage of property ownership. However, he seems an intelligent as well as a wealthy man. He states that his experience is that the incumbent, i.e. you, will care for the house and surround better than any new tenant, and, with this in mind, is prepared to charge a rental of only fifty per cent of market rental value. His purchase is undoubtedly more as a long term investment expecting property prices to appreciate well in this area."

"I would strongly recommend serious consideration of this, knowing as I do, that you would prefer to stay there rather than move. You could invest the proceeds of the house in safe bonds to realise close to the rent he is asking without making any further inroads into your savings."

"Thanks, Charles. Sally will love to hear this. I`ll call you tomorrow when we have had a talk about it" said Chris.

TEN

THEN

From the day Chris and Sally decided to become tenants of Kirkhaven House, things began to improve for them. It started with their finances. Charles helped them to invest the bulk of the receipts from the sale into a range of safe and income earning investments, as he had done with Chris` lump sum award when he left the Corps. He launched a Trust Fund for Greg and found suitable Trustees for them. The income was to be paid quarterly for their running domestic expenses, and it was predicted to be well above the generous rental being asked by the American. The rental agreement was for full internal maintenance by the tenant and for external repairs and maintenance to be paid for by the landlord. They felt obliged to allocate some of their perceived rent saving to keeping a high standard internally, and hoped that one day soon, they may be able to show off their work to the owner. Maggie told them they were `potty` to do this, but they continued to do it, to make themselves feel good, something that had not happened since Chris` misfortune in Bosnia.

The next piece of good news was that Erik was back. He had decided to stay at the pub in the village, the Kings Arms.

Sally thought this must be so that he didn`t compromise Maggie, whose parents lived in the other half of the farm with the stables. Although it could have been for a number of reasons. Maybe he had turned up unannounced and found Bodmin`s toothbrush in the bathroom. Erik sought out Greg and checked his school schedule. They agreed to play golf on the drier Saturdays and Sundays because Greg was at school throughout the daylight hours in the week.

The final piece of good fortune to finish November was Alan`s return from Iraq. Alan and Chris had been best mates through their training and had worked together in a number of skirmishes throughout the world, and also many policing duties in troubled countries. The British Royal Marines are regarded as probably the best political police force in the world. Alan had just been posted back to CTC (Commando Training Centre) at Lympstone as an instructor for the last six months of his service career. He began to spend a lot of time with Chris in the house and on cliff top walks, something Chris had not done on his own since moving there. He confided in Sally that he had a plan to pull Chris out of the quicksand and for them to do something constructive together in six months' time when he retired. Sally was pleased and secretly hoped that this was nothing to do with open `mercenary` activities in Africa or South America in which she had heard other retired forces people had become involved.

Greg`s golf handicap was now down to eight, and Erik, playing less than he should, was struggling to keep to his three. Consequently, the world series was now eighteen to fifteen in Greg`s favour. The Christmas term`s school report was better than his parents had anticipated. They knew he was doing well. Parent Teacher evenings in October had confirmed this, and he was now in the top set for everything except music. He could drop music next year if he wished.

Chris was now only drinking on Friday nights when Alan

took him out in Exmouth and they finished in a club until crashing out in Alan`s pad at three in the morning. Alan`s deal was that there was no drinking at home (Christmas excepted) but that they had one major bash every Friday. Sally was thrilled and had already decided on a special Christmas gift for Alan. What he had not yet told her was that the old acquaintances he was meeting with Chris were destined for the same project. The Sultan of Oman was becoming increasingly concerned by the threat of minority groups in the region. His was not a particularly oil rich country, but it was beautiful and had a right to remain free of conflict and harbouring terrorist training zones like some other mid-Eastern countries. Through his Defence Minister he had agreed to recruit a team of highly experienced ex-Royal Marines to train his own forces to a high level, not only in combat but also in policing. Alan was determined to include his long term friend in this bonanza, and this possibility was enhanced when he himself was made the final recruitment arbiter. Firstly, though, Chris had to lose twenty kilos in weight and become fit enough to cope with the desert conditions and also to look good again in a uniform. He saw Chris as one of the principal trainers in the `policing department` and they both accepted that weapon or conflict training was no longer possible on Chris` agenda. Alan tactfully left Chris to tell Sally of the plan for her husband to work in Oman, and unaccompanied, at least for the first stages of their contract.

Erik bought a gas space heater to warm the Barn studio to enable him to spend a few hours with his much loved palette. Sally endeavoured to feed him lunch, although he insisted on eating a banana for breakfast and having dinner in the Kings Arms. He and Chris drove over to Ottery every day to the gym in the Sports Centre, which was opened early by Emma, the cleaner, who had special permission to do so by the Manager. The privacy gave them both a chance to indulge in training techniques that, as professionals, suited their individual needs. Chris used a combination of extreme endurance exercises and muscle growth in particular areas to compensate for his amputations. By now he had come to regard his prostheses as genuine body parts, and he and Erik were similar in that Erik looked at his tennis racquet as a genuine extension of his arm.

Sally, meanwhile, was writing of her own mixed emotions. Deep love for Chris, who only she knew had had to come to terms with his enforced impotence. There was genuine affection for Alan, whom she had known for years and respected hugely. And a weird and disturbing warm contraction of her tummy muscles every time she saw Erik`s lopsided grin, his long sun bleached blond curly hair, or even hearing of his latest selfless deed. She wondered what any reader of her diary would make of her situation amongst these three Alpha males.

The Alpha Female finally appeared clad in a full length ermine coat with matching hat! Maggie looked like a James Bond film lead and swept into the house:

"Is he here or in the studio?"

"Who?"

"You know who. His car is in the drive."

"You mean Alan." Sally was deliberately playing dumb

"No! The Viking object of desire`"

"He`s in the Barn. Why are you dressed for Après Ski?"

"It`s good isn`t it? My mother was given this outfit by a grateful prince in Chamonix."

"Crikey! He must have been grateful. Is it a case of `like mother - like daughter`?"

"No. They didn`t invent sex until the sixties. Men were eternally grateful for a quick flash of calf in those days. I expect she gave him a couple of those."

"Well. Take it off and sit down. I have great things to tell you."

"Not now, Sal. I have come to be sacrificed on a Scandinavian altar! Anyway, I can`t take it off, there is nothing much underneath."

"Mags. You really are a hoot. He will have an emotional disturbance right in the middle of his painting."

"I do hope so. The bastard has not been to see me in all the time he has been here."

"Really! I thought you two were an item."

"An item of derision more likely. It will take a crow bar to lever off his tennis shorts. Have you got a spare key to the cottage? I`ll go and wait over there and give him a big surprise."

"You certainly will. No one has been in there since about 1980 when they had servants here and gardeners and flunkies."

"Isn`t he living there?"

"No. I think he is in the King`s Arms."

"It`s all gone wrong. He should be in my arms, not the bloody kings."

Maggie decided that she would go for the Barn and set off down the path looking hilarious as her heels wobbled on the gravel surface.

The barn door swung open to reveal Maggie.

"Hello Mr Swedish Man", said the husky voice.

"Maggie! I thought it was a woolly mammoth!"

"Have you forgotten all about me?"

"There are some people you remember, and others it is difficult to forget."

"I suppose you Vikings have been going around the world again, plundering, pillaging and raping!"

"Just a little pillaging this year, Miss Oversexed Horseperson."

"I have come to shock you back to your most basic

instincts", said Maggie, removing the fur coat and standing inside the closing door in just a hat and a G string.

"I am visually impressed! Come and stand more in the middle whilst I finish the plumage on this chaffinch."

Maggie moved to the centre of the barn under the main light, with mother`s ermine folded over one arm. Erik mixed a light orange wash and began to paint it on the canvas attached to his easel.

"God. Hurry up! It`s bloody freezing in here!" said Maggie. "I`m getting goose pimples all over my extremities."

"If you are going to make it as an artist`s model, you have to be prepared to pose in all conditions."

"My nipples are standing up in the cold."

"Good. They look much more paintable like that."

Erik cleaned his brush in the jar of water.

"Now, what was it you wanted ?"

Erik took the coat off her arm and put it around her shoulders, then propelled her towards the space heater and stood her there to warm up. He then turned her to face him, and said:

"Maggie. If you come to me again starkers, or even half starkers, in the vicinity of vulnerable kids, or the general public, I really will give you a memorable spanking! Go home, get some normal clothes on and I`ll meet you in the bar of the Kings Arms at seven o`clock."

"But, it`s already half past six."

"Then, you better get a move on!"

He held open the door and she tottered back to her car, and drove fast down the driveway.

Erik switched off the heater and lights and closed up the studio. He strolled up to the house door, and knocked twice, then twice again - his identity code.

"Come in Erik."

He stood looking blankly at Sally, who could contain herself no longer and burst into laughter. Erik put the kettle on to boil and leant back on the worktop.

109

"Did you put her up to that stunt?" he asked.

"Goodness no. She turned up like that all on her little ownsome."

"Did Greg see any of the show in here ?"

"He`s in his room I think. She didn`t show anything here except a tasteful ermine coat."

"I thought ermine was only worn these days in your House of Lords?"

"She certainly would cause a titter if she turned up there in mother`s coat. Was she wearing anything else?"

"Not a lot! What she did have was growing icicles after a few minutes. I was painting a little bird at the time."

"It had to be a blue tit" said Sally, and then needed to sit down.

Chris walked in and his face was damp with perspiration from a power walk to the harbour and back. They told him about Maggie`s latest performance until tears joined the drips of sweat rolling down his cheeks.

"Get into the shower, Chris. Sally get changed. I`m buying Maggie dinner at the pub and you`re in too. Greg will be OK, won`t he?" said Erik.

They both nodded and went upstairs. Erik read the daily paper after washing his face in the downstairs cloakroom. As do most men, he began with the Sports` pages at the back. The inside back pages usually covered sports other than football. There was an old photo of him with Monika, winning the Wimbledon Mixed Doubles last summer above the headline:

`Is the Snooty Beauty to marry Joel ? `

This rumour had begun in the locker room late in September and was now being considered by the tennis press. It was one of the reasons he had dropped out of the last tournament of the year in early November to escape to his bolt hole, deep in the West Country. Monika, tall, elegant and aloof, had won her nickname more than two years ago.

She disliked the press and avoided them, so they made up stories to compensate for lack of genuine information.

Chris and Sally appeared at the same time, playfully fighting each other for priority on the stairs.

"If we can fold Sally into the back we can take the Porsche" said Erik. "It will mean you can both enjoy a drink."

"We go in the old Octavia" said Chris. "I don`t drink now except on Friday, so I drive."

Maggie was not very happy to find she was not alone with Erik, but soon settled into the fun of the evening. The Kings Arms was full of locals at this time of year. They all came out of hibernation in October after the end of the holiday season and the village became a community again.

"Erik is the only `grockle` in here tonight" said Sally. She waved to the lady who ran the corner shop.

'What`s a `grockle`?" Erik asked.

Chris explained that it`s a slightly derogatory term for a holidaymaker or second-home-owner in Devon. "In Cornwall they call them `Emmets`, which means `ants`!"

"We should be popular. We create jobs and bring down loads of money every year" offered Erik.

"True, but the downside is the second home situation putting up house prices so much that the local kids can`t afford them on the salaries they can earn down here." Maggie added.

"Because the boys all have to go away to get good jobs, did you know there are twice as many girls in their early twenties in Exeter as there are boys?" said Sally seriously. Chris and Erik drank an enthusiastic toast to that statistic.

The pub was packed and, as the evening progressed, the kitchen was half an hour behind the order in producing each meal. Everyone drank a little more than they had planned. The Salvation Army came in - just three of them to collect for their Christmas support of the less fortunate.

"That could eventually have been us," said Chris, "If

it hadn`t been for a generous American and a bucket of good fortune, we were all going down the pan? "He put ten pounds in the collecting box. Sally nodded in approval. With two large glasses of chardonnay already inside her she added,

"We are so grateful to our American that when he comes over here, we definitely will not call him a `grockle` and we shall take him to the best restaurant in the whole area for meals."

Their food arrived and Sally noticed that the crush had forced Erik`s leg firmly against hers. The side of the alcove seat prevented her from moving further away. The meal was good and Erik bought more wine for all but Chris to enjoy. The red gingham patterned tablecloth only reached six inches beyond the table top on each side, and Sally could see Maggie trying to entwine her legs around Erik's`. She giggled. No one passed her the potatoes and Erik was in deep conversation with Chris in the noisy, smoke-filled room. She reached across Erik to pick up the tureen and noticed there was a foot of space on the other side of his seat.

In her giggly, happy state Sally suddenly realised that his firm muscular leg did not need to be pressed so tightly against hers. She went very quiet and asked for a glass of water. In contrast Maggie became louder and her riske comments and horsey stories captured the attention of both men and of the four people at the next table as well. The inanimate leg stayed in its place. It didn`t move closer or further away. It didn`t caress or show any interest in her. The denim jean didn`t move at all against her bare calf or thigh. And yet it didn`t have to be there!

Sally lay in bed that night unsure in her wine-fogged mind whether it had been Chris` prosthetic leg or one of Erik`s. She finally fell asleep at midnight.

Two days later, when Erik was eating his morning banana

and leaving the gym with Chris, a new Mercedes Sports pulled up beside them, narrowly avoiding the children going to the school next door.

"Monika" said Erik incredulously. Chris looked on as the six foot tall blonde ignored him.

"I`ve come to take you back for our engagement party."

"We are not engaged. I have not asked you to be my wife. Chris, this is my mixed doubles partner, Monika - possibly ex-mixed doubles partner!" Monika did not look back at Chris.

"How did you find me?" asked Erik.

"You should not have told Georgiou where you were going when you collected your car. The lady at the house told me you had come here with her husband."

"I think you should drive straight back to London."

"I am taking you with me. My statement to the Daily Telegraph and to Le Monde confirming our engagement will be printed tomorrow and the celebration is on Saturday for four hundred on a Thames Riverboat.

PART TWO

ELEVEN

THEN - TWO AND A HALF YEARS LATER

Greg had one of his GCSE exams left to take and he was watching his favourite tennis players on the No 2 Court at Wimbledon at the beginning of the second week of the tournament. Joel (Erik) was seeded seventh and expected to beat Leander Paes of India, who was seeded twenty three and a doubles specialist. The BBC were only showing part of the match but, because the No 2 Court was now known amongst players as the `Graveyard Court` for seeds, there was extra interest and especially as Paes had just won the second set to level at one set each, and now had broken Erik's serve in the first game of the third set.

Greg had kept Erik's secret now for almost three years and, amazingly, so had Granny Dawn, who was probably hoping to receive another garment of Erik's to boost the raffle takings at the Women's` Institute. Sally was still not teaching permanently and had just finished as GCSE adjudicator at a school in Broadclyst, near Exeter. She walked into the living room having enjoyed an hour sitting on the garden bench and writing her `life's diary` as she called it.

"Mum. Come and sit down. I have something to tell you," said Greg from the sofa.

Sally poured a cold drink and came to sit next to her now tall son in front of the television.

"I want you to watch some of Wimbledon with me."

"But darling, I have no interest in sport. You know that."

"Just for ten minutes whilst I show you something that will be a surprise." added Greg to keep her there.

"Mum. When did you last see Erik?"

"Let`s see. It was just before Christmas in the year we sold the house. About two and a half years ago."

The TV producer changed the cameras on Court No 2 again. Erik had broken back to now lead 2 - 1 in the third set.

"Look hard. Recognise anybody?"

Erik had whipped a backhand return down the line prompting a close-up from the nearby courtside camera.

"That....that`s Erik....or his brother!" Sally sat forward on the sofa and strained to see the now more distant shot of the curly blond hair and the white headband.

"Yes Mum. It actually is Erik!" said Greg.

He watched his Mum concentrate, her hands over her mouth.

"The football season is over and he has started playing tennis?" she half asked.

Patiently Greg helped the penny to drop.

"No Mum. He never played football, or golf professionally. He was, and is, a top tennis player."

A long pause ensued whilst, with the help of a few errors by his opponent Erik/Joel went into a two sets to one lead. The cameras changed back to Centre Court.

"How long have you known and kept it to yourself, you despicable child?" Sally half scolded him.

'Only about three years. He asked me to keep it quiet, so I did. Gran knows.I thought she would tell you."

"But he used to come down in the football `off` season," said Sally.

"It was a quiet time for top tennis too. He also came in November/December, and that was when football is in full swing."

Sally thought back more and, still staring at the TV, which was showing a different match with Pete Sampras,

"What about that fiasco with that rude `footballers wife` or groupie who came here and they went off together?"

"That was not a footballer's wife. It was his mixed doubles partner, Monika Kristensen, daughter of a Danish Minister. They didn`t get married you know."

"I do know that because he wrote to tell me and apologise for her and for leaving so abruptly," said Sally.

Sally went into the hallway and picked up the phone, and dialled a local number.

"Mags. What are you doing now?"

"Well, I was rubbing down Nimrod when the phone went."

"Drop everything and meet me in Oliver's in half an hour. I have astounding news!"

"It must be three or four months since anyone has uttered those words. Or the first part anyway," said Maggie.

"I will be there anytime you say."

"Oliver was being outrageous to a group of eight ladies from a coach outing. The driver had arranged a day visit from their hotel in Dorchester. They had come from Sunderland earlier in the week and were objecting to his black and white striped braces, which were Newcastle colours.

"Now look here you bunch of slappers, I can`t foretell what my Saville Row tailor chooses to make `brace of the year` can I ? I have to stay at the forefront of sartorial elegance to keep my Michelin Stars in this superb restaurant", he was saying as Sally came in and joined Maggie.

"Hallo Girls", said Oliver moving across to their table, the four bracelets on his left wrist jangling.

"I like your jewellery, Oliver", said Sally.

"Had them for years, ducky. Given to me by an Egyptian, whom I helped find his true calling."

Having served the coach party Oliver hung about. Sally could contain herself no longer.

"I have just found out that our Erik is called Joel something and is a top tennis player. In fact he was on the TV just before I left home."

"Of course he is" said Maggie. "Just won his way into the quarter finals."

"Won in four sets this time. Six-love in the fourth set and in the `Graveyard`" added Oliver.

"You both knew" said Sally, astounded.

"I was listening to it on the radio when you called. Even Nimrod was rooting for him." Maggie replied.

"And I had to keep rushing back to the kitchen to keep up with the score" added Oliver again.

Sally berated them both for not having told her. They were equally stunned to discover that she didn`t know.

"When he told me he played for Sweden I assumed it was football rather than tennis and never suspected I was wrong."

"Swedish Davis Cup team. He is their No 2 singles player and one of the doubles pair" Oliver answered knowledgeably.

"How on earth didn't I manage to find out? I suppose I put him at the back of my mind when he went off to marry Monika that day."

They thought she must have followed the public saga of the bogus engagement in the papers and the later court case in Denmark for something like `breach of promise`.

"How did you miss it all? It was all over the tabloids. They loved it. Maggie used to come in here and we would bet each other on the next revelation or on the verdict of the Court."

"It kept us going during that awful winter last year, when I had to keep the horses inside for weeks."

"Greg and even my mother knew, for goodness sake. I suppose I was rather tied up with Chris` new job and the teaching."

They enquired after Chris and his role in Oman and heard that he had begun a new two year contract, but wouldn`t return for a whole year for his next leave. Sultan Qaboos was very pleased with his army`s progress, much of which was down to the training by the team of ex-Royal Marines. He had written a paper that his Ambassador had read in the United Nations General Assembly that, after thirty years of his reign, he reckoned that he had the best and most capable police force in the Gulf. Chris was a completely rejuvenated, confident guy again and loving the Omani people and the work. Sally thought Greg missed Chris a lot, and, without Erik visiting, was in need of a strong male lead for the next two years until he cleared `A` levels.

"Send him to me. I`ll sort him out and teach him worldly things that those two hunks will never have heard of" said Oliver to a gale of laughter from the women at both tables. He minced back to the counter in mock offence.

Sally discovered that neither of them had been keeping in regular contact with Erik since he left. Oliver often sent him encouraging texts on his new mobile phone but only received one word replies. All their information came from the papers and from magazine articles or from their monthly issues of the `exclusively tennis` magazines. George Mercer had told Oliver that `Nasty` had not been in the water for two summers and Erik had told him that he would like her floated and fully checked this year. It was bad for any boat to be kept out of the environment for which it was designed for very long, in this case the sea water.

Erik/Joel lost to Andre Agassi on the Wednesday. He played well but Agassi was in good form winning by three sets to one. On Friday, together with his Swedish Davis Cup partner he won the Men's Doubles Quarter Final and then lost the semi-final on Saturday morning (played then due to a rain delay) to Bhupati and Paes.

Chris and Sally had extended their lease on Kirkhaven House already twice, each time for a further year. The rent had stayed at half the market level. With both people in employment, albeit Sally only some of the time, money worries had faded into the distant past. The old Octavia had been replaced with a new Skoda Fabia, this time a diesel which was proving even more economical as fuel prices began to rise. Arthur delivered a letter one morning from solicitor Charles, who was acting as intermediary now between landlord and tenant. The American had dispensed with his US lawyer, preferring to use a British letting agent. Charles wrote that he had bought, at the same time as the house, the tall square water tower that stood in a small compound at the junction of their hedge and George Lee's nearest field. He had bought it for a song from the Water Board, which had no further use for it. In the last two years Mr Eriksson had leased space on it to the ever growing mobile phone companies to fix masts to its side.

The survey on the small one bedroom cottage had been bad last year and he had decided to close or even demolish it. He would like, however, to make a bedsit out of the square water tower and wanted their approval before commissioning an architect to design an unique holiday let. It would have an outstanding view across the River Axe and out to sea. Charles was asking them to let him know their decision, stating that planning approval was far from certain in view of the unusual property. Without consulting Chris, Sally wrote back her approval, adding that they very much appreciated being consulted and wishing the American owner well.

Greg completed his French exam and had most of the

next fortnight off as post exam leave. The teachers didn`t want a hundred teenagers inside the school letting off all the pent-up steam that they had accumulated prior to their important GCSE exams. Greg had made the cricket team this year and they still had two matches to play plus Sports Day in which he was competing, like most of his friends in Year 10. Sophie had become a `thing of the past` and now Emily and Cassandra were competing for his attention. Sally knew Cassie`s father was on the District Council Planning committee and had a fearsome reputation for rejecting applications. She thought Greg had plans for Cassie and doubted her father would approve those either.

Arthur rang the doorbell at eight am and Sally threw on a thin bath robe and ran barefoot down the stairs to answer the door. Greg was still in his room enjoying his second day of freedom.

"Sign here please Mrs Shaunessy."

"Thank you, Arthur." Sally took the small parcel.

"The painter`s here again I see. Up the drive, asleep in his car."

Only half awake Sally took the parcel inside and remembered that she hadn`t ordered anything to be decorated. Realisation hit her with a resounding blow. The Painter - Erik! In the way any other woman would, she bounded back up the stairs two at a time, wishing she had washed her hair last night instead of writing her `diary`. She washed the sleep out of her eyes and applied some make up.

"This eye pencil is bad. It just makes blobs," she cursed.

Last week she had bought an eggshell blue T shirt with butterflies all over the front. She was going to take it back - it being a size too small. However, this seemed a good time to wear it! A few days sunbathing in the garden had made her legs a nice brown for July in England. She pulled out her favourite shorts. They were short denim cut-offs with an inch of frayed hemline. She swiftly brushed her hair and went down to the kitchen. There was still no sign of Erik so Sally laid the breakfast table with placemats and an array of condiments, marmalade and a cheeseboard. She had Erik`s favourite muesli because Greg now also liked it for breakfast as well as a snack after jogging. There were two croissants left from the six she had bought yesterday in the corner shop in the village. She put the only banana Greg had not eaten in Erik`s place and the muesli with a bowl next to it. Next she found her cafetiere at the back of a cupboard and some coffee - opening a new pack - and put the kettle on.

Nobody came to the door. Sally wondered if she had jumped to entirely the wrong conclusion, and wished she had asked Arthur to be more explicit. She slipped on a pair of flip-flops, kept for wearing in the house in the summer and went out of the front door. Walking along the side of the driveway, so as not to crunch the gravel she quietly reached the bend and peered around the hedge. The corner of the white Porsche Carrera was clearly visible parked just inside the gateway to one side, leaving room for another vehicle to pass. As she was straining to see if anyone was in the car, a figure, the exact size of Erik, stood up from a crouching position three yards in front of her and from behind the hedge just around the bend. He threw his arms around her in a bear hug and kissed her neck so passionately that she gasped aloud. It was two full minutes before he relented enough for her to take a breath.

Erik stood back and said,

"I heard you coming as I was halfway towards the house." He held her at arm's length. "You look absolutely sensational. I could eat you for breakfast!"

"Come inside" said Sally, still regaining her composure. "Why did you sleep in the car when you only had to knock on the door?"

"I arrived at around five am. It was just full light so I went down to the river and watched the birds feeding at low tide. It is so good to be back after the Wimbledon circus and the whole tennis merry-go-round. I have really missed all this tranquillity. I only sat back in the car and drove up here about an hour ago. I dozed off for a while and then the postman came in, but I didn't think it was fair to wake you all so early. They walked up the drive hand in hand and in through the open front door. Sally grabbed a bath towel from the pile of completed ironing left in the kitchen and pushed Erik towards the stairs. He decided to jog back to the car and collect a washbag, and brought the car up to the house. Fifteen minutes later a clean-shaven Erik re-appeared in clean clothes and with the inevitable lop-sided grin. He came up behind Sally who was taking croissants from the microwave.

"How about another hug from a cleaner man?"

They held each other again for far too long and began to look into each other's eyes. The magic was broken by a heavy footstep at the top of the stairs as a bleary teenager gravitated towards his feeding trough! Erik put down his mother and went to hug Greg who was speechless and yet returned the warm greeting readily. They sat down to breakfast. Erik noticed that the banana and muesli, and even the croissants had already been prepared.

"Did you know I was coming today?" he asked.

"You said later 'in the week' and only `possibly`, replied Greg, not realising that Erik`s special preferences were on the table and that the question was aimed at his mother.

"Arthur rang the bell and told me, so I anticipated your surprise a little" said Sally.

"Are there no secrets in this village? I thought you must have got out of bed looking like Miss U.K."

"Did you really know Erik was likely to come down again, Greg?" asked Sally.

Greg looked at Erik who nodded.

"Yes, Mum. He did say he may have the time."

Sally explained that she had only just been told a few days ago that he was in the country and that he played tennis and not football. She glanced sheepishly at Erik who looked as amazed as anyone could with a mouthful of muesli! Greg thought he should add some more to this topic.

"I kept you in the dark about a couple of things, Mum. We both kept quiet about the e mails between us because Erik asked me to. He didn`t know you still thought he was a footballer or a golfer, and I knew your lack of interest in sport meant that the only way you would eventually find out was through friends. But months went by and they didn`t and you didn`t, so I kept it going. It saved you and Dad having to read all the rubbish in the papers about `Snooty Beauty and the Beast` and the other stupid headlines.

Sally sniggered and looked at `the Beast`. He did look rather like an albino gorilla, sitting opposite her with his sun-bleached hair and a banana in one hand. She put her right hand over her mouth to prevent laughing out loud as he and Greg both now had serious expressions.

"What other stupid headlines?"

"Boys toys: Joel is still playing with Monika!" and "Will his case be in the Centre Court" and.....and" Greg paused. Erik muttered into his napkin. `Joel has a different Danish Pastry for breakfast."

"Oh Yes" said Greg "With a photo of you playing in the French with Hannah Nystrom."

Sally roared with laughter.

"They didn`t? I missed all the fun."

"Not much fun over on this side of the net" said Erik "It cost me about 200,000 dollars and my untarnished reputation."

Both Sally and Greg were laughing now and Greg mentioned that Erik had sent him an e mail saying he had got off lightly.

"Erik will tell you the rest. I am going for a run" said Greg.

Erik had hardly taken his eyes off Sally all through breakfast. He picked up her hand and kissed the end of her middle finger. She looked away and made to move, but he held on to her hand for a moment until she sat down again.

"Where`s Chris today? Last I heard from Greg was that he was here on leave."

"He went back last week. This time it has to be a year before he gets paid leave. There is some new regional policing network that he has to introduce and supervise." Sally went on "Why are you looking at me like that - and in such a loving way? Just because Chris is away I am not going become another one of your willing conquests, another notch on your bedpost, another string to your tennis racket!"

"No Sally. Definitely not. You are extra special." Erik replied with a most intense expression.

There was a pause when neither of them seemed to have anything to say.

"I had better clear away before Greg returns."

In the kitchen she said:

"What happens to all your cast off women? Do they float away on the tide, distraught and rudderless? Or are there so many in the queue that you are always moving on to the next one and you don't notice?"

"Sally, one day I will tell you everything that goes on inside my head and how little it has to do with passing fancies."

"And Maggie. Is she waiting expectantly up at her stables?"

"Only if Arthur has reached there on his post round. Certainly not information that has come from me. I will tell you one thing though. All these women approach me. I have not made the first advance on a girl since I was fifteen years old. But I do have a deep respect and affection for you."

TWELVE

NOW – TWO YEARS LATER

"Mummy, Mummy!"

"What is it, Lucy? Did you have a good day at school?"

"Mummy. Alex has got beef burgers."

"Oh, that`s nice. Did he give you one?

"No Mummy. Don`t be silly. It`s a disease. I overheard his mum telling Mrs Kellogg. She said that the doctor had told her that Alex had got `beef burgers' and that the children must be kind to him and not make him angry."

"Sit down, Sweetheart. Would you like a drink?"

"But Mum. It`s serious. He won`t die will he?" Helen poured her a glass of apple juice.

"It is called `Asperger's' and it is not a disease and it`s not serious, and he definitely won`t die. In fact he will seem just the same for most of the time. Lots of children and lots of grownups have it and we never know. It is a good thing to be kind to everyone, and it is good to be kind to people who sometimes do or say things that you wouldn`t say. Alex could get upset over little disagreements or things that go wrong, so his mum is right to ask the children not to make him angry."

"I was really worried, Mum. What`s for tea?"

"Go and play or do your homework. Tea is not for another hour."

It hardly seemed two years since all the emotional strain of her divorce. She had been amazed at how rapidly divorce could become absolute. No word had come about Peter`s marriage to Rose and nothing was printed in his Company`s Newsletter, which they were still sending to his old address. She looked at the `hatches, matches and dispatches` page every time, before adding it to the recycling. Perhaps Rose didn`t like the bed socks any more than she had! Peter kept up the payments and was supposed to come down on alternate weekends to take Lucy out for the day or the whole weekend. The settlement had included his right of access to Callum too, but he had never offered to spend any time with Callum, nor would Callum have agreed to meet him anyway. For two years Peter`s visits from Swindon had been monthly rather than fortnightly. Lucy had seemed quite happy with this. After the first year he stopped taking her back for the weekend and resorted to a single day out or an event or a play area, and back home by 6pm. Helen assumed this was to save a double trip of over two hundred miles.

Helen had used her Economics degree and an expensive mini dress to secure a job in a local bank, part time for three days a week. This boosted her income and prepared her for the time when Callum was over the minimum school-leaving age and Peter no longer had to contribute to his expenses.

Everyone knew and loved Bronwen and the village was looking forward to her wedding to Andre in June. They all had already invited themselves and were planning hats and marquees on the cricket pitch.

Erik was supervising the spring re-launch of Viti-Levu, which was looking smart and shining after a winter`s spell in the boatyard/car park and a new coat of varnish on her on-board woodwork. He and Callum were planning adventurous trips this year, weather permitting, along the South Coast. Erik was to move his few travel belongings on board within the week. This last winter Viti-Levu had stayed on a cradle and Phil Mercer was now reversing the trailer and cradle down the harbour slipway into the water. The harbour, which is tidal, was around two thirds full and rising. Erik, already on board, let her float backwards off the cradle and then started the small inboard engine. He motored gently out to the mooring that he had now rented for twenty years. He secured her to the mooring with a loose chain and gave George, watching from back in the yard, a thumbs up sign. Phil did most of the heavy work these days as George had developed an arthritic hand early in life. Erik went below and swept up the last of the shavings and superfluous nails from the re-fit. He folded the sails carefully and stowed them, looking forward to his crew member and partner breaking up for half -term. It was near the end of May and his was one of the last craft to be secured to a permanent mooring that spring. He had been commentating at the French Open at Roland Garros and was grabbing a few days in his beloved `bolt-hole` until Queens and Wimbledon weeks from mid-June

He continued to tidy and wipe surfaces inside Viti-Leva's cabin and prepare the port side bunk for his head to lay on tomorrow. Then he drove to Kirkhaven House to collect Lucy to take her to her last indoor session of the season with the tennis group at the Ottery St Mary Sports Centre. She had progressed well in the two winters since Henrietta`s Mum had first suggested Lucy went there. Lucy was ready and waiting with her little Adidas bag and the racket that Erik had measured her for last summer and brought down a few days later from London. They drove to Ottery in the Porsche and Erik heard all about how to behave with someone diagnosed with `Asperger`s!

'You don`t actually have to mention it to them at all`, he was informed.

On arrival he took from the back of his car a brand new Yonnex tennis bag and gave it to Coralie, the coach, to thank her for what she had done for Lucy and for keeping quiet about his identity for two years.

"There are half a dozen autographs along the top you may recognise" he said.

"Thank you so much" she said, kissing his unshaven cheek and reading off the names of Nadal and Murray, Gasquet and Lopez, Petra Kvitova and Li Na. In correspondence with Erik Coralie had moved her on to full tennis, together with Paul, a local Ottery lad, who went to the school next door and was a year older than Lucy. After tonight they would move outdoors during the summer. The principal concentration was on ground strokes. Erik was content just to watch Coralie working with guidance and gentle encouragement. He wondered what stamina the little girl had naturally because he liked her movement and stroke fluidity, and the anticipation was there still - a split second ahead of average.

Poppy Chocolatiere was thriving with its local trade all winter and its appeal to the holidaymakers in summer, being a nice walk from the town of Seaton, where they stayed or used the car park. It was the only place, other than the pub, where one could sit and buy a drink or snack after the first half of the walk. The legendary Devon cream tea had become a major item on the menu and there were even instructions on its history and how to make one, printed on card attached to the walls inside the little cafe. These had been written `tongue in cheek` by Poppy herself, who had put on a stone or two in weight since opening her venture.

Reliable, blunt Deirdre had continued to support Helen for over two years and was experienced in cooking all their favourite meals. She had been working the originally agreed two days a week and prepared cooked meals on her Mondays and Thursdays and left quiches and pies, crumbles and home-made soups in the fridge or freezer for Helen's use on the in-between days. Bill was still the gardener for a school in Lyme Regis and their Maisie had qualified as a NVQ3 Carer for a family business with three nursing homes in East Devon. Maisie's battle to avoid the Brigadier, as she waited for the early bus to work, was known throughout the village and, more than once, her boyfriend had come over from Axminster to challenge Roper the Groper to 'swords or pistols at dawn' or the twenty first century equivalent!

"Ugh, ugh" Helen hopped into the house on Thursday morning having walked barefoot back from her garden bench. "Ugh. I've trodden on a slug and it's horrible. I've squished it between my toes." She hopped into the cloakroom loo and held her raised foot under the basin tap. "I can't get all the slime off." She climbed the stairs with difficulty, putting her weight on one foot and then on the heel of the other and then thoroughly scrubbed at the problem in the bidet.

"Serves you right. I've told you before not to go running around with bare feet" said a familiar voice from the kitchen as she descended the stairs

"It's so good to have you back, Deirdre. No one has been here to throw abuse at me since you left!"

Deirdre had been having an operation and was recovering from what Lucy called 'her hysterical ectomy' and now had returned to take care of Helen and the children. She viewed her role, not as a paid job, but as a duty. Peter's behaviour, in her eyes, had left their 'poor girl' with a burden that needed to be shared. Deirdre's first opinion had been that Helen was an over privileged, overindulged city type who needed to do a good day's work and find out what really went on in the world. Since then Helen had become a favourite in the village and found herself a job as well as caring alone for two lively children.

From time to time since he had spent a whole Saturday showing Helen, Callum, Lucy and `Etta` around his organic farm, George Lee called round to have a chat. They found it easy talking to each other and comparing their children's progress. He had retained Mary Yvonne, who kept house immaculately and was good for Luke and Robin in most ways. He had confided to Helen that he now had a bolt on the inside of his bedroom door and they both had laughed about him defending his `honour`. Today George arrived, quite agitated.

"They told me in Poppy`s that you had a run-in with Mary Yvonne last week. Has she been giving you a hard time?"

"Nothing I can`t handle" said Helen.

"What was it about?"

"No need for you to get involved. You have enough on your mind with the veg. contracts. We had a little disagreement over your choice of one of your friends."

"Really. Who?"

"Me."

"Oh dear! What did she say?"

"Just a few things about the amount of time you spend with me, and apparently talking about me. And a lot of things in French that may not have been too complimentary,"

"Michael said you had a biscuit fight!"

"Only a small battle - and I paid him for the biscuits. She ran out of words and started throwing Crawford's cream crackers, not very accurately. I have been throwing a cricket ball to Callum recently and I caught her off-guard, right between the eyes with a packet of six Wagon Wheels. She sort of gave up then and flounced out of Spar into her car.

"God, Helen. I am so sorry."

"It`s all forgotten. I had a lovely half-hour in Poppy's, afterwards, telling them all before they heard an exaggerated version later from the shoppers around us. They found it hilarious."

"I can`t have her assaulting my friends."

Helen decided that the rest of the conversation may be better held out on the garden seat as she had noticed everything in the kitchen had been quiet for a few minutes. They took their drinks out into the spring sunshine.

"Let me take you to dinner tonight by way of apology" said George.

"You can take me out because you want to, if you like, but no apology is needed," she replied.

"Pick you up at seven thirty pm. How`s that?"

"Good. I`ll call you before if I can`t get a babysitter," said Helen.

Deirdre said that Maisie would do the babysitting if she could bring her `young man`. Helen agreed and they arrived on his motor bike just after seven o`clock.

George and Helen enjoyed a happy evening at the Hare and Hounds Pub Restaurant above Honiton and watched `Morris Dancers` playing and dancing for their beer. They sat in the tall Range Rover and talked for nearly an hour in the driveway back at home, before Helen got out. She walked around the car and kissed him on the mouth through the open driver`s door window. George looked pleasantly surprised and said:

"I`m glad I wound down the window."

He watched her go inside the house and drove slowly home.

Erik brought Lucy back after the first outdoor session of the springtime. She was red in the face after a vigorous hour with Coralie and chasing Paul`s heavier shots down the lines of the full sized court. He said `goodnight` and walked around to the Barn Studio. He had found his copy of the key in his car glove compartment. He noted that the salt from the winter seas and wind had left a film around the hasp and padlock. Erik switched on both lights and walked pointedly across to the paintings on the floor in the corner. He removed the cardboard protection and pulled out the `girl by the river`. Taking it to his pile of art materials he set up the main easel and placed the canvas on the horizontal support. Standing back two paces he studied the painting, letting his mind take him back again to the days of its creation and a depth of emotion. After a seeming pause in the time of the universe he went to find his `barn stool`, dusted off the seat with his hand, and returned to the painting. A tear followed the line of his nose joining his cheek and crept around the corner of his mouth to silently drop from his chin to the floor.

Five or maybe ten minutes passed. Erik went over to the canvas again and, with his thumb nail, gently peeled a small piece of bird dropping from the shoulder of the girl. He took the painting back to its hidden place and replaced others around it and the cardboard covers. Leaving the easel and stool he took another set of keys from above one of the wall timbers, left and locked the studio. Erik walked along an overgrown path at the back of the nicely laid garden and through a small wood to a wooden gate in the hedge. The gate was secured with a chain and padlock attached. He found the key and, with difficulty, released the padlock and opened the gate. It led into a small compound that was full of scattered leaves and twigs. The flagstones to the tower staircase led to a second gate and the road. A once carefully designed garden of flower beds and climbing roses had been badly neglected for a number of years. The staircase was wide and led to a landing about fifteen feet above the ground. The stairs were metal and looked sound but badly in need of a good clean. He went up to the landing. A second, narrower stair stretched to a smaller level area. He went up again. The small landing was beside a long room that had been cleverly hung from the metal girders of the huge square concrete water container above. A second key let him into the bathroom/toilet. All the water had been shut off with a lever on the mains supply line. A lightweight aluminium ladder lay on its side inside the room. Erik took this and placed the two prongs at one end firmly into the locating holes underneath a wide hatchway. The other end of the ladder rested on the level metal landing below.

He produced a third key on the keyring. It was wrong. He tried a fourth, berating himself for having forgotten. The key released a spring holding the hatch frame tightly shut. A gentle push against the counterweight inside and the hatch itself and a folding solid wooden ladder behind it came easily down to replace the, now removed, steps from the bathroom. Eric hesitated and leant against the rail. It was a year since he had last asked Phil Mercer and his wife, Cathy, to check the `Umpire`s Chair` and almost seventeen years since he himself had been inside. Those final six steps were very intimidating. For two years, since returning to his `bolt-hole` he had been building his mental strength and determination to take those last steps. He summoned his courage and went upwards.......

THIRTEEN

NOW

The musty smell was the first thing to hit Erik as he emerged into the large bedsitting room. He walked across to the single picture window and the safety catches opened easily allowing him to slide one side across and for the sea air to enter this south-west aspect. Looking around, nothing seemed to have moved since he was last there and he began to wonder how often she had come back after he had left.

The power points looked out of date now and the radiators which had been updated years ago. The posters on the wall, one of El Cortes, the Spanish bullfighter of the sixties, a Nike poster picturing Erik and Samuraja (Sammy) in a doubles match in Australia and the blown up photo of Maggie, Sally and Aurelia up to no good at Bath Rugby Club. He surveyed the old sofa, with the rebel spring that always seemed to be exactly where you were sitting; the double bed they had taken up in sections and built together before it could be placed, then replaced, then argued over, then moved again. There was their kettle with its cracked power connection and asthmatic whistle and all the familiar coffee mugs in their glass cabinet over the tiny sink. The fridge stood lonely and with its door open.

Erik sat in the dark wooden rocking chair and his weight tore a line across the old, frayed cushion at the back, releasing a handful of white padding. The chair seemed sound enough. He rocked back and forth looking across the sea towards distant Berry Head and Brixham. After maybe twenty minutes he thought he was in the rocking chair with her on his lap and her arms around his neck, her clean-smelling hair against his cheek.

He woke out of the half-dream, slapped his thigh and stood up.

"This is daft, Joel, you are going to send yourself into an asylum for heartbroken lovers. Snap out of it! She is not coming back. Not after all this time. Lay this ghost and think clearly," he said to himself.

He went to the writing desk she had bought from the brigadier and pulled down the flap at the top. Inside were biros, pencils and a rubber. A few single pages of lined foolscap papers and a loose pack of scrap paper cut offs with its perished rubber band looked back at him. Sliding open the top drawer underneath the flap there came a strong smell of her perfume. He sat down on the floor and silently wept. He used to bring her `J`adore` perfume and body lotion when he passed through the duty-free shops at airports. Of course, that was the drawer she used to keep a small make-up bag. Inside there was still a hairbrush and a pair of dainty earrings like swinging stars.

Erik put the earrings in his pocket and closed the drawer. He retraced his steps locking everything and leaving the `Umpire`s Chair` as he had found it. He drove down to the pub in the village. Sitting in a corner on his own he drank three pints of Heineken lager during the next hour and a half. Two women came and sat at the next table jogging him back to reality. He walked along the riverside bank back to the harbour and his bunk bed on Viti Levu and the soporific rocking of the wind and the river flow.

To the amazement of historians and the displeasure of her Bishop, the Rev. Poppy had displayed a poster on the wall of her Chocolatiere Cafe with accompanying tea towels `for sale` printed:-

The History of the Devon Cream Tea

- It was the year 877 AD and early in the reign of Alfred King of Wessex. In an attempt to come closer to his subjects, he enrolled on a catering course in Devon, the western limit of the kingdom (the Cornish being a bunch of savages.)

- Alfred won the academy`s Master Chef prize with superb scones topped with local produce. - strawberries and thick cream from Devon cows.

- He was overwhelmed by the accolade and then nearly overwhelmed by the invading Danes.

- The Wessex army had run out of ammunition, just along the road at the Battle of Lustleigh Cleave. Alfred remembered his reserve batch of scones, now cooked to a cinder in the oven. Distributed through the army the soldiers let loose volley after volley of the rock hard missiles, pummelling the Danes into submission.

- He was forthwith acclaimed as Alfred the Great but merely remembered historically for his catering oversight - burning the scones!

- The men of Devon began to thrive on a daily Cream Tea and for hundreds of years they became the feared backbone of the British Navy.

Someone had written at the bottom of the poster in biro `they all died of heart attacks before the age of thirty`, which had proven difficult to erase.

There were also instructions how to eat your Devon scone - i.e. `cream first then jam`, unlike the Cornish, who got it the wrong way around. There was a recipe with photos of a perfect finished display.

Poppy`s Bishop had vented his anger at the historical inaccuracy and blatant commercialism of the posters and suggested that it was not appropriate for a member of the clergy to be so involved with the retail trade. Poppy had respectfully replied that there was nothing in the Bible stating that God`s representatives should not make chocolate or sell cream teas, and had he recently taken a look at the trinkets and souvenirs in the foyer at Exeter Cathedral. He had not been back for over a year.

For several months Helen had been compiling a collection of Deirdre`s clever soup recipes with view to publishing them in a book with a ring binder, and selling them locally for both Deirdre and a charity. She had written up all her notes and was waiting for the cook`s return for more gems to appear. With Deirdre back in the kitchen Helen was able to return to her relaxation of reading. She had recently found the book by Sally Shaunessy that she had put down a couple of years before. It had been put into one of the bookshelves

Helen thought she would begin the Shaunessy book again because she had forgotten some of the names and their relation to each other. Half term came and Lucy went to stay with Peter`s parents in Haslemere for a few days whilst Peter commuted the thirty or so miles into work and came back to them early enough to spend some time with Lucy in the light evenings.

"I think Daddy sort of lives here now" said Lucy during

her daily phone call to Helen. After a few seconds of whispering and scuffling Peter`s mother took the phone and said that Lucy had gone to the toilet and would call again later.

"Interesting" thought Helen.

Co-incidentally during Helen`s regular meeting with Bronwen and Rachel at Poppy's, Rachel said

"Your husband was in here at the weekend. He had come early for Lucy and I served him a kind of brunch. He was asking a lot about you. Don`t you tell him anything?"

"No more than I have to - in the twenty seconds he waits whilst delivering or collecting Lucy about once a month. Also he is my ex - husband," answered Helen.

"Sure" said Rachel. That`s why I didn`t give much away."

Bronwen laughed and said, "All your lovers. and the job with the new manager, who looks like Johnny Depp."

"Basil? He`s not my type at all - well I don`t think so. I`ve never really thought of him with me. Actually he`s not too bad, I suppose."

"There you are. Another one to add to your list."

"What other lovers do you mean ?"

Rachel began, "There`s Erik, who has a Porsche and likes you best of all we admirers. There`s George and his Range Rover. Then there is Brigadier Roper who would give you the furniture in his entire shop for one little grope in the shadows. There`s Keith who sits down here in a daze if you even walk past the door, and of course, now there`s Johnny Depp in the Bank. All desperate for you."

"Do you think I would go off with the Brigadier. Or out for an illicit country drive with Keith in his bus? And what makes you think George fancies me ?"

"Only a candlelit dinner at the Hare and Hounds the other evening and `Do come in for a coffee George! ` and we all know what that means" said Rachel. His Range Rover was there for two hours. Wow! My Jim only managed to stay for half-an-hour, even when Mum had gone to stay with her sister."

'That`s not fair. It was only an hour and we sat in the car all the time."

"You can put all the seats flat in those new four by fours, Andre told me," added Bronwen.

"Ah! So he has plans for you as well," said Rachel.

"He definitely does! On honeymoon somewhere exotic" Bronwen said excitedly "and quite soon."

"How do you know all about George and me?" asked Helen.

"We are the brains of the spy network, you know. We protect the safety of the villagers and special friends."

Rachel went to brew more drinks.

"What was Peter asking?"

"Just appearing interested in who you are with - I mean men. Do you go away and leave the children? And had that ancient beachcomber ever been back to the village ? I asked him who he meant, although knowing full well. He said the one who wanted to paint nude portraits of you. I didn`t know that, Helen. I mean, did he ?"

Helen went scarlet. "No he doesn`t …. didn't! I am not sure how Peter knows, but Erik does paint naked women."

"I`ll do it. I`ll do It." shouted Poppy coming in from the kitchen with a tray of newly made chocolates for display.

"I can see the headlines in the Sunday Mirror" said Rachel "Naked Vicar says she would do it again. The Reverend Poppy, forty two, of East Devon tells our reporter that, if God had intended us to be covered, we would have been born wearing clothes. PS This photo was taken with a wide lens camera."

"Hey, hey, that`s no way to speak about the Boss. Anyway I am only forty one, and the extra weight is temporary."

Callum broke his own record for changing from school clothes to casual and rode his bike down the hill, along by the river and past new lambs, now half-grown, grazing in the field that slopes up to the edge of the golf-course from the harbour. He hailed Viti Levu and then noticed that the skiff was moored outside the yard opposite. He rode over the bridge and up to the boatyard and past the sign which said `Trespassers will be spifflicated` with `prosecuted` crossed out. He had done this himself a year ago, using a word his uncle would say to him when he was naughty and around five years old. Erik was talking to Phil about the tower, but broke off to greet Callum with the established `high five` handshake that sportsmen and others used these days.

"We`ll talk more tomorrow, Phil. I want to make some headway with the rigging in the daylight."

Erik and Callum were beginning to work as a team. They each understood what the other was doing. The boat was a lot older than the ketch on which he had taught Greg, but good equipment made one yacht much the same, in general, as another. Callum was keen to get out on the water. He had the same independent nature that Erik enjoyed himself and unlike most of his school friends, didn`t need to be forever in the peer group.

They finished fitting all the ropes and prepared the sails for ease of hauling. The mainsail was folded around the boom and the boom ready to spin as the sail was pulled up the mast. Callum cycled home with a promise of a sail tomorrow if the weather followed the forecast.

By the time Erik had returned from the Seaton Co-op supermarket it was seven thirty am and Callum was already on board. He sculled the skiff back to shore to pick up Erik and two bags of food. They ate a quite different breakfast. Callum fried eggs and tomatoes and mopped them up with pieces of fresh baguette. Erik had found some pickled herring and ate it with black bread and black coffee. Erik was still trialling and running-in the re-bored inboard engine that he had not had the use of for the first two years on Viti

Levu, and they motored out with the first of the ebb tide. It was eight ten am and they were well ahead of the holiday sailors on this May Bank holiday weekend. This May half-term week at the end of the month was a first peak week in the holiday business in the South West. Families with children at school took it as an extra vacation week to their main holiday, which would usually be reserved for the school summer holidays in late July and August. The business owners liked this week because it tested their new seasonal staff to the limit. By the end of the week they knew who would make it through the season and who would not.

If the sun shone, everyone who loved the rivers, or the lakes or the sea, would be on them or in them. All shapes and sizes of craft would make appearances, often with new, untrained and wobbly owners. The locals stayed at home or went out very early, that is those few who were not working hard to support the visitors. Viti Levu sailed a half mile out to sea on a broad reach using the light south-westerly breeze and then she ran before the wind along the coast past Lyme Regis and Golden Cap hill separating Charmouth and Chideok. Erik loved this unpressured life and a chance to talk `sailing` all the way to his young student. Callum took out his mobile and called Helen to explain what they were doing. He explained to Erik that he had forgotten to leave a note for his Mum about lunch. They ate lunch as they sailed and Erik told him how the tinned corn beef had become an important food item during the Second World War for the troops abroad - much of it coming from South America. He went on to tell this geography/history lover why Sweden did not enter the war. Sometimes a country has to do what it considers best for its own people. They discussed the advantages and disadvantages of this to Sweden during and after 1945 and how it affected the rest of Europe. Erik changed the topic to sailing and outdoor adventure.

"How would you like to go on a junior adventure fortnight this summer?"

"What would I do?" asked Callum.

"There are a number of different courses in several parts of the UK You could go rock climbing in Scotland or Wales, trekking in Ireland, Scotland, the Lake District, or to a sea school in Wales or Scotland. Some places offer a mixture of activities, and there are many in different countries in Europe too."

"I don`t think Mum has any spare money for me to go on expensive adventures."

"If she did or I paid for part of it, would you want to go?"

"I thought last year that I would like to try crewing on a topsail schooner - one of the Tall Ships in the race, but now I would choose a mixture of land and sea, maybe trekking on a pony and then sea-canoeing," said Callum.

"I`ll see what I can find that is still available."

They brought Viti Levu into harbour slowly on the jib and the motor and moored her on her lime green buoy. Callum cycled home, talking to people he knew along the way. Cycling around the bend in the drive he saw the Seaton florist delivering a large display of flowers to Helen, who was taking them and trying to read the card at the same time.

"They are from your Dad," she said as he took off his trainers in the porch. He said nothing and went straight upstairs to his room. Later Callum came down and joined her for the evening meal. It was a fisherman`s pie with a tasty topping preceded by another of Deirdre`s unusual soups.

"Those flowers are lovely aren`t they ?" asked Helen.

"What soup is this? It looks green and horrible, but it tastes great," said Callum.

"It`s courgette."

"But I hate courgettes. Mum what have you done?" He made a sour expression and pushed the bowl away.

"Courgette, cream of coconut, onion, carrot, potato, salt, pepper and a dollop of single cream. All liquidised and made with love. I thought you said it was great."

"Yes it is. But courgette is a swear word! Like broccoli." He pulled back the bowl and continued spooning the soup enthusiastically. "Peter Walker is a `broccoli` if he comes inside this house ever again."

Peter came inside the house a few days later. He returned Lucy after her week with his parents.

"Helen, can I come in? I need to talk to you about something important."

Helen pulled out a chair in the kitchen for him to sit on, but leant against the fridge, arms folded.

"Helen. I have been thinking. It is crazy - all this to-ing and fro-ing with Lucy, and you have to go out to work when the children need you at home. You and I having to pay two house rents when it could only be one. Why don`t we forget our previous difficulties and get together again?"

FOURTEEN

NOW

Helen decided to listen to Peter as he sat in her kitchen on the second Sunday and the last day of school half-term. She thought he looked quite fit and smart. No doubt two years of chasing Rose around the bedroom had kept his weight down. Whilst he was talking she remembered how much they had enjoyed sex in the early years of their marriage. It must have been around the beginning of the affair with Rose in Qatar that it began to become just an inevitable routine, on Thursday nights before the Qatari Muslim weekend and after parties and a few drinks

Peter`s relationship with Rose had already broken down or was going through a bad patch. The flowers, the questions at Poppy`s and the Dragon`s intervention in Lucy`s phone call together told the tale. He wants you back! Mother is not going to iron his shirts for much longer and he may have to find somewhere to live. Why pay another rent? I think he actually just said that. She tuned in again to the monologue.

"......his business failed, you know. Womaniser!

".....his wife couldn`t stand it any longer and went off. Since then he has had a string of young women in there on

147

the pretext of mothering the kids. Word is the latest one has seen he has his eye on you and is about to go."

Helen`s silence gave Peter the extra confidence to stand up and pace the kitchen floor.

"And then we come to the frightening scenario of the Scandinavian. Of course you know where he got his money from to buy this place. He was a second rate tennis player years ago and overpaid by a sponsor......."

Helen spoke for the first time.

"I don`t know who owns the house, except that he has been very kind to us."

"Of course he has. It`s the easy way to get access to Callum."

Helen looked puzzled.

"My man says he bought the house years ago and abused a teenager shortly afterwards. The family couldn`t prove anything and moved away. He lets the house to families with teenage boys that he can groom for his own pleasure."

"But he hasn`t shown up in the two years we have lived here."

"Don`t be daft. It`s that Erik bloke using a different name as a cover." Peter went to look for the whisky decanter. Shock registered all over Helen`s face. Not Erik surely. She sat down and thought back to the beginning. Erik had be-friended Callum before Helen had even met him - yes - he had picked Callum up when he played truant, somewhere down by the river. There was the strange, come to think of it, episode of their buying a boat together. And they spend hours on it alone with `heaven knows what` going on in Erik`s cabin, his bedroom! God, what had she done, letting her young son become a victim of a known predator or pae-dophile? How had her intuition let her down? Why hadn`t anyone warned her? And Lucy - he takes Lucy to Ottery! What do they do there? She says it`s all tennis and she likes him a lot. Is Erik after both of them or is one a cover for the other? What do I do now.....? All these thoughts were running through her head........

"Where`s the whisky in this house?" called Peter.

"We don`t have any. I don`t drink very often these days. There may be a bottle of red wine in the cupboard under the stairs," said Helen.

"What the hell is it doing there?"

"I think I hid it from the babysitters!" Helen said distractedly, thinking she must talk to Rev. Poppy.

Peter found the wine and poured himself a glass, sipped it and screwed up his face.

"So, as Callum`s father I have come to ensure his safety. Also, Lucy tells me she misses me so much she cries herself to sleep at night. It all makes sense that we should be back together, get away from the country bumpkins and the dodgy landlord and find somewhere more civilised to bring up our children. I brought a few things with me so I could stay and take care of you tonight. We can sort out the detail in the morning. I don`t have to be back in the office until Thursday."

Helen jumped herself back into reality and stared Peter straight in the eye.

"In the last two years I have become my own person and make my own decisions. I will speak quietly because both the children are upstairs. Thank you for the information. I will consider it seriously. Leave me your mobile number and I will call you after I finish work either tomorrow or Tuesday."

"But you may be in danger tonight. I have the responsibility to care for Callum."

"He is fourteen now. If you don`t begin that for another two days, I doubt it will make any difference. I see you have finished your wine. Now please go. I will tell Callum of your sudden interest."

Without actually pushing, but standing close behind him, Helen ushered Peter out through the porch.

"I have very strong feelings still for you.......and I will make up for my past indiscretions.......you won`t need to work ever again...we even......"

"GO NOW PETER!" She didn`t mean to have shouted but the words came out like three bullets from a gun.

Peter jumped back and headed straight for the car. Helen closed the front door immediately in case he came back, and watched the car leave from the kitchen window out of the corner of her eye, pretending she was only interested in the sink.

A few minutes later she decided to go upstairs and hug both children before beginning a daunting inquisition about their time with Erik. Lucy and Callum were sitting side by side on the top stair, probably having heard everything. Thinking quickly, Helen said:

"Come down here both of you. Let`s go out in the garden and spend a few minutes together. Callum, bring us each a drink will you. Lemonade for me please."

"Mum, you were brill!" said Lucy, walking beside her.

"Didn`t you want Dad to stay?"

"No, no. We want you to marry Erik!"

Helen sat on the garden seat with one arm round each of them, looking at the Peace roses which were releasing a wonderful scent into the evening air. As they silently finished their drinks, a male blackbird began to sing from the topmost branch of the old cherry tree

"Go and have a bath, darling, and wash your hair. I`ll come and help you get all the shampoo out in a moment." Lucy kissed her and went towards the house.

"Mum." "Yes, dear."

"Just because a man wants to a help a boy or a girl it doesn`t mean he is going to try to have sex with them always does it?" asked Callum.

"No. Nearly always it is just a kindness to teach or help them. But there are a few people who have a problem and plan everything so that they can take advantage of a child or teenager."

"How can you tell which they are?"

"It is best to stay in a group until your parents get to know them well. Don`t be alone with the person. Listen to what they say. Do they talk about your body or ask you to take any clothes off. Does it feel right to be near them? Be aware of all these things. Listen to rumours about their past. but don`t necessarily believe the rumours. Tell where you are going and with whom. Those are the main things to be aware of.

"You didn`t check Erik out when he first spoke to me."

"No I was very wrong and a bad mother not to do that. Has he ever said or done any of the things I spoke about?"

"No. Nothing. He teaches me a lot of things, but not about my body. What did Peter mean about him doing this before?"

"I don`t know. I think it would be a good idea to stay away from Erik for a few days while I find out some more."

"I am sure he`s OK, Mum. I`ll stay away this week, then he goes to watch the tennis at Queen`s Club. He is a tennis pro, Mum. Last week we were playing tennis on the sports afternoon and I asked Mr Johnson again about Erik and said that he watched a lot of tennis. We looked up a website of all the tennis pros in the last twenty years and their photos. It was back in the 1990s and he is called Joel Eriksson. He was really good and won Grand Slam Doubles titles. He got up to No 7 in the world in Singles too. It said he now is a tennis correspondent and has a number of charity interests."

"Thanks, darling. Now we know he is not a rich foot-baller. You didn`t think that anyway, did you? Did you hear Dad say he wanted to come back and live with us?"

"Not if you want me to stay in this house "

Callum went inside the house. Helen stretched and

finished her glass of lemonade. She got up to join Lucy in the bathroom.

"There's shampoo in my eyes. Wash it off! Wash it off! It stings," was Lucy's welcome to her mother.

"Etta says that her dad told her that the ladies in the Masai tribe in East Africa put cow's poo in their hair. I told her we do the same only it's 'pretend poo'. They use real poo and we use sham poo! Ha, ha, ha, ha."

Helen grinned at her lively daughter and hoped for the best in the next five minutes.

"Does Erik ever touch you when you two go off to play tennis?"

"Oh, yes. Lots of times!" said Lucy, still with eyes closed as the shower spray wavered in Helen's hand and sprayed more curtain than Lucy.

"Concentrate, Mum, concentrate! That's what Erik says to me and Paul on the court."

In trepidation Helen added, "Where does he touch you, darling?"

"Beside the tennis court."

"Where on your body?"

"He stands behind me and puts his left hand on my shoulder and his right hand holds my wrist and we swing the racket together."

"Right. Thanks, darling. Does he ever touch you in the car, or when no one else is around?"

"No. Coralie and Paul are always watching. Paul is learning too and I think Coralie loves Erik."

Lucy climbed out of the bath and Helen wrapped her in a large green bath towel.

"Has Erik ever seen you like this with no clothes on?"

"Mummy, really! I am nearly a lady now and I shan't show my lady bits until I am married. Saskia thinks I can then show them to anybody, even the doctor when I am having babies."

Lucy ran off to her room and Helen sat on the bath, partly relieved and partly envious of the wonderful innocence of her daughter.

Lucy ran back. "Erik kissed me once. Just there," pointing to her forehead. He was going away and Coralie was jealous. Ha ha." She ran back to her bed, an innocent night`s sleep ahead, and clean clothes already laid out ready for her morning at the local primary school.

On the way back from the farm suppliers that evening, George parked his car and trailer in the bus layby in the village. He went into Spar to buy a loaf of bread for Mary Yvonne to make the children's` school packed lunches. Peter, driving through, after leaving Kirkhaven House, saw him and leant out of his car window as George passed.

"You`re the fellow who owns the farm next to my house." George held out his hand, "George Lee. Pleased to meet you."

Peter didn`t take his hand but merely said:

"My wife is no longer available. We have decided to get together again and will be moving away at the end of the month." He pulled away leaving George speechless standing in the middle of the road.

Helen phoned Poppy from work and asked to see her in her `counselling` role preferably in private. Poppy invited her to the vicarage at 2 pm, before Helen would have to be home to meet Lucy, as Deirdre has asked to come on Tuesday that week. Poppy had made the imposing limestone vicarage less imposing by planting Virginia creeper and letting it climb all over the front of the house.

"Amazing maroon colour in October," she said welcoming Helen inside and guiding her into the large living room.

Helen explained that Peter had returned with a proposal for them to become family again. She didn`t need any guidance in that department, but was perturbed by what he had said about Erik. Poppy asked all the questions she may have expected about Callum`s and Lucy`s personal experiences of one to one contacts with Erik. She enquired about the sources of Peter`s information and whether there was anything to substantiate the allegations he was making. Then she said:

"We are women and all women seem to have a better developed intuition than men. It has been a safeguard during aeons of male domination. What does your intuition tell you about Erik?" Helen shrugged, "All good things. Sexy man. Strong character, kind and gentle. Unusually secretive. A loner."

"No. Your intuition. The feeling that has no reason. Good or bad?"

"Good."

"Nothing creepy about him?"

"Nothing creepy. Lots of mystery though."

"I am the same about him," said Poppy and so are all the women in the village. In my experience, when there is a man or woman around with anti-social or abusive sexual energy, women sense it and at least one or two voice it. Now I can tell you a little more about our Erik. I needed to hear what you were saying first in case anything had changed. When he first came to the village and immediately latched on to your Callum I was not a happy clergy person, so I asked around. First to the police patrol boys who drink my tea whether I am open or closed. They cannot say outright if there is a known predator or registered paedophile on our patch, but they have a list of permanents, i.e. residents, back in the station and are updated regarding the movements of those on holiday. When I asked them they said they were likely to be more interested in the roving ambition of a certain retired army officer! This was their way of saying `nothing known`.

"Then I quizzed some locals because I had heard he was here at another time. It turned out it was a long time ago. ...before the millennium. I was not here. Spar was a small corner shop. The pub has changed hands and the White Horse closed. But Arthur the postman was here and the Brigadier, and most knowledgeable of all was Phil Mercer from Seaton - you know - he and George, his dad, run the Boatyard. To put it all together it seems Erik was a useful tennis player and, although Arthur didn`t say much, he said he had a lot of well-known friends. Brigadier Roper admitted selling him some furniture. Now Phil knows a lot but keeps much of it quiet. Erik was a great help to them after a yard fire and helped them rebuild. He came down about three times a year to his boat and played a lot of golf. He owns that tower next to you, that water tower with the window in it. Maybe you have never looked at it. The window is on the side away from the road and it is all closed up. And there was something they all hinted at - a sort of love triangle linked with abroad."

"I am rambling. The most important thing is that the son of the family that lived in your house was distraught and suicidal at the loss of his friend (road accident). Erik worked on him and he recovered. Now they used to go out on Erik`s boat a lot, but no one ever suggested anything bad about the friendship, just Erik doing a good `counselling` job, if you like."

"Thanks Poppy. Thanks for being so open and clearing my mind of some questions. I have a few new ones now. The boat is a mystery. Erik and Callum bought one together recently. Maybe he bought his own boat back. Now I must go home and be there for Lucy," said Helen.

Lucy always arrived home before Callum. The Lyme Regis school bus dropped Callum in the village and he walked home up the hill. After Lucy had unloaded the daily social dramas from school, Helen asked her whether she had cried herself to sleep last night because she missed Daddy.

"No, Mummy. I only did that once when Daddy went away first and I thought when parents did that you never saw them again."

"Daddy said last night that you did it often."

"He asked me in the car last night whether I missed him and I said `Yes`. Well, I do, but I would rather it was Erik. Then he said did I ever cry when I missed him and I said, `Yes. Once I cried myself asleep.` Well it was true, Mum, I did. Can I go and see if the hedgehog is still at the end of the garden with its babies?"

"Change your clothes first, and trainers, not school shoes." Helen wondered if she would get `life` or just a few years for cutting her ex-husband into small pieces and feeding him to the buzzards.

Her last meeting in the interrogation process, after Peter's `revelations` was to be with Erik himself. His car was in the drive so he must be in the barn studio. She grasped the nettle and strode down the path. She knocked on the door and strode inside at the same time. Erik looked as though he was punching an imaginary opponent and then stopped in a `freeze- frame` stance.

"What on earth are you doing?" asked Helen.

"Tai Chi," he replied.

"I've heard of it, but never seen anyone doing it before."

"Come. I'll show you. Ah, you have on the wrong clothes. You do look very business-like in your Bank uniform. It suits you. I would give you my money," said Erik.

"That's no good. We want to lend you money at interest, not receive it."

'Damn. In ten seconds he has taken away your serious approach. Try again.'

"I need to talk to you. Can we go somewhere?"

"A walk along the cliff path? Tea for two in Honiton? A pony trek on Woodbury Common?"

They settled for the garden seat - the site of many recent confidences. Callum looked out of his bedroom window just after he had hidden the book going round the class and it was his turn to read. He decided that he had better not join them on the seat in view of yesterday evening`s events.

"Erik, you know I am very fond of you?"

"No" he replied

"The girls in Poppy`s think I have a long list of lovers and you are the first on the list."

"So you want me to make passionate love tonight to authenticate the village survey?"

"Erik. Are you making improper advances to my children?" He sat bolt upright, thought for a minute, then replied:

"You will expect me to say, `No`, but how improper do you mean? Do you mean sexual advances or simply that they do things without consulting you?"

"I meant mild sexual," said Helen hesitantly.

"No. Most certainly not. Can you tell me what is leading you to ask the question, without compromising your mistaken informer ?" he asked.

"Yes, I can. It`s my ex-husband. He seems to have been employing a Private Eye to check out my multifarious lovers and the abusers of my children."

"I know him. I bought him a pint two years ago in the Kings Arms because he seemed to recognise me from somewhere. He was around again a week ago asking Phil who shared my cabin. I was going to give him a PR leaflet that my current manager has dreamed up, to save him trouble."

"Are you really our landlord, and, if you are, why not say so. Why change your name? Peter says it is a cover for you to get access to children."

"Yes, Helen. I am the owner of the house. The reason I changed my name and the reason I say little about myself is that for some years, I was the victim of my own success.

I played a reasonable game of tennis and it earnt me a lot of money and my name became widely known. I needed a place to get away from constant publicity and people wanting a piece of me. So I would come and stay and sail my boat here during the year. Usually three visits - two sailing and all three for golf with a young lad who needed some guidance and aim in life when I met his Mum one summer. It's a coincidence about the boys but I was a lucky teenager who was rescued, if you like, by a mentor, and it has been a chance to balance the books."

"He said you were abusing the boy. The family couldn`t prove anything so they moved away," said Helen.

"Nonsense. He and I are in touch every month. He is in charge of a charity that is clearing the debris dragged into the sea in Sri Lanka after the tsunami wave withdrew in 2004. They are doing good work enabling inshore fishermen to be able to fish again without breaking their nets. The family moved away for quite a different reason. Your husband, ex-husband, is making a number of allegations that are motivated by a desire to influence you against me for some reason."

"Yes. He wants me back! Because his mistress - or current wife - I don`t know what she is - has thrown him out, or he has lost interest in her. Erik, I am not sure what to do. I am scared he could use all this to try to take custody of the children. I believe you, but would a Judge ?"

"Has anyone at any time told you that I have done anything that could be construed as an attempt to take sexual advantage of a child?"

"No."

"It is all speculation then, based on nothing, and designed to frighten you and for you to take him back into your home. No court would entertain the `claim`."

There was a long pause. They both started talking together. Helen continued:

"Did you buy back your old boat?"

"What. Viti Levu? No, she is thirty years older than `Nasty`. `Nasty` was a new ketch when I bought her in 1997. I sailed her down from the Hamble with Samuraja, my doubles partner. Bought her with some of our winnings. We had cleaned up in three consecutive tournaments earlier that year."

"Nasty?" exclaimed Helen.

"Yes. He was the most naturally fluent and gifted player I have ever seen. Ilie Nastase from Romania. The Aussies called him that, but he was quite nice. And you would have found his jet black hair and gypsy looks very attractive!"

"Does he know you named your boat after him?"

"I doubt it. He wouldn`t mind. Probably ask to spend a weekend on her. I sold her and many other memories of that time in haste after the Millennium. That`s another story. Look, I go to Queens and Wimbledon at the end of the week. I`ll go now instead. It would be better. It will give you some time to sort out the rumours and the truth. Ask Callum to keep his usual daily check going on Viti Levu until after Wimbledon please."

"Erik. Thank you for not evicting me when Peter didn`t pay the rent."

"Thank you for believing my story and not Peter`s. I guess that makes us even. Wait, though. Am I still top of the Helen seduction list?"

"Maybe."

Helen went into the house and Erik returned to pack up his paints in the Barn Studio.

"Mummy"

"Yes, my darling Lucy"

"I couldn`t find the little hedgehogs, but I have found the mother in Erik`s studio. He has done a fabulous painting of her today. The paint is still wet. I touched it to see. Then I crept out and came back to the house while he was chatting you up in the garden."

159

FIFTEEN

THEN

`SPY TOWER` was the headline on the front page of the local journal, followed in smaller, but heavy black print by `Millionaire applies for planning to spy on Axe Valley`. Their reporter had been reading the applications to the Council Planning Committee for alterations and new building proposals at their next meeting. There were rumblings in the pub that evening:

"Don`t want no wealthy git looking over my back garden."

"Why?. What do you do out there in secret then?"

"Not him. It`s his Missus with the postman."

"She must be feeling neglected to go for Arthur."

"Serious though, he`ll know everything that goes on in the village."

"Only got to ask Aggie in the shop. She`ll tell ee all the gossip."

"That salmon you caught underweight last week - he`ll see through his telescope and have the Fisheries Board on you."

"I don`t like it. They`ll throw it out won`t they?"

"Dunno. He`s rich they say. Few quid in the right places. You know how it is."

"Well, I think it`s good idea" said Maisie from behind the bar. "That tower has been an eyesore for years. All they phone masts stuck on the side and the paint peeling off. I heard he is only going to use it for painting pictures" she added.

"He`ll be watching you sunbathing up the top field and painting you. Next thing you`ll be on sale in Branscombe Gallery!"

"Jumble sale more like...need a bloody wide canvas."

Maisie hit the last contributor with her tea towel and knocked his beer over the guy sitting on the next stool. Chaos reigned for a few minutes and then they moved on to the usual topics of weather, the price of cattle at recent markets and cars towing caravans.

The summer had moved into the family holiday time and `Outrageous Oliver`s was thriving. The name drew many in to see what was outrageous in this conservative community. The older generation, some homophobic, others beyond humour, would not come down until mid-September after the children had gone back for the start of the new school year. Oliver had hired Danny who was eighteen and on summer vacation from South Devon Catering College in Torquay. He was supposed to be the cook. His parents had known Oliver since he had opened his original `Harbour Cafe`. Mandy lived in Seaton and was a working Mum and part-time waitress on the busy summer days. They gave as good as they got from Oliver, and added to the `outrageous` atmosphere of the place. Sally took Erik down to the cafe at the first opportunity.

"Look who`s back Oliver." He and Erik embraced just inside the doorway. For once Oliver was without words.

"Thank you for all the encouraging texts, my friend" said Erik.

"We followed your every shot, ducky. George told us on Sunday he had a message to give `Nasty` a special buff up and we hoped that meant you would come down this week. Maggie has been wetting herself in here every time your name has been mentioned, and had a catfight with someone who thought you were past it. Verbal one - not croissants at ten paces or anything like that!"

"Maggie is still single then?" asked Erik. Sally nodded.

"Danny. Black coffee and a cappuccino. Look at him! I pay him massive wages and he stares into space all the time. Go on! Go on!"

Danny brought the drinks on a tray together with a glass of water for Oliver.

"I was going to employ his sister. She would have been much better. Where is it she`s gone?" asked Oliver

"As far away from you as possible" said Danny. "On an archeological expedition to all the old forts in Southern Algeria. In the Sahara" Danny qualified.

"Probably come back with Legionnaire`s disease" said Oliver.

"You haven`t improved since I left Mr........What is your other name Oliver?" said Erik.

"It`s Out-rageous" said a small boy from two tables away. The whole family had been listening in. "It says so on the front of the cafe"

"Quite right, young man, but it`s a restaurant not a mere cafe. Remember in future please" said Oliver.

"Now darling, have you won lots of money this year? Maggie and I are sort of management for you now. We look after your interests in the West Country and were wondering when you were planning to pay our fees!" he asked Erik.

"I am a little short of funds this week. I expect Maggie will hope to be paid in kind, but you will have to wait, Oliver."

"People have been known to change their orientation" said Oliver hopefully, and then winked at Sally.

"Sorry, not me. Not even to get Maggie off my tail" said Erik.

"That`s where she hopes to be" added Sally.

"There`s a digital padlock on my chastity belt and I have forgotten the code numbers" said Erik drinking some coffee.

"Mmm, have you changed your coffee brand this year, Oliver?"

"No" said Danny from the counter. "It`s last year`s dregs re-cycled. He does the same with tea bags. Dries them off and re-uses them. He reckons he can make one tea bag last a Bank holiday weekend."

"Get back into the kitchen immediately" said Oliver.

The family near Sally were now laughing openly and enjoying the banter. Another family of four came in and sat down followed by Mandy, carrying one shoe with a broken heel.

"Serves you right. Told you not to buy new shoes" said Oliver.

"Get them from the charity shop like the rest of us. Bet you paid about forty for those and they don`t even match your bag. I got these Gucci pumps in Sue Ryders for three quid and they`re perfect for the summer.

"They`re womens` shoes" said the same boy.

"What do you know small trousers? Is your Dad in the footwear business?" Dad shook his head, grinning. "Well shut your face or a flying cheesecake could be heading for it!"

The family stood up to leave. "See you next year" said Dad. "We paid the Chef."

"Chef! Chef!" said Oliver. "I had to teach him how to boil water."

"Is Greg up to speed with his `A` level work?" Erik asked Sally.

"I think so. He doesn`t say much and tries to give me the impression that he is only muddling through. Whenever I see one of his teachers though I hear cautious optimism and no sense of there being a problem."

"What about his golf? Is he playing at all?"

"You may have a surprise. He won the men`s monthly medal a couple of weeks ago and they cut his handicap again" said Sally.

"My goodness. What is he now? I thought his letters had been missing that information."

"I`m not saying. You`ll have to ask him."

"Here comes my handicap" said Oliver for Mandy`s benefit. Late for work, one shoe, we are preparing for lunch and she`s watering the plants."

"If I didn`t, no other bugger would" retaliated Mandy.

"Sir here couldn`t give a toss about my plants but the customers tell me they make the place almost tolerable."

"I agree, Mandy, they are lovely and the perfume from the lilies and that stephanotis is much nicer than the smell of cooking" said Sally.

"He hasn`t a clue about flowers" said Mandy. "He thought Stefanotis was a Greek Restaurant owner. You`d think that being a .....well a......"

Oliver interrupted "A refined gentleman of a more discerning persuasion, was the term you were looking for."

"Well, yes, one of them......you`d expect him to be great with flowers and things," continued Mandy.

After having lunch with Oliver and checking `Nasty` at the boatyard, Erik and Sally returned to Kirkhaven House to be there when Greg came in from school. He and Erik greeted each other with a `high five handshake` and began to talk about Greg`s new grips on his golf clubs. They loaded their clubs into the car and set off to play at the nearby cliff-top golf course. Sally watched them go with a smile, knowing how much Greg had missed Erik`s companionship.

While they were waiting on the seventh tee for the pair in front to finish putting, Greg began telling Erik about a visit he had made today with his tutor group. As part of his new `life skills and experience` course, they had visited the crematorium in Exeter. After a tour of the chapels and an explanation of the process of the deceased person through the system, he was impressed with the great care the staff took to ensure every aspect was completed with reverence and provision of all the supporting services the family would desire. They then went into the large memorial garden where all the group were able to see the variety of plaques left by relatives, with appropriate words for their loved ones. The most poignant moment of the day came when the group found the tribute to their colleague, Michael, Greg`s best friend, who had been killed in the school bus incident three years before. The plate simply said:

`MICHAEL. LOVED AND FOREVER REMEM-BERED`

The journey back in the school minibus had been in silence.

They went back to Viti Levu after the game and sat enjoying the evening light, eating beans on toast with a fried egg on top.

"Can`t eat this when I am on the circuit" said Erik.

"Erik, what do you think happens when we die?"

"My mother told me when I was small that the person became a star in the sky. There are so many up there on a clear night in Sweden that I could easily believe that."

"Do you think Mike is up there watching me?"

They both looked at the only star visible in the evening light, the planet Jupiter.

"Doubt he is that one; that will be Ghandi or Lord Buddha I expect. What do you think happens? Do we continue in some form?"

Greg and his sixth form friends had all agreed that life

continues afterdeath. It didn't make sense to them that the intangible mind should just stop. Erik explained that death is so final and there is no way yet discovered of continuation one way or another. He had come to some conclusions after talking to people who think they know. He suggested to Greg that he keep an open mind and read around the subject and make a point of visiting churches and individuals who could have their own ideas, and then find out why they do.

"Who could I ask?" said Greg.

"People who have to console families after a death of someone close; church leaders, funeral directors. Borrow books from the library. Older people are best because they will all have had to think about it. Most of those over fifty will have lost a parent or aunt or uncle and wondered, maybe even thought a lot about whether they are still somewhere," Erik replied.

"What about you? Do you think you know?"

"I have some ideas that make sense to me and I pitch them against things I read and hear. I went to a meeting of Spiritualists once and listened to a lady passing messages from men and women who had died to others in the audience who were hoping for some link. Some were specifically about topics the medium could not have known, unless it was a fix. I thought it couldn't be a fraud because neither the medium (the person with the gift of hearing), nor the recipient had anything to gain from fixing it. They have small churches in every big town if you want to go and watch one day."

"Say it is genuine and part of us continues and we leave the body behind, sort of like getting out of a car and walking away never to come back again. Where does that bit of us go?"

"That is the big mystery. No one seems to know in a way they can prove or demonstrate" said Erik. "Lots of religious people think they know. Do what I do. If some of what you hear makes sense to you, place it in a file in your head. Add all the items in your file together after a while and come to a conclusion. Then through your life, balance that conclusion against anything new you hear or read, and alter the conclusion if necessary. You may be able to meet Michael again one day and resume your friendship in another dimension."

Erik changed the subject, "Have you got a summer holiday job?"

"Yes. I thought I would run a small business cleaning golfers` clubs and their bags and trolleys. I have bought some special types of cleaner for metal and plastic and rubber. The Club Secretary said it would be OK and I could do it beside the clubhouse."

They talked about how much to charge for each job.

"I may have some work for you too," said Erik and told Greg about the tower plans if he managed to obtain planning approval.

East Devon Council Planning Committee discussed the plan at length. Although there had been many rumblings in the pubs and cafes, shops and over garden fences, there had been no letters of complaint in response to the planning application posters on the gate and telegraph pole outside the tower compound. The Committee members speculated upon what activities may be watched from such a commanding outlook until the Chairman brought the mirth under control.

Approval was given with restrictions on the position of windows preventing viewing over nearby Kirkhaven House on one side and the Farmhouse on the other side. Also there had to be off-road parking for residents due to the narrow nature of the lane. The committee agreed with the Council Surveyor that any improvement to the present state of the water tower would be good.

Erik began to contact two local builders with his architect's design for the changes to the tower, and one from Bristol recommended by the architect, because they had built a suspended room successfully before. The venture was going to cost a lot of money. It would be an unique creation and a good investment and could bean ideal site and quiet studio for a wealthy bachelor artist. Both the London-based architect and the Bristol Builder saw the tower project as one which would enhance their reputations for original design and structural

innovation. They won the contract, made themselves available swiftly and work began within days. The Bristol builders brought a team of men to stay in the immediate area and work overtime in the good summer weather and long daylight hours.

The water tower was drained and cleaned. Straight metal staircases were delivered and fixed in place with platforms at two levels. They were wide to facilitate the initial building work, and later to enable furniture to be taken upwards. A large hole was cut in the base with half to be filled by the folding ladder to be used as the final stage of ascending into the room above. The other half was pannelled with pieces that could be taken up when a larger space was needed to move furniture from below. The South West aspect wall was opened and a huge picture window installed and broad skylights inserted into the roof. The whole of the room that had been created was plastered and a wooden floor fixed to wooden joists. The builders took great pride then in installing steel girders to partially suspend a smaller room below to become a bathroom. This was supported on one central pillar which took all the plumbing and electricity cables to and from both rooms; the waste leading to a new septic tank at the edge of the next door field.

Erik arranged for a new fence to surround the property with two gates – one from the road, wide enough to allow a single car to enter and park under the tower and one leading through to the wood and then down to Kirkhaven House. He was pleased with the result and watched the builders finish their part of the refurbishment by painting the whole structure shamrock green to blend with the range of greens in the surrounding vegetation and trees. He signed two bank drafts drawn on his `property account` in the Cayman Islands for large sums, one to the architect and the other to a happy finance manager of the Bristol firm. Each knew he would use photographs of their work to advertise the skills of their respective businesses for years to come.

The old water tower, standing slightly higher than the surrounding tree line, and now painted a colour which blended into the environment, was no longer a blot on the landscape. It overlooked part of the village and provided a spectacular view of the coastline towards Torbay and the famous Devon red cliffs. Erik and Sally began to decorate the inside of the main room. There was a small kitchen corner with sink and drainer, short work surface and cupboards above and below. A new microwave oven and the kettle from the Barn Studio stood ready for use.

Since finding out that Erik was the American landlord and realising that he was paying Chris and Sally rent for using his own barn, Sally had kept this money in a separate account. Now she insisted upon using the balance to buy furniture for the new venture.

Most artists in the world live and work in poor surroundings. They make do with studios in garages, lofts, outhouses or barns, often living in the same space as they paint or sculpt. The bohemian existence has become part of the public image. Coming from an affluent past, and having accumulated his own wealth from sponsorship and prize money, Erik however, was enthusiastic about adopting better, but still more `lived in` surroundings for his hobby. This tallied with the limited sum that Sally had to furnish the tower.

They spent two days touring the second-hand shops, a charity furniture store and attending an auction in Honiton. They bought a sofa, table and two chairs, a four foot wide bed and mattress, an ottoman box, a rocking chair and several stools and lamps. None of the lamps or lampshades matched each other.

"You could write while I paint, if you come up here when the household chores and family food preparation was over" said Erik. He was increasingly aware of a rapport with Sally that helped create the relaxation and change he needed from the pressure of tennis and the media circus around the tournaments.

"I have been taking time out to sit in my bedroom at the window overlooking the garden, and writing when I have been in the mood. You have the perfect environment up there for inspiration, but my presence may cramp your style" said Sally.

"Let`s share the inspiration. Two forms of creativity in the same place. We don`t have to speak whilst we work." The idea became more attractive the more they both thought about it.

They decorated the tower room in light pastel shades of paint to maximise the size of the single room and give a light open feeling. An artist`s studio is reckoned to be best using a northern aspect for its light source. Erik was happy to enjoy his light entering through the wide skylight with its horizontal blind and the south west window with the prospect of beautiful sunsets. To encourage Sally to share the room Erik asked Brigadier Roper to find a writing desk that would be practical as well as an antique. The hundred and twenty year old rosewood desk with drawers and a good sized writing table, that folded upwards to conceal smaller drawers and open inset compartments, made a perfect thirty seventh birthday present for Sally. The Brigadier delivered the desk, wrapped in old carpets for protection, to Kirkhaven House with `Roper`s Antiques of Quality` inscribed in gold letters along the side of his estate car. He insisted upon sitting Sally at the desk and showing her each of its features with his arm around her and his hand pawing at her bare shoulder. It reminded her of her first date with Anthony Williams when she was just fourteen. His arm had crept into the same position and had begun clutching and releasing her shoulder in the back row of the Odeon Cinema.

Remembering where Anthony`s hands had progressed later in the film she stood up quite abruptly clouting the Brigadier under the chin with the other shoulder. They said their farewells in pain with the Brigadier holding his face and Sally nursing her shoulder. The expensive present decided Sally to join Erik in his new studio.

SIXTEEN

NOW

Reverend Poppy phoned Helen the next evening and asked how she had got on with the `Erik` conversation. She then suggested the name of a friend, an old and experienced solicitor in Taunton. He had advised some of her parishioners before from here and from her previous appointment in Tiverton. The proposal was that Helen met Peter on formal ground to deliver her decisions with both a witness and qualified referee. Peter agreed to the meeting under the impression it was to build a case against Erik. He had jumped to the conclusion that Helen had believed everything he had told her on the Sunday evening visit and was acting responsibly to protect Callum and Lucy. He had added that any personal changes in their relationship would be much better discussed amicably at home after he had moved back in.

They met at Godfrey Spencer`s office in the centre of Taunton a week later. The solicitor began by discussing the allegations against Erik (Joel Eriksson) and future implications for their children. He listened to Peter`s long repetition of much of the character assassination of Erik that he had given Helen on the Sunday. He then heard Helen explaining the results of her discussions with each of the children, with constant interruptions from Peter.

Mr Spencer was used to chairing sometimes difficult and acrimonious discussions between married couples; his speciality being `Family Law` and he was known to be fair and firm. His business was based on fact rather than emotion. He ignored the interruptions, and let Helen give her full account. Although Peter had not expected this, Mr Spencer was willing to explore the personal differences between them. But only after they had dealt fully with the criminal allegations. Peter had based his conclusions about Erik on the report from his Private Investigator, and supposition, conveniently slotting them into his plans to regain Helen and the children. He had expected the responses of Callum and Lucy to be negative to his ambition because they would have been frightened of a bad reaction from the perpetrator. However, he chipped in with derogatory remarks about Callum, his `unreliable` character and `history of telling lies`, in an attempt to reduce the responses to minimal effect.

Mr Spencer apologised for being called away to take an urgent telephone call and asked his secretary to bring a tray of tea, as well as to become a third person in a room that was revealing some inharmonious prospects.

"Why do you always put Callum down?" asked Helen.

"He is a useless lump who needs a firm hand."

"You have made little attempt to play a part in his childhood development from as far back as I can remember, and favoured Lucy in a very obvious way. There must be some quirk in your nature to be so adamantly dismissive of your only son."

"Not my son" Peter said almost imperceptively.

"Just because we are divorced does not make him any less your son."

"Would you like me to top up your tea?" interposed a worried secretary.

"Rose agrees. He is no son of mine."

"What on earth do you mean?. You were present at his birth."

"Look at him. Ginger hair. Thousands of grotty freckles. Already taller than me at thirteen or fourteen or whatever he is. Obstinate nature. Argumentative. How much more different than me could he be?" He continued, "I have black hair - and he is bloody ginger.

What more proof do you want?"

"You are saying you are not his biological father?" asked Helen quietly.

"Now come along Mr and Mrs Walker. It`s better that we talk about nicer things until Mr Spencer returns. Did you see that photo of Prince Harry playing wheelchair basketball?"

"Stupid Prat" said Peter.

"Really Mr Walker. There`s no need to.........."

"Not you, Miss. That royal idiot" said Peter.

"I suppose you are going to suggest that there is something odd about his birth because he has red hair" said Helen

"Look Helen. It was well known that you had a fling with Ben Evans, the Compound Manager, before Callum was born. I was the butt of all the jokes for ages, because I had to keep going away to Dubai and Kuwait. Even Rose, who joined the company years later, heard the rumours. I, being a dutiful husband, kept my head down to protect your reputation."

"You pompous fool! I was devoted to you. Ben was kind and helpful whenever I was alone, as he was to all wives or wives and children when their partners were away. He had a happy marriage to Emily. He was just doing his job well."

Godfrey Spencer returned and poured himself a half cup of tea and his secretary left the room.

"Sorry, that was a genuine emergency. Now, where were we? Yes. Mr Eriksson. It seems very straightforward. All the evidence or information you have presented, Mr Walker, is speculative. Without something more definite from a connected source there is no case for Mr Eriksson to answer or for the police to investigate at this time."

"So the only way for me to protect my son is to do it myself. To move back in with Helen and do the Authorities job for them" said Peter in his most manipulative tone."

"Mrs Walker. I believe you have something to say on that particular domestic situation." said Godfrey Spencer looking meaningfully at Helen.

Helen took a folded piece of A4 paper from her handbag.

"Peter. I have come to a decision regarding your proposal when you visited me a few days ago."

Peter interrupted "We agreed to sort out all the details out in private at home."

"You suggested that in your usual bullying way, without waiting for my reply. We were divorced two years, no about one and a half years ago, and I was given custody and daily responsibility to care for both children to remain with me. Since then, nothing has changed. I do not wish to alter that court decision, nor to invite you through my door again."

"Lucy cries for me, and the door is our door because I pay for it.

Helen continued "You told me a lie about Lucy`s desire to be with you. She cried once only - on the day you walked out to live with your lover." She glanced at her page of notes.

"You have tried to ruin the name and reputation of a kind man with whom I have definitely not had a physical relationship and who turns out to be our previously anonymous landlord. When you defaulted on the payment of rent he resisted our eviction from his house and the difficulties you would have created for the children with moving, change of schools etc.

"You plead concern for Callum`s welfare with Erik, yet, in front of Miss......Mr Spencer`s secretary, you claim he is not your biological child. Something I could refute with a simple DNA test. You have made no attempt to see him or ask after him, in the period since the divorce settlement.

"If you attempt to enter my home again I will apply to the Court for a Restriction Order` to be placed on you and your representatives. You have used a tasteless piece of tittle tattle to try to get your own way because Rose has probably thrown you out and your horrid mother is refusing to let you sponge off her any longer and, another thing......."

"I think we have covered all the relevant decisions you have justifiably legally made, Mrs Walker. We will avoid the emotion....."

"But I love you, Helen. You are my Angel. I made a terrible mistake - I admit, but now I have repented......"

"OK, Mr Walker. This interview is now over......."

"It would be wonderful for all of us. We could have another child......."

Helen stood up, shook Godfrey Spencer`s hand, and headed for the door. Peter remained seated, slouched in his chair.

"I suppose he has offered you regular sex to stay in the house. Has he told you about his wife in Sweden?"

Poppy knew this was a testing day for Helen and kept it to herself. The three women were having a frivolous morning in Poppy Chocolatiere while Rachel served happy holiday-makers who had rambled along the riverside, and ramblers who had walked miles downstream from where the River Axe was more of a `piddle` than a river. There had been a lot of laughter about the `chocolate disaster` with one party suggesting recipes for a `chocolate dilemma` and a `Jasper Carrot cake`. Four more ramblers joined them. They had the sensible walking boots with thick socks, lightweight rainproof anoraks with hoods and the compulsory mini backpack.

They began to relate funny tales to the room. How the bridge collapsed over the Western Canal and two of them were rescued by a longboat full of sightseers. They read the posters on the wall behind their table on the History of the Devon Cream Tea.

"There really is a Lustleigh Cleave, you know. We`ve been there" said one.

"Yes" answered Rachel carrying their tray of assorted goodies.

"But the Danes weren`t rambling around there. Poppy says they were at Edington in the general area of Cheltenham."

"I once was clobbered by a hockey stick from a girl from Cheltenham" said another at the table. "Posh public school we were playing. She probably thought I was one of the family`s servant girls"

And so it had gone on, until the cafe area emptied and they settled back to their favourite topic.

"He`s gone to commentate on Wimbledon" said Rachel to Bronwen`s enquiry. "It`s not on yet" said Bronwen. "It's two weeks away. I knew he was a tennis player when I saw him first."

"You didn`t tell us" said Poppy who had looked in to see if Rachel was coping.

"You can always tell. Enormous strong forearms, bronzed with an inch of bleached hair on each one and pigeon toes!"

"Why always pigeon toes?" asked Rachel from behind the cake display, which she was refilling. She sneaked a look downwards. She had often been called pigeon-chested at school and the word pigeon still rankled.

"It`s the way they stand at the service line and practise for hours and hours throwing their bodies at the ball but also letting it strain against the foot to avoid foot faults" said Bronwen. "I read it in one of our library books. Also the stops and sudden turns push the feet inwards."

"We had better ask Helen. She is the one likely to have seen him without his shoes and socks." Rachel led the laughter at her own remark.

Helen had gone straight home. Deirdre had been looking after Lucy and Callum and they were sampling her latest soup creation as a starter for tea.

"Not bad," Lucy the official taster was saying. "Not bad. Six out of ten."

"Only six" said Deirdre. "I thought it was at least an eight."

"I don`t like to mark too high early in the competition" said Lucy. "Like Craig in Strictly."

"I didn`t realise it was a competition" muttered Deirdre.

"Yes. A competition for the English Souper-Cook ...soup, super....get it?"

"We get it" said Callum. "I`ll give it an eight."

"Only the official food taster`s marks go forward" said Lucy. Helen didn`t join them. She changed into gardening clothes and went to put her hands into some earth. A wise woman had once told Helen`s mother that, if she had a deep spiritual experience or a highly emotional encounter, she should then consciously `ground herself`.

One of the best methods of doing that is to go gardening and plunge your hands into the soil. Helen was wiped out after the `stage act` she had performed that afternoon. She had hardly slept the previous night and had needed to force herself to drive the car to Taunton, and then steel herself to climb the stairs and enter Godfrey Spencer`s front office. The morning phone call from Poppy and the moral support from Mr Spencer carried her through. Afterwards, returning to the car, she had to wait and unwind in the driver`s seat. Her fingers finally stopped tingling and she drove home feeling drained.

There was no mental cohesion left for her to step on to the familiar stage of being a mother and the reliable, unwavering pillar for the children, just yet. So she took refuge in her garden, remembering the recipe for grounding her emotions. There were sweet peas to be planted. It was far too late in the year for their best blooms, but Helen had designated a place for the frame and now began to dig over the rectangular bed of bare soil. After each spadefull she bent down and broke up the lumps with her hands. No gloves today in order to get the best earth contact.

Helen`s principal hobby in Qatar had been pencil sketching and occasionally painting with water colours. Friends had viewed her finished articles and made pleasant remarks. She remembered no one being ecstatic or heralding her work as an artistic breakthrough.

Peter had made a point of not looking or commenting until he gave her an unpleasant `put down` when they arrived at Kirkhaven. After seeing the exceptional use of colour and attention to detail of some of Erik`s work, and that of the artist who had used the Barn before, she had decided to hang up her pencil and find another hobby to which she was better suited and could enjoy showing off to a few friends. At some time in the recent history of Kirkhaven House there had been either a tenant who cared for the garden or one who employed a gardener. There were mature shrubs at the front in a semi circle facing the house, sitting in overgrown beds with a gap between the two arms for the driveway to pass through. They had been planted knowledgeably with the big tall rhododendrons at the rear and smaller flowering bushes and plants graded towards the turning circle of the parking area. The house and its front door completed the outer circle. To one side there was a smaller exit for a wide path leading around the house, wide enough to take a vehicle to the barn and broken-down cottage some distance into the rear garden.

The rear had been largely put to grass with several fruit trees to one side, dominated by a mature cherry tree with a `once well cared for` lawn surrounding it. When Helen arrived there had been no actual flower beds, although many flowers peered through the grass during the long Devon growing year. Random clumps and fairy rings of crocuses, snowdrops, polyanthus, daffodils and narcissi welcomed her new day vista from her bedroom window, reminding her how much she loved living in the countryside. The strong elm bench seat had become a good friend once she had cleaned and treated it, as it sat in the shade of one of the few oak trees that had escaped the Seaton and Lyme Regis Elizabethan shipbuilders. They were recorded as having provided three of the support craft for Drake`s pursuit of the Spanish Armada in the sixteenth century.

Fields adjoined the rear garden which had mature beech hedges and boundaries with one gate leading to a cliff top path. A small wood, as unkempt as the rest when the family arrived, ran from the driveway to a compound owned separately she assumed by the Water Board, and dominated by a huge water storage tower now no longer in use but with a dirt-covered window on the side.

After Peter left and when he finally decided to pay his part of their expenses, Deirdre suggested that her Bill would borrow the `sit on tractor` from his job in the school grounds and, when Helen could afford to pay him for an hour, cut the grass in the back garden. He had been doing this for over a year and kindly taking the grass cuttings back to Lyme for the school composting system to absorb.

Consigning her art ambitions to the waste bin and putting aside her sedentary pastime of reading, Helen had begun a year after moving in, to become a gardener. She bought some gardening tools and a wheelbarrow and tidied up the front area around the drive and turning circle. It looked much better than before. Taking time whenever she could from domestic chores and more recently between days at work, she had moved on to cut beds alongside the grassed rear, with some help from Callum to take up the heavy grass turfs. There were now four well-stocked beds along one side of the garden facing the oak tree and seat. The sweet peas should have been established by now.

Helen was now physically tired out as well, having bent and dug, dug and bent for twenty minutes. She put the tools back in their small shed and, brushing away wisps of her dark hair that clung to the perspiration on her face, headed for the house. Callum had ridden out on his bike and Lucy was on the phone to a friend.

Deirdre ushered Helen into the kitchen.

"What happened then? Did you sort him out?"

"He will not be back without an order being slapped on him to keep away."

"You are a lovely girl. You deserve better than him."

"Yes. I agree. But I don`t need another man remotely like Peter.

Thanks for caring for the children, and doing tea."

"I saw you come in and realised you needed a bit of quiet after all that court stuff."

"It was only a meeting with a solicitor" said Helen.

"Same thing, isn`t it?" stated Deirdre. "Now you sit down and I`ll make you a big mug of tea."

Helen decided that she was not yet ready to take Callum and Lucy into her confidence about the afternoon`s meeting and her decisions. She was still unsure about Lucy and whether or not Peter would continue to come down to meet her and spend a day with his daughter. She phoned and thanked Poppy, who complimented her on making a plan and sticking to it. Helen did not feel like eating anything so just nibbled on a ryvita and some cream cheese.

The phone rang at eight o`clock.

"I suppose you are now satisfied, you brazen hussy. You`ve

had the best years of Peter`s life lavished on you, his help in paying to bring up another man`s child and now you can live in the lap of luxury at his expense whilst sleeping with criminals and anyone you please. You young women are all the same, after all he has done for you and Rosemary. As soon as you`ve got all you want you just kick him out of his home......... At this point, Helen realised she had only said one word. "Hallo" she said, putting on an accent. "I think you have the wrong number. This is........" She changed one digit in the number and slammed down the phone, went to the wall socket and removed the connecting plug. So Rose has seen the light as well. 'Good for her. I may phone one day and compare notes with her. Poor honest, open Rose. Not so innocent and naive anymore.' Neither of them would be rabbits caught in the headlights again.

"Mummy, I can`t sleep. The full moon is shining into my room and making it like daylight."

"You could pull the curtains, darling."

"But that would spoil seeing it full for the only night of the month."

'Lucy logic' Helen said to herself. "Mum. Mrs Carnegie said that all the Buddhists call the full moon day `Poya Day` and they take the day off work. Will you phone the school tomorrow and tell them Lucy Walker has become a Buddhist and so will not be going to school today? If they don`t understand, tell the school secretary to ask Mrs Carnegie." Helen pulled her naughty daughter onto her lap and cuddled her warm slim, shape tightly.

"Do you know how much I love you Lucy logic? I love you with such a brightness that it shines like the full moon all over the world, so everyone knows."

"That`s quite a lot" said a sleepy voice. They slept together for two hours in the armchair.

The next morning, on the way to work, Helen stopped in a layby and texted Erik. She was not quite sure where he was today. Probably having breakfast with old tennis friends at one of their London haunts.

"Erik. Come back soon. Now if you can. Problem over. I miss you. Callum misses you. Everyone does. Love Helen."

The reply came quickly. She read it in the Bank car park.

"Lovely message. Thanks. Will return a.s.a.p. Swedish public awaiting my garbled summaries. Nice surprise for Callum coming. Love from Erik Eriksson."

Finals day at Wimbledon was two days before and Novak Djokovic had triumphed again and should have danced the first dance at the Players` Ball with Petra Kvitova the Ladies Champion if they still followed the tradition. Rachel had tuned in to Swedish TV somehow, and listened to Erik`s summing up between games.

"After three days of trying to find the right station I finally got it and then couldn`t understand a bloody word" she said to the three other members of the Erik fan club. They had gathered early at 9 am to look at photos of wedding dresses brought in by Bronwen.

"What is a brazen hussy?" asked Helen. "I have always thought it sounded like something you polished and hung in the fireplace. Anyway, I was called it a fortnight ago."

"Sounds correct. It`s somebody who is getting more than her share of the available hunk" said Bronwen.

"Definitely suits you, Helen, with your list of lovers and your ability to make everyone jealous - especially me" Poppy added from the kitchen doorway, a smudge of white chocolate on her nose.

"I`m not brazen" said Helen. "Brassed off, maybe, but definitely not brazen. The Dragon Woman of Haslemere phoned to give me a piece of her mind after I had my altercation with Peter and called me that."

"I hope you replied in similar terms" said Rachel.

"No. I retained my dignity. I told her in an Irish accent that she had the wrong number and pulled the phone cord out of the wall. I then took out the only photo I had of her - at our wedding with a stupid hat - pinned it to the cork noticeboard in the hall and threw Callum`s darts at it for five minutes."

"Nice one" said Bronwen. "That`s her out of your system."

"Now come on, I haven`t got all day. Let`s look at these wedding gowns." Poppy washed her hands and joined them at the table.

"Will there be a sign outside the church saying `Marriage today conducted by Reverend Poppy`?" asked Helen.

"If you came to church occasionally you would have seen that I am officially the Reverend Penelope Mildred Duguid, pronounced `Do Good`. No. Don`t say it. Everyone has since I was ordained."

"OK. But Mildred!" said Helen

"Named after my mother`s headteacher."

"St. Trinian`s. Wasn`t he/she called Mildred?" asked Rachel. They circulated the photos and brochures, and inevitably chose three different designs to confuse Bronwen more than she already was. The women in the library had preferred two others making five.

"Try them all on. Have a wonderful day out and pick the one you like, ignoring everyone else`s choice" said Poppy with authority.

SEVENTEEN

THEN

"How long has he been here did you say?" Maggie had said when Erik first arrived.

"Three weeks" said Sally.

"THREE WEEKS!" Maggie shouted back down the phone. Sally put the phone back against her ear.

"I did ask if he had seen you yet."

"Of all the inconsiderate Swedish Viking Scandinavian pigs. When I think of all the texts of encouragement, all the shouting at the TV I did to help him win his matches. Where is he now?"

"Probably at his boat" guessed Sally.

"Grrr. I am going down there now to sort him out."

Ten minutes later there was a loud hissing sound coming from the side of a white sports car parked in the lane beside the edge of the harbour.

"Are you in difficulty, Miss?" asked a helpful passer-by.

"No, but the rat who owns this car will be when he gets off his yacht." replied Maggie having let down all four tyres of Erik`s car.

"Crikey. What did he do to you?" said the man.

"Nothing. That`s the trouble. All promise, but no delivery."

Maggie jumped back in her car and took up a sheet of A4 paper and a black felt pen. She leant on the bonnet and wrote:

`DEFLATED BY MISS DOPPORTUNITY`

She put the page under the windscreen wiper and drove away. Later that evening Sally phoned Maggie because she had seen nothing of Erik nor heard from Maggie and was intrigued to find out how the confrontation had gone.

"I let down all the tyres on his bloody car" said Maggie.

"What did he say?"

"I didn`t see him. I`m not going to run after him. If he wants the prize, he will have to win me over."

"What about all the running you were doing before? You know, fur coat and blatant suggestive remarks. Hardly playing hard to get" said Sally.

"I have to show a little dignity. Anyway, do you know where he is going to be tomorrow?"

"He will be at the Golf Club in the morning setting up Greg`s club-cleaning stall. Greg is trying to start a summer business cleaning clubs and equipment for the Club Members and the visiting golfers.

They are meeting there at 8 am" said Sally. "The weather is forecasted as really hot, so there will be lots of golfers there."

Maggie parked her car away from the harbour and peered over the wall alongside the road, noticing that Erik`s inflatable dinghy was tied to the post beside the lane. The tyres of the Porsche were still flat but the message had gone from the windscreen. She looked around to check that Erik was not in the boatyard talking to George Mercer, or anywhere to be seen.

There was a metal ladder reaching vertically from the lane down the harbour wall to below the water line. The inflatable was moored beside the ladder. Wearing a shirt and shorts over her bikini and plimsolls, Maggie lowered herself down the ladder and, producing two pieces of baler twine from a pocket, tied one piece to each of the bungs in the back of the two main inflated sides of the dinghy. The other end of the twine, she tied firmly to the part of the ladder under the water. With the incoming tide, these ends of the blue twine would soon be well obscured.

Across the harbour in the boatyard, young Phil Mercer was preparing a road boat trailer for a customer and was amused to see Maggie`s activity down the ladder. She saw him and walked around to the yard.

"Phil. If I give you a fiver, will you keep quiet about what you just saw, and let me borrow a small wooden dinghy to get out to Erik`s boat?" asked Maggie in a conspiratorial voice.

"Surely will. Dad hasn`t paid me this week yet."

Maggie rowed out to `Nasty` and climbed aboard with her bag. She went inside the open cabin and took an apple from the food hoard. A few minutes later she had laid a towel on the foredeck and positioned herself at an angle from which she could sunbathe and see the moored inflatable dinghy against the harbour wall.

It was over an hour before Erik strolled down the slope from the Golf Clubhouse situated halfway up the cliff driveway to the Course. He joined the two retired dog walkers leaning on the road bridge, enjoying the sight of the scantily clad Maggie sunbathing on the deck of his ketch.

"Did you let my car tyres down?" Erik called from the bridge.

"That was me" grinned Maggie. "Your penalty for neglect."

"I shall not neglect you this morning, Miss Oversexed Horseperson.

He walked down to the dinghy moored next to the metal ladder, untied its mooring rope and climbed in. Taking an oar in each hand he pulled strongly away from the wall. The initial impetus of the tug stretched taut the two lengths of twine connected to the rubber bungs at the rear of the dinghy. They popped out of the rear of the parallel floats simultaneously, releasing the air and deflating each one. Erik had rowed another four strokes before he realised what had happened. Helpless in the middle of the small harbour he and the dinghy sank gracefully like Cambridge once did in the Boat Race.

Phil and George watched this after Phil had quietly told his Dad of Maggie`s earlier work. And now Phil started the outboard engine attached to the wooden dinghy by the yard to come to Erik`s aid.

Maggie was helpless with laughter and sat with legs hanging over the side of the ketch. A soggy Erik salvaged the inflatable, now floating just below the surface of the water, and left it attached to Phil`s craft to be towed back to the yard. On the way, Erik jumped on to `Nasty` and squelched his way to the cabin. Jeans, shirt, jacket and trainers poured water in all directions. Whilst Erik dried off and changed his clothes, Maggie made her way along the deck and down into the well behind the cabin.

"Did you have a nice swim?" asked Maggie and burst out laughing again.

"Did you fix my dinghy as well as the car?" asked Erik from the cabin. Maggie nodded, speechless with laughter.

He stepped out of the cabin and grabbed Maggie`s wrist. Then he sat down on the bench seat in the steering well as she struggled to get free. Although she was strong from her horse handling he too was fit and strong. He pulled her across his knee and grabbed the nearest suitable implement, which was his small camping frying pan and, to the amusement of the two pensioners still on the bridge, walloped Maggie`s bottom with her legs kicking and cries of pain and abuse coming from her head which was now partly inside the cabin. Maggie rolled onto the floor and stood up red-faced.

"You horrible bully. You, you `skitstovel`" calling him the only Swedish swearword she knew.

"What did you call me?" said Erik

"Skitstovel"

"Do you know what it means?"

"Yes." She had no idea what it meant.

This time he dragged her into the cabin out of sight of the bridge.

There was a squeal and two more whacks with the frying pan.

Maggie stormed out of the cabin, climbed on to the deck and retrieved her towel and beach bag. She then climbed down into her wooden dinghy and paddled, more than rowed, back to the boatyard, scowled at a grinning Phil Mercer and strode off to her car.

In the pub that evening George, Phil`s dad was holding forth at the bar to an interested audience of locals.

"All I could see was the frying pan from where I was standing.

As he lifted it up it caught the metal rail around the steering well making a `ding` noise. So all I heard was `Ding, thump, yell`. Ding, thump, you bastard`, ding, thump, yell.` It was the funniest thing I`ve seen down the harbour for years."

The next morning Sally`s phone rang. It was a subdued Maggie.

"Sal. I need your advice."

"What about?"

"Whether to charge that Swedish bully with assault."

"Erik? Why what has he done?" Sally sat down to listen.

"He beat me up. All I did was let his tyres down and he grabbed me and beat me up."

"Oh God, Maggie. Are you all right?"

"No. I am having to speak to you standing up and I can`t ride any of the horses out." Maggie sniffed away her tears.

"What on earth did he do to you?"

"In front of everyone at the harbour, he pulled me across his knee and beat me. I had been sunbathing on his silly boat and he came back and attacked me with a metal object."

"It sounds very out of character for Erik to attack a woman. What sort of metal object?"

"A great big frying pan."

"He spanked you with his little aluminium frying pan?"

"Yes, but it`s heavy and I was only wearing my bikini. Then I said something else and he dragged me into the cabin and with my face shoved in his dirty washing, he pulled down my pants and battered my bare bum again with his bloody frying pan."

Sally was unable to reply and shaking with trying to suppress her giggles. She could only squeak placatory noises into the phone.

Maggie went on "I have spent twenty minutes trying to look at my red backside in the mirror to see whether the name of the frying pan manufacturer is printed on it." Sally collapsed on the carpet.

Then she pulled herself together and suggested they go down to Olivers and discuss it over a coffee without delay.

Oliver of course already had a version of the previous morning`s events. The two pensioners were regulars at the cafe and had tied their dogs to the rail outside and related the story of yesterday morning over tea and slices of cake. There was a sea mist and a light drizzle falling as the two women arrived at Olivers. The cafe was empty. Most holidaymakers had stayed indoors today in the miserable weather. Oliver listened with a serious face to the full tale of Maggie`s ordeal and delivered his verdict on the charge of assault and whether to take it further. He agreed with Maggie that it definitely was an `assault` with the possibility of compensation for injury and even restriction of trade as Maggie couldn`t ride her horses. He suggested that, as it was quiet, they enact the likely court scene and consider its coverage in the local press.

Danny and he pulled two tables together and Oliver sat Danny at one end with a tea cosy on his head as the Judge. Oliver himself was the defence counsel and Mandy was instructed to play Maggie.

Sally was to be a witness and Maggie was told to sit quietly with a large latte.

Danny: "All stand in respect of the office of the Judge - me."

Everyone stood up.

Danny: "In the case of The Queen versus Eriksson, the Defence Counsel may continue."

Oliver: "Now, Miss Soames. You say that you merely let the tyres down on Mr Eriksson`s over-the-top expensive sports car?"

Mandy: "Yes, and it was a chance in a million that the baler twine used to pull the plug out of his little boat was the same brand that I use at my stables to tie up bunches of hay for the horses."

Oliver: "Are you saying that you had no part in dunking the Defendant in the cold smelly harbour?"

Mandy: "I was sitting on the boat, unable to do anything except laugh."

Oliver: "And he sank into the water holding onto the oars whilst still trying to row."

Mandy: "He was pulling them out of those curly things they sit in so he didn`t lose them as well as the boat."

Sally: "Rowlocks"

Mandy: "Well, if you`re going to be like that, I`m not staying here to give evidence."

Danny: "Order in Court. Any more interruptions and I will have the courtroom cleared!"

191

Oliver: "Then you claim Mr Eriksson climbed aboard, picked you up and put you across his knee and then whacked you with a kitchen utensil?"

Mandy: "It was a frying pan. Empty. No bacon and eggs or things in it. And he spanked my bum with it."

Oliver: "Were you wearing your famous fur coat when this happened?"

Maggie: "How does he know about that? Did you tell him?"

Sally: "Not me, but I expect it went round the village."

Danny: "Silence in Court."

Mandy: "I only had on a bikini because I was sunbathing."

Danny: "Was that the full extent of the assault?"

Mandy: "No, your Honour. He then pushed me into the cabin so no one could see, pulled down my drawers and hit me again with his frying pan."

Oliver: "Is it true that you now have `Carmichael`s Kitchenware, Wigan, Lancs.` imprinted on your bottom?"

Mandy: "Yes. In two places, though the town`s name is not very clear in one of them."

There was a pause to allow the hysterical laughter to subside.

Danny: "Can the Court see photographic evidence of this?"

Mandy: "Yes. Here you are yer honour" handing over four paper napkins."

Danny: "Mmm. Nice bum. Can I keep this one?"

Maggie: "It`s not funny. It hurts to sit down on your hard chairs."

Oliver: "Finally Miss Soames, the prosecution have implied that you provoked Mr Eriksson with your release of air in his car tyres and sinking his dignity in the harbour. Also that by trespassing on and sunbathing on his boat in nothing more than a drawstring and a fanbelt you provoked him sexually. Would you say you are sexually active?

Mandy: "Well. No your honour. I just sort of lie there!"

This time Maggie was laughing as much as the others. Danny said,

"Case dismissed" and they dispersed to cater for the couple who had just entered the cafe.

"Mandy, you were brilliant as Maggie" said Sally, and Oliver added, "She is ideal for the part because she is rehearsing for the local amateur operatic`s `Oklahoma` and playing Ado Annie, the girl who can`t say `no`. But, Maggie, just imagine how the case would be reported in the papers. You would be a local joke for years to come."

"I think I already am" said Maggie with a glum expression.

Maggie gave Oliver a big hug and thanked him for cheering her up.

She and Sally went back to Kirkhaven House and sat in the dining room as the garden was still wet from the rain. Another cup of coffee later the doorbell rang with Erik`s ring code.

"Do you want to see him?"

"Not really" said Maggie "I`ll hide somewhere." Sally answered the door. Erik was there with another man, equally attractive, tall, Asian-looking with deep brown, almost black eyes.

"Sally, meet Samuraja. My good friend Sammy."

"How do you do, Sally. I have heard so much about you this year, and I can see it is all true" said Sammy.

Rather flattered, Sally asked them both in and took them into the sitting room, noticing that Maggie had made herself scarce.

"I don`t like your English weather" said Sammy. "When Erik called yesterday he said it was hot and sunny, but not to come down then because he was dealing with a naughty child. Now look how it has changed for my visit!"

"Coffee, Sammy, or something else? Tea, juice?" asked Sally.

"Just a glass of water, please."

"Black coffee for me" added Erik.

Maggie peered through the gap in the open door where the hinges were, and, attracted by the prospect of meeting Samuraja, Erik`s doubles partner, she made an entrance. "I am the naughty child he was dealing with" she said.

"Ah, really? said Sammy, "And how old are you little girl?"

"Old enough to teach you a few new tricks" she replied.

"Come and sit down, Maggie......if you can" Erik grinned.

"Bastard."

"That`s better than what you called me yesterday."

Sally re-appeared. "Ignore these two, Sammy. They are having a running battle. How long can you stay?"

"Just a few days. I am in the country to make a few appearances at functions for my sponsors. The next one is not until Thursday."

"Where are you staying?" she asked.

"Not sure yet. Probably at the pub if there is a room."

"Sammy is a very good horseman. He keeps polo ponies on his estate near Bangalore" said Erik.

"Maggie, maybe you could take Sammy for a ride along the cliffs to enjoy our Devon scenery when the rain stops" said Sally.

"Nothing would please me better," said Maggie looking meaningfully at Erik. "But it maybe a day or two before I can ride with you because I am recovering from an unfortunate injury. I have a spare room at the Stables. Why don`t you come and stay with me? Then you can ride out every day."

"Don`t you have an appointment in Bodmin later?" asked Sally with a knowing look.

"No. He`s not.......I don`t have to pursue my business in that direction for the foreseeable future" answered Maggie quickly.

"Ok. You will have to show me where you live" said Sammy.

Erik suggested they all meet for dinner at the pub and go home from there. "Bring Greg too" he added "and maybe his new girl."

"Who is that?" asked Sally.

"You had better ask Greg yourself."

Greg now rode a scooter and had passed his test first time. He picked Caroline up from her home in Musbury and they joined the others in the local pub for dinner.

EIGHTEEN

NOW

Erik had arrived back as they were meeting in the cafe. He parked the trusty Porsche in its usual place and knocked on the front door. Deirdre answered, covered in flour and with a mouth full.

She beckoned him in and quickly produced the black coffee he enjoyed in the mornings.

"You must have left London early."

"To avoid the traffic."

"Helen has gone for a gossip with that mad vicar and Bronwen from the Library. She`ll be back soon. I know she is desperate to get sweet peas in the ground before the day is out, though what she sees in they things is beyond me. Give me roses and dahlias and solid flowers any day."

"Deirdre, if I were your lover, I would send you champagne and strawberries for every breakfast."

"You are a one, Mr Erik. Imagine having my weetabix soaked in champagne."

"I`ll be in the barn this morning. I have a female hedgehog with only half her bristles shivering inside there and I need to finish her off today."

"Try to save her. She`s probably got babies in the hedge at this time of year" said Deirdre in her most caring voice.

"I`ll do my best." Erik took the carton of milk she handed him, without giving the game away, and thought it would be good for a mid-morning cup of tea.

He did not, in fact, reach the Barn Studio.

On the way he saw the patch that Helen had dug over and left for two weeks. She had long before decided it was a waste of time planting the sweet peas and had been using her efforts to prepare the bed for a range of new plants. For the first week, every time she thought of Peter`s scheme, she went out and dug it over again.

Today she had woken up remembering a dream of Peter dragging Callum and Lucy along the bed of a stream and being herself caught helpless in quicksand. She had told Deirdre that later she would be sorting out the sweet pea patch.

Helen returned, chuckling to herself at some of the coffee conversation and was delighted to see the white car in its parking space. She put her head around the kitchen door to hear "He`s in the Barn" and went swiftly up the stairs to put on some better make-up and change into more flattering clothes. Erik greeted her before she reached his Studio. He had made two large wigwams from a pile of bamboo canes leaning against the garden shed and was beginning a third. She looked up and first saw him when she was quite close and her stomach flipped at his unique grin.

"You should be in gardening clothes" he said. Without explanation, Helen coyly just said, "Thank you for the frames" and moved towards the garden seat.

"I feel so bad about you leaving early and the things I asked you, and worse, even wondering whether they could be true."

"And I am angry with myself for not having told you more about me and the ideas I had for adding spice to the childrens` lives. I have always been a loner and make my own way usually without asking others first. You were perfectly right to ask those questions and I should have anticipated peoples` raised eyebrows at my actions."

"Can we put it behind us? I have given Peter the complete brush-off with legal threats and have no intention of ever having a relationship with him, or anyone like him."

"Today is the beginning of a new episode of this countryside soap opera and it starts now. May I send Callum on a two week expedition course with mountains and rivers in mid-Wales in the school summer holidays?"

"He would love it. How much will it cost me? Or do I have to surrender my body to your voracious appetite for females, like my ex-husband suspects" she grinned.

Erik looked at her sideways. Helen was on a roll. "And if I do, please can we live here rent-free and have gold plated bannisters and a diamond newel post in the house?"

"You would have to be pretty amazing and more than once a day to warrant all that. And what`s a newel post?"

"The knob that stops you falling off when you slide down the bannisters."

Erik winced loudly and Helen started laughing and laughing. When she had wiped her eyes and blown her nose Erik said, "The course is already paid for. I had to book it last week to get the place for him. I chanced you would approve. How about I pay for the course and you buy any gear he will need to take with him?" She agreed and thanked him.

"How long have you been married to your wife in Sweden?"

"Have you been reading old copies of French tennis magazines?"

"Peter`s Private Investigator probably was the source."

"Peter needs a refund of his fees. A few times since my mid-twenties this rumour appears, often with photos. My sister Anya lived in an apartment in Kristiansand on the south coast of Norway and I would often stay with her and we would go out together in the evenings. We would find photographers snapping us and later the pictures would appear of Joel with his wife. We think the wife idea began because she was unmarried and had the same name.

Now Anya has married Henrik and they have two children and live in Stockholm. Kristiansand was where I learned to sail properly. The Norwegians are famous for their sailing. Even the King and Prince won medals in Olympic Games fifty years ago."

"Isn`t it unbelievable what some newspapers will print without getting their facts accurate?"

"Helen, there is no way the victim can reply effectively. Like the story Peter brought about me and my history. If you had not investigated it and I had stayed away, it may have been believed in the village forever. All people in the public eye can do is patiently wait until someone refutes the rumours in future interviews or articles."

"Yes" said Helen "It`s not a good situation."

"I have been married once though" Erik added.

Helen turned and looked at Erik and thought it would have been very surprising if such a handsome, strong character and masculine man, who was over forty, had not married at least once.

"Do you want to tell me more, or is it too painful?"

"Not at all. In some ways it is a happy memory. It was a long time ago. I had a bad year in tennis when I was twenty-one and had a mixed partner, Lindsay, from New Zealand, who also had gone through a losing time. We had occasionally discussed that, as children, we had dreamed of living on a South Seas Island" said Erik looking across the fields. They had decided after one particularly bad tennis month, to draw out all their money from the Banks, pack a bag and go to the Solomon Islands in the Pacific. Lindsay had an Aunt living in the capital Honiara. The Solomons are made up of dozens of islands, many uninhabited. They decided to go and live on one of the outer islands and applied for a licence to live there. One of the requirements for acceptance was that they had to be married.

Auntie arranged a traditional Solomon Island wedding with all her friends and they set off by boat amongst other passengers, for their own virgin island. Joel and Lindsay were the last on the boat after it had stopped at several other places, and the crew took them ashore in a small dinghy from outside the lagoon`s narrow entrance. They slept on the beach the first night, then set about making a temporary home. Lindsay found fruit everywhere growing wild whilst Joel built a house of sorts with timbers from some bamboo and tarai trees and the few tools they had in their possession.

It was idyllic! Swimming and fishing in the lagoon, exploring the tiny island, making a boat with an outrigger like Lindsay had done in teenage adventures in New Zealand. For a whole month they had their perfect dream and kept out of touch with the world.

They missed their friends and craved cheese and polo mints. They enjoyed each other without inhibition on day or night, grassy hinterland or beach, or in the sea, ate healthily fish and wild fruit. The only problem was mosquitos. After dusk the mozzy ruled!

They tried creams and sprays that had been bought in anticipation.

These didn`t really make much difference and soon ran out. They then tried their own creations of any plant or fruit with a strong smell rubbed on the skin. None was successful. They slept wrapped in their clothes and found they sweated profusely in the thirty degrees heat and high humidity and Mozzy found his way inside at sometime during the night. Last resort was to lie in the water at the edge of the lagoon. That worked, but they hardly slept. After a month, they packed up and, with sadness, left on the same boat that had delivered them, which had made a pre-arranged monthly visit to check them out and deliver cheese and a few other essentials. They found their first polo mints in Auckland airport where Lindsay went home via an internal flight, and Joel flew Air New Zealand back to Europe.

"We stayed in touch for some years. Lindsay became a teacher and I went back to the trusty racket" finished Erik.

"Are you still married?" asked Helen.

"We both signed a piece of paper which seemed to be enough to satisfy her parents. She is probably happily spliced to a hairy Kiwi farmer now, so I guess the paper was enough for the church or authorities in New Zealand."

"What a delightful dream to make real. Only spoilt by the mosquito, the smallest wild animal and one of the worst in the world. Tell Callum your story, he would love to hear it. He wants to go to Fiji one day and studies all he can find about the islands in the Fiji group.

"Yes. He told me. That`s why our boat is called Viti Levu. I thought fourteen was a little early to tell him of Lindsay and me making love in the lagoon." Erik replied.

Later in the morning Phil Mercer met Erik outside the roadside gate of the water tower compound. They used the final key of the bunch in Erik`s hand to release the padlock and chain securing the gate. Phil said "I`ll not have any time to do this up myself, Erik, but Cathy will clean it up and she and her sister can paint it."

"I`ll be able to do a lot" said Erik "And I can check or change all the electrics and water connections."

"You`ll need a qualified `Electrical OK` these days. There`s a new man in Seaton. He was in the pub last night. I`ll ask him to come and help. He wasn`t got much work yet in the town" said Phil. They climbed up into the large room.

"You going to holiday let it?" asked Phil.

"This summer I want to paint up here. Get more inspiration from the view and, you know, the old memories." He looked at Phil.

Phil picked up the message and said: "I was only a tacker but I knowed you loved her. All your money and you had all they willing women longing to help you spend it."

"It`s an old American folk song and I always love to hear Dee Morrison sing it: `There`s only two things that money can`t buy. And that`s true love and home grown tomatoes!`

Erik looked out of the window, not trusting his voice any longer.

"Take a bit of money to buy this view. You could charge the earth and be booked up all season as a holiday home" said Phil.

"Maybe next year. I want to open up the two sides with more windows. I may need planning approval for that and it can be done over the winter."

"I`ll be your letting agent" Phil said jokingly.

"Why not? I owe you for not talking my private life all over Devon and if, as you say, it will be very popular, it should be easy. We`ll advertise it in a couple of upmarket magazines and all you will need is your mobile switched on while you work in the Yard and Cathy to arrange the cleaning for a Friday or Saturday changeover."

"Yeah." Phil began to think this was good news.

"I`ll pay you the going agent`s percentage and we`ll put the proceeds into my Charity`s project of the moment."

"All righty. I`ll get Bronwen to find me a book on the legal bit."

"Google it" said Erik.

"Dad does all that on his PC. He can do that" said Phil.

"What will you call it?" asked Phil.

"We`ll keep her name for it" decided Erik. "The Umpire`s Chair."

Helen was unable to read more of Sally Shaunessy`s book because someone had put in a request for it into the library and she had returned it to Bronwen. Helen put herself back on the `next borrower`s` section of the library computer record in order to get the book back yet again. When Erik collected Callum from the house after one of his sixty second clothes changes, Callum said:

"Mum. I forgot to tell you. Carole phoned early this morning when you were in the shower. Can she come and visit? Her number is on the phone pad."

"When? When does she want to come?" No answer from the closed door of the moving Porsche because Callum was trying to pull on his shoes from the cramped angle at which he found himself sitting. Erik and Callum had gone boating/fishing. There was little wind so it would be motor mainly and three or four fishing lines trailing from Viti Levu`s sides and stern.

"Carole. Hello it`s Helen. Callum only five minutes ago told me you had called. Can you come the day after tomorrow for the day ? I have a job now and I am working all morning tomorrow. No. If tomorrow would be better, come after two pm when I get home. Great."

Carole was one of many hundreds of visitors to Devon who stayed with their parents who had retired to their chosen final residence. Most were delighted to see their sons, daughters and grandchildren because the most recent meeting was probably at Christmas. It suited Carole`s generation too because holidays with children were expensive. Accommodation in the spare room of their parents` flat or bungalow was cramped but free, and Grandma or Grandpa would usually pick up the bill for outings, and supply most of the food. Carole usually came without her husband, who was something in the city of Manchester, and stayed three times a year with her parents in Sidmouth. She had been a CS (Cabin Supervisor) with Qatar Airways and had met her husband, Damian, on one of her flights from Doha to Manchester. She and Helen had become friends from around the time Lucy was born in Qatar, where Carole lived in the cabin crew accommodation in the middle of Doha.

Carole had two boys, Gregory and Clement, nine and eight respectively. They had graduated from being `little sods` in Helen`s early meetings with them, to `horrible large sods` and were rapidly approaching the `thoroughly obnoxious shit` category of developing child males. Carrying names that resembled those of medieval popes there was a danger of assuming, at first glance, that they were pious and godlike in nature. Then by accident, you read in a history book of some of the anti-social and devious acts of actual medieval popes, and began to come to the conclusion that the boys` names were inspired!

When Helen arrived back from work the next day, Carole and the two boys had already arrived. With no sign of them in the house, she quickly changed clothes in her bedroom. Bloodcurdling Dracula yells caused her to look out of the window. There, sitting on her garden seat was Carole with one hand on Erik`s arm and gazing attentively into his eyes. Helen sped into the garden, stopping just quickly enough to be able to saunter around the corner and give the impression that the world was rosy. There was an exchange of `wonderful to see you darlings` and a cool `Hello Erik` before Erik unfolded a camping chair. As a gentleman, Erik kept the chair and tried to sit on it. He looked like a five year old sitting on a potty designed for someone aged only two! Helen pulled the chair off his body, and sat herself down in it. This of course, put Erik next to Carole again on the garden seat. Carole replaced her hand on his arm. "Tell me more, Joel, about you and Pete Agassi" in the voice she used to reserve for the Business Class passengers.

"It is Pete Sampras and Andre Agassi. And I am generally known down here as Erik" said Erik patiently.

There was an unusual thump and then a crackly noise on the barn side of the garden. Erik went to investigate and discovered two small boys throwing lumps of earth at the Barn Studio door. Gregory was making lumps to throw and Clement was just throwing handfuls of soil with small stones in it. The blue door and surrounding brickwork was splattered with soil lumps stuck to it or streaked with brown earth.

"Why are you attacking my Studio?" Erik asked quietly. They stopped, hands and arms dirty with earth and one face with a brown neck and chin.

"We can`t get in, so he got angry" Clement pointed at Gregory.

"Doors are locked usually because the owner doesn`t want other people to go in without permission."

"We want to" replied Gregory.

Erik unlocked the Barn and reached for a broom and dustpan and brush. He gave the broom to Gregory, the taller, and the dustpan to Clement.

"You brush down the earth and you sweep it into the pan and put it back in the flower bed."

"Don`t want to" said Gregory and headed for the un-latched door. Erik grabbed his arm and thrust the broom back into his hand.

"When it is cleaned, I may let you go inside."

He watched as they swept up the soil in the disorganised way reluctant operators do. Clement ran around to Carole after the first dustpan of soil had been poured back amongst the begonias. When Gregory finished the rest, Erik took him back to the doorway.

"What would you like to do now?" he asked.

"I want to go inside." Erik waited until the penny dropped.

"Please" said a muffled voice. He showed Gregory the paintings and the unfinished hedgehog, and then the boxes of oil tubes and colours

"That is all there is in my Studio."

"I don`t like birds. They crap all over everything."

"They have to go somewhere and there are no bird lavatories for them to use!"

"Well there should be" said Gregory.

"They also make many beautiful songs to brighten up the countryside" said Erik.

"My Dad says they made a bloody awful racket that wakes him up."

They locked up again and went to join Carole and Helen. Carole looked up from her mobile, from which she had been showing photos to Helen.

"Clement says you have been beastly to him and made him cry. Go now darling and Joel will show you inside his Studio."

"No, Joel will not" said Erik. "He had the chance to come inside but refused to clean up the damage he had done. Gregory cleaned for both of them and I showed him around."

"He`s only a little boy. He doesn`t understand sometimes." Erik did not pursue the conversation but heard Gregory say, as the two ran off again, "It was only a lot of crappy animal drawings."

Helen noticed that Carole`s already short skirt had managed to creep further up her smooth brown thighs for Erik`s benefit and found herself reluctant to leave and make drinks.

Lucy returned from her day at school.

"Hallo Auntie Carole. Hallo Erik. Mummy, Gregory and Clement are throwing stones at the birds in the cherry tree."

"Oh dear" said Carole without moving an inch. Erik nodded at Helen and followed Lucy to the cherry tree.

"Stop it" said Lucy "or Erik will put you on the bonfire and set fire to it." She caught Erik`s glance and laughed behind her hand.

"Come here please." The boys dropped the stones in their hands and came slowly over. "Sit down. You too Lucy." He told them all that a country without birds would be a sad and quiet place, and Lucy added that it would be like night time with no sounds in the sky. People who are old or are lonely love to have birds to keep them company and they put out food to keep them close. These birds are eating the cherries to take to their babies that are growing up in nests in the hedges and trees.

"The cherries should be for us" said Gregory.

"Some for us. Some for them" said Lucy.

"Should be all for us" stated Clement.

Erik explained that birds and cherry trees were living and growing on Earth before we were, so perhaps we should share our fruit with them. There are many different species of birds in England and even more varied and exotic ones abroad. Whilst they are on holiday, he suggested they should see how many types they could count and then ask their Mum to buy a book about them. Lucy offered to show them a bird website on her laptop. They took the opportunity to go indoors with her - and away from Erik.

Erik went to finish his hedgehog`s frame. He was quite pleased and thought that it should sell later for the standard one hundred pounds, when he had looked at it enough. Carole and Helen settled to a leisurely tea indoors, but the topic would not change from an enquiry about Erik. Rather than catch up on each others` lives, Helen began enjoying the analysis.

"I thought you were happily married" stated Helen.

"I am, but I`m also on holiday, and variety is spicy. It helps you to appreciate what you leave behind and are going to resume in a fortnight."

"How can you have a roll in the hay when you have children in tow?" asked Helen.

"Tire them out, leave them with Mum and Dad to feed

and babysit. You`re doing the same, I`m sure. In between work days, and while the children are at school, you must be learning the most enjoyable Swedish love techniques."

"Everyone seems to assume I am his personal ball girl."

"Exactly, darling, and why not. In your case you have nothing to lose and everything to gain."

"Mummy" said Lucy, appearing from the laptop bird search upstairs and looking for a drink. "Boys do have funny willies, don`t they?"

"Oh no, he hasn`t has he? I am sorry, Helen. Gregory can`t seem to keep it to himself. Damian thinks he will become a famous `flasher` one day."

Helen was tempted to link the genes more with Gregory`s mother.

She asked Lucy to stay downstairs and help her prepare tea for them all.

As with parents all over the world, they had named their children after months of discussion with friends and reading `baby names` books. Almost invariably the name chosen remained unabridged for them. Jonathan was Jonathan, although he was Jon or Nathan to everyone else. Henrietta was Henrietta, not Hen or Etta. Charles was Charles, though he preferred Charlie or Chas. No Gregs or Clems inside their boundary.

"Clement, eat up your fish fingers" said Carole.

"I don`t like fish fingers."

Carole looked to her left, "Gregory, you took two sandwiches, now you must eat them."

"I don`t like brown bread, and this has got bits of stuff in it as well." He picked a seed from the granary slice and held it up. Lucy went into the kitchen and brought out the plate of white bread sandwiches she had made, guessing that Helen`s attempt to give the boys healthier sandwiches wouldn`t work. Helen smiled to herself and said to Carole

"I`ll boil Clement an egg instead of his fish fingers." Carole continued to look out of the window towards the Barn.

Helen returned with an egg for Clement and one each for the others.

Clement said, " I don`t like eggs." Helen bit her lip and made a silent prayer of thanks that this was not Deirdre`s day, imagining on which part of the boy`s anatomy she would have cracked the egg, and seeing in her imagination the yolk dripping out of his hair and down his face.

"Look at all the lovely food Auntie Helen has made that you have wasted" said Carole cutting a piece of chocolate cake for each of them. "Can I have some crisps, Mum?" said Clement. Carole looked at Helen.

"Sorry. We haven`t any in the house" Helen lied.

"We`ll buy some on the way home, darling" said Carole. The boys waited in their chairs because they had seen the strawberry jelly as they passed the kitchen door on the way to the table. As Carole gazed out of the window again, Lucy wrote `jelly and ice cream` on her napkin and passed it around the end of the table to Helen. Helen shook her head so violently one of her clip-on earrings fell on the floor.

Callum arrived, greeted everyone, sat down amongst them and demolished all the sandwiches, four fish fingers and a cold boiled egg, two glasses of orange juice and a piece of chocolate cake.

Helen, proud of her son and his perfect but accidental timing, said in mock embarrassment, "I think he is in a growing phase!"

To hasten their departure, Helen looking at her watch said, "We`re going to have to hurry Lucy, to get you to your tennis practice on time. Carole, it`s been lovely to see you again. I do hope the weather will stay good for the rest of your holiday. Carole ushered the boys away from the table to the front door.

"But Mum, there`s jelly...." said Gregory. Carole was

taking a printed card from her Prada bag and was not listening. "Give this to Joel will you, or have I got time to pop round to say goodbye?"

"I`ll give it to him. He doesn`t like to be disturbed while he is being creative" said Helen quickly.

"You will definitely know more about that than me" Carole added with a hint of envy. "Come on boys. Out of the kitchen please and into the car. Say thank you to Auntie Helen." The only sound came from Clement "s'not fair" as Helen and Lucy waved from the doorway and went back inside as the car drove away.

"Mum, you fibber. Three fibs, one after the other."

"Really. You must be mistaken" grinned Helen as she dropped Carole`s card into the waste bin. "You can have the jelly now and there`s a new tub of ice cream in the freezer."

NINETEEN

NOW

Erik spent the middle of July re-furbishing the Tower and trying to erase some of the material reminders of fifteen years before. Although they were fully occupied with the demands of their three small children, Cathy Mercer and sister Tracey cleaned and scrubbed every surface of the room and the stairs leading to it. There was no mention of `Her` in their conversation and no `knowing` looks when past use of the tower was discussed. Erik was working near them for much of the time, changing and testing plugs and points and light fittings, and all the plumbing to sink and separate bathroom, before being verified by an expert. There was also no mention of the unwritten agreement between Phil and Erik for the Mercers to be the future letting and cleaning agents. Erik realised that Phil had said nothing about past events to his close family members and was waiting until closer to its launch to talk about the `holiday let`. Phil`s memories would have made a popular topic in the pub and around the family meal table. Erik placed Phil even higher in his estimation and was grateful for his discretion and privacy.

Phil took away a trailer-load of leaves and small tree branches that cluttered the compound rectangle at the bottom of the stairs. When they had finished Erik locked up the road gate again and left the gate in Kirkhaven`s hedge as the only easy access. He moved all his painting gear up the stairs and the batch of four canvasses secreted in the corner of the Barn. The other paintings he left decorating the walls of the old Barn with the largest ones still on the floor resting against the cob walls. It was a poignant moment, he felt, in his life to erect his easel in the tower and place a blank white canvas on it. He gazed out of the newly cleaned wide windows towards the coastal headlands of South Devon, black coffee in hand.

Now perhaps he could turn self-pity and regret into joyful experience and artistic inspiration.

Two weeks later he and Helen met Callum from the train at Exeter and heard his enthusiastic tales of the adventure course in mid-Wales. He told about expeditions into the Cader Idris mountains area about scree running and the amazing cwms at the base of each high hill. Tales of sleeping under the canvas sails of an old whaleboat; the sails suspended in the branches of a tree. They had sailed the boat with its `lower and dip` rig along the Welsh coast from the mouth of the River Dovey up to and into the River Mawddach when they had rowed upstream to camp in the field site. Dinner was cooked in a large pot over an open fire and everything they had was added to make a vast stew.

By the time they reached home, Helen and Erik had barely uttered a word and they both knew that this adventure had been a great success.

Erik knew that if had decided to sleep in the Umpire`s Chair, it would be too emotional at this early stage of his occupation, so he returned each night to Viti Levu and was gently rocked to sleep by the water beneath her. Callum however was still keyed up after his course and had slept a little on the train. Just after midnight he heard a crunch of gravel under foot. It was one of the rare still nights on the Devon Coast, windless and warm. He crept downstairs. Lucy and his mother`s bedroom doors were still closed.

Leaving all the house lights off he was scared to see a dim torchlight going out through the wooded area towards the road. It came back again as he watched, hidden in the dark behind the window. It headed towards the Barn. He could see the build of the man was not that of Erik and he wore a baseball cap. Erik`s thick curly hair didn`t ever suit a hat. The dim torch came back again and Callum`s eyes, now better accustomed to the dark, could see the man was carrying something.

He thought about waking Helen, but realised she would be frightened as much as he was. What could she do anyway? He phoned the police and answered all their questions, explaining why he had left his mother sleeping and that the visitor/intruder was definitely not entitled to be there. A patrol car arrived in ten minutes, having driven fast from Ottery St Mary. Callum didn`t realize they had come, half expecting a film-style appearance with flashing lights and loudspeakers. He saw two new figures walk slowly to the house and then stand still in the shadow of the trees whilst they watched the intruder make his latest journey towards the road. They simply followed. Callum quickly returned to his room and pulled on some jeans and a T shirt, trainers on his feet and debated again waking Helen. Deciding against it he left the house to see two uniformed policemen and one WPC escorting a, now hatless, man towards the Barn. He followed. The WPC looked back before she went in and saw Callum. She came towards him. "Who are you?"

"I called you. I`m Callum Walker."

"Come and sit down Callum." They sat on the garden seat.

"I think you have made a mistake. The man says he is the tenant and all this is his property."

Callum looked puzzled thinking it couldn`t be Erik. "My Mum is the tenant and the house is owned by a man called Erik who is Joel Eriksson, who used to be a tennis player."

"Come and see whether you recognise the man." She led him back to the Barn Studio, which now had all its lights switched on.

All the paintings were now piled on the floor and two had tears across the centre.

"I have been tenant here for almost three years and therefore all these belong to me..." He saw Callum in the doorway next to the policewoman. "You are responsible for this. My useless son can never get anything right" said Peter Walker. One of the policemen was beginning to apologise to him, and adding that it was a strange time to be moving paintings around.

Callum quietly said to the WPC, "He is my Father but he left my Mum two years ago and she is now the tenant. The paintings all belong to Erik, the owner."

"Charlie, hold on a minute. There`s more to this. You need to hear what the lad has to say" said the policewoman.

"Don`t believe anything he tells you" said Peter. "He makes it up as he goes along, and hates me. Always has."

Charlie took over. "Take Mr Walker to the police car and keep his own car keys" he said to his colleague. "Gina, you and I will go into the house and talk to Callum. Is your Mum at home?"

Helen was standing clad in a bathrobe, in the porch, as Callum pushed open the door followed by the police.

"What is happening, darling? Are you in trouble?" she asked, looking worried and still only half awake. "I saw the lights and lots of people around the Barn."

"Good evening - morning. Are you Mrs Walker?" said Charlie.

"Yes. I`m Mrs Walker. What have you done, Callum?"

"I think I`ve shopped Peter." Callum still refused to say `Dad`.

The police established the ownership of the house and its current tenant and confirmed that Erik owned his own paintings.

They said they would need to see the lease in due course and check things out with Mr Eriksson tomorrow. They would take Peter in the car in case charges were made. They offered to let WPC Gina stay for the rest of the night if Helen and Callum were still worried. Helen thanked them and declined the offer.

It was three thirty pm before they got back to bed after Callum had related the story and they discussed what would happen next. On the way to bed Helen looked into Lucy`s room. Lucy was half under the covers and holding Rupert Rabbit in her hand, fast asleep and oblivious to the events of the night. Erik and Helen made police statements the next day and Erik refused to prefer charges against Peter although the police advised him to seriously consider doing so, and to claim damages for the torn paintings.

The Sergeant kept saying the painting of the girl was not there and he had only come to see that one.

"It was only one of the canvasses. I had moved it to my new studio. He must have seen it before. He thinks I only paint naked women and am some sort of pervert" said Erik.

"He seems to reckon it is valuable" said the Sergeant.

"It is to me. Thanks for what you all did last night."

"Would you autograph this for me before you go, Mr Eriksson? It`s not for me, you understand. My wife used to watch you play."

"Mummy, I can speak six languages" said Lucy suddenly.

"Amazing. Did you learn them quickly, or did it take a long time" answered Helen.

"I suppose you could say it took about eight years."

"Which languages are they?"

"I thought you would never ask. They are English, American, Australian, New Zealand, Canadian and Jibberish!"

Helen laughed. "You are certainly fluent in the last one."

"Bye, Mummy. I`ll try my hardest." Lucy was off with Erik to play in the Exeter and District Junior Tennis Tournament. It was only open for local players and had an Under 12 and Under 14 event as well as others for older players.. Erik had entered Lucy for each of these, both to have fun and see how she compared with the Exeter girls, some of whom played at school as well as in Clubs.

Helen headed for Poppy Chocolatiere. Poppy was away at a conference of clergy. Helen waited until the little cafe was half empty and Bronwen had arrived before going inside. A bag of shopping from Spar now sat in the shade inside her Ford Focus. Helen related the events of the last twenty four hours. The girls, for once, were speechless.

"He thought he could get a lot of money for Erik`s work. Good quality paintings, the type you would buy and keep on the wall of your sitting room and an artist with a famous name. He had noticed them before and found a painting of a boat that Erik would have sold for a hundred pounds in a London Gallery with one thousand five hundred being asked." She didn`t tell the about the mysterious conversation with the policeman about a painting of a girl.

"I thought you said he only painted naked women" said Rachel.

"That`s what he told me when I first asked him" Helen replied.

"Now he is up in the tower and shut away from the public gaze, perhaps he will start again!"

"Bet you`ll be the first candidate" Bronwen said.

"I wouldn`t mind if it was just for me to keep and look at when I am too old to remember when I had no wrinkles.

But I don`t fancy being leered at in a gallery or sold for a song on the Portobello road. Just for me and my husband, if I had one."

"He won`t be wanting us" said Rachel "Little and Large."

"I don`t think artists always look for the perfect figure in a woman. In Rembrandt`s time it was always the ones with a fat bum and a large waist" Helen offered.

"Go on" said Bronwen "I like this line of enquiry."

Helen continued "They look for character in their models." Rachel picked up a round tray and a fork and pretended to be a painter holding palette and brush "Bonjour Mademoiselle. Je m`appelle Rembrandt. He was Belgian,, wasn`t he?"

"No. Dutch."

"Sorry. Goedemorgen. I`m Rembrandt the famous artist. I am particularly interested to represent your personality and character in this oil painting. So please take off all your clothes so that I can see these qualities better."

"All right" Helen gave up "I suppose they were men as well."

"George Lee was here yesterday." Rachel changed the subject. He was asking if I knew how much longer you would be staying at Kirkhaven House. I told him I thought you would always be there. You`re not leaving the village are you?"

"No" replied Helen somewhat puzzled.

"He said that a man had told him you were getting back together with your husband and leaving soon."

"That`s odd. Think of it I haven`t seen George recently" said Helen.

"George? Oh good, I thought I may get you in the evening. It`s Helen. Have you been very busy with your harvesting?"

"Yes. Quite busy. How is everything going?"

"The usual round of children's transport, housework and undiluted fun" Helen joked.

"How much longer do you have here in Devon?"

"The rest of my life, I hope" She had expected this question. There was a pause, then George said,

"Your husband stopped me in the village and said you were getting back together and that he was taking you back to London."

"Really, when? I mean that's nonsense. Was he in a police car?"

"No. Alone in his own car. He warned me away from you."

"Yesterday?"

"No. Weeks ago. Not long after our date" said George.

George accepted Helen's offer of a drink later that evening. He came over after dinner when his and Helen's children had gone to bed. She explained her battle with Peter, her decisions and even his latest attempt to profit from Erik's paintings. George noticeably lightened up during the revelation, not only from the beer he had consumed.

"We can still be good friends?" he enquired.

"Of course. I am sorry for Peter's selfish actions."

"It sounds as though he has a deep rooted problem."

"He has a chip on his shoulder about not having been sent to Winchester School like his brother, and I found out recently that he thinks Callum is not his son." George was not sure whether to ask but Helen continued "He is, of course, and Peter could have checked by DNA test long ago. Instead he has been a bad father and left Callum with almost a hatred of his Dad."

"Perhaps if Callum could get the monkey off his back and Peter could get the chip off his shoulder, family harmony could be restored." George was definitely relaxing now.

"The monkey may like chips" Helen grinned and sipped her wine

218

"They could be banana chips" George was right into it now.

"Or the monkey could be a chippanzee!"

George groaned and said, "Could you break out of the cage tomorrow evening and walk over the field to my place? I could cook us `monkey and chips`. I`ve never made it before or very much else in the kitchen, but I was a legend at College for my boiled eggs."

"All right, but I`ll cook the monkey" said Helen.

"My ex-wife used to say that everyone knew when I was trying to cook something because the burning smell went all down the road

Before this frivolity went much further Helen wanted to clarify his relationship with her opponent in the `battle of the biscuits`.

"Are you and Mary Yvonne an item now?" she asked.

He shook his head. "I can`t get her off my back."

"Well. That`s original" said Helen, or the wine spoke the words.

"You`re quite naughty aren`t you" said George.

"It has been on my CV. Listen, I have an idea. We would need to have a drink before we act the parts to make it look realistic.

When I come round to you, we could pretend we are lovers whenever Mary Yvonne is listening or in the same room. Perhaps if she thought you were in another relationship, she would back off and just care for the boys. George poured another can of lager into his glass.   "I`m not much good at acting, but I`ll give it a try. I`ve only ever been on stage once. In the Christmas Nativity at Primary School. I played a sheep. I was brilliant - at least my Grandma said so."

"This is a major role. You will have to stay in character all the time. You may even have to kiss me in full view of the audience."

"Now I`m really nervous! We need to rehearse." He

moved to sit on the arm of her chair, which wobbled and turned over sideways dumping George on the floor and Helen on top of him.

He hung on to her and said, in a slurred voice

"I must be too heavy for the chair, or slightly pissed." Helen was speechless with laughter.

Callum heard the crash, woke up thinking there was another break-in and appeared in the doorway to see his mother on top of George on the floor. For a split second he thought she had tackled the burglar and was winning the fight. The giggling pair both looked at Callum standing in nothing but his boxer shorts. Realisation hit him as to what they were doing, and he gave them a disapproving parental type stare and then turned and went back upstairs to bed.

"I had better go home" said George.

"You had better go home" repeated Helen.

"I`ll leave the car and walk" said George.

"I think you should leave the car and walk" repeated Helen.

"You will have to get off me" said George.

"I suppose I ought to climb off you" said Helen.

They untangled, and, at the third attempt, righted the chair.

Helen sat in it and said "Bye George Sheep".

George tucked his shirt into his trousers, deliberately and purposefully put the car keys on the sideboard and headed for the door. "I`ll collect the tractor tomorrow" he said.

"You came in the car" called Helen, eyes closed.

"I`ll collect the car at the same time then."

Helen came downstairs dressed and ready for work to find Erik in the kitchen drinking his inevitable black coffee.

"You`re here early" she said, the headache making it sound more abrupt than she meant.

"If you drink strong, black coffee you will never be `latte`" said Erik. "I came in because the front door was open. Lucy did quite well yesterday. She is in the semis of the Under 12 and has had easy games. They play only one set. She had a good tussle in the under 14 third round and won in three sets. Her opponents are stronger there and serve harder. We have only concentrated on ground strokes with Lucy so far. Callum is coming as well today, to give her some support.

Callum and Lucy came downstairs together. Callum looked at Helen and said nothing. His freckles had come out in dozens in the sunny weather which he hated almost as much as his ginger hair.

Lucy looked very good in her tennis outfit, and Helen thought she must search for tennis dresses soon, instead of shirt and skirt. Her blue racquet cover even matched the stripes on her socks and tennis shoes. Helen kissed her as they left after breakfast all at the same time in separate cars. Helen stopped next to Deirdre who was coming in the gate with beads of perspiration on her forehead.

"There are a few unwashed glasses and the breakfast things and its only the children for tea this evening."

"Out on the razzle, are you?" said Deirdre. "Hope he`s worth it."

She moved on towards the house. Helen laughed. She was enjoying herself more than she had for years.

"You never think of your Mum being attractive to men, do you?"

Callum was talking to Erik standing outside the tennis court wire netting watching Lucy annihilate her slightly overweight opponent in the semi final of the event for the youngest girls. They were only playing one set. Her opponent`s family were all there. At least three generations were gathered together shouting their encouragement and cheering every point she won. Sadly, for her, she won only a few and lost six one. Erik gave Lucy some money to follow the tradition that winner buys loser the after match drink. Callum went on to air his thoughts to his trusted friend, but without going into the events of last night.

"You don`t said Erik. I remember being surprised when men spoke of my mother being young and pretty. And my sister too, because I would never look at her as being desirable to me, it used to be surprising when I found my school friends fancying her. They were after Anya, not my mother. But you knew that" he smiled

"One of the boys in the year above is crazy about our history teacher. She must be ten or eleven years older" said Callum.

"That`s not the same" said Erik. "Many men fancy older women and have happy long marriages or relationships. They don`t start as young as your schoolmate because of the law, but the emotions and the feelings can begin at any time from teenage onwards."

Lucy was quite exhausted after losing her quarter final to a thirteen year old in the older event. She had chased every shot until her legs felt like a wobbly jelly. They had played two long sets and many long rallies. Callum encouraged her when she came back from the drinks caravan.

"You played very well kid sister, I thought you were going to win the second set when you went four two up." Erik had told her she had done well. In a year or two you will be able to gain advantage with the serve Coralie will teach you. You will be heavier and stronger and be able to hit the ball past her before she can reach it.

"In tennis we learn most from the matches we lose, so there are times its good to lose. Lose - think - learn - change - win. Come out on the boat with us this evening and try a different sport. Callum will teach you how to sail. Mum called me. She is out for the evening. We`ll bag up the tea Deirdre has made and eat it on board Viti Levu. Then I will stay until Mum returns."

They checked with the Referee the times of the finals on Saturday and found Lucy`s was the first event on court, next to the final of the boys under 12 event. Two matches were on courts side by side.

Erik took them to watch her final opponent who was now playing in the under 14 event. He asked Lucy in the car how she thought it best to play the next match. They agreed that the other girl had a good forehand but her backhand was definitely weaker. They would talk some more about it on Saturday on the way to the game.

Helen was not so sure about the plan to fool Mary Yvonne in the cold light of day and without the numbness of alcohol to shut off the common sense braincells. She couldn`t change her mind because she had forgotten to ask George for his mobile number and expected to have Mary Yvonne to answer the land line phone. She decided to go for it as part of the new positive Helen who was rising from the ashes of a marriage. Packing an overnight bag, she thought, would add spice to the role of a visiting lover. She wore a thin summer dress. Its low cut front and the uplifting bra emphasising two of her assets that had proven popular over the years with the men and a means of turning brown eyes green amongst the women. Her summer tanned legs were still shapely but would never be long enough in her estimation. However, they were good enough to rival Carole`s and her dress's hemline was far enough above the knee to bring a headmistress out in a cold sweat.

Because Satan`s brother `Blotto` had ruled at the end of the evening, no time had been fixed. No call, or confirmation had come from George who was probably overwhelmed, cutting organic sweetcorn and nursing a hangover. Helen thought seven thirty pm was a fairly benign time to appear. It would be close to the boys bedtime and Mary Yvonne would be preoccupied finding pyjamas and washing faces. The brothers were used to seeing Helen wrapped against the weather waiting for Lucy in the school playground. She didn`t think they needed to see her naughty bits falling out of their inadequate harness. That was for Mary Yvonne`s eyes to calculate.

Carefully negotiating a route along the road down to the farm, without treading on one of the fresh cow pats that randomly led to the milking parlour, Helen used the enormous brass knocker to bang on the door, seconds before she noticed the bell push.

George answered the door wearing a white shirt and patterned bowtie, striped dark trousers and his wavy dark hair gelled and glossy, holding an open bottle of champagne. He smiled in delight and said in a loud voice,

"Hello darling. So glad you could come."

God, he sounds like Noel Coward thought Helen.

"You could have used the bell" George said.

'I have always preferred knockers" said Helen equally loudly.

"So have I" George whispered. His eyes being allowed to follow the natural path of vision they had been craving since he first opened the door. Helen turned scarlet, having realised what she had just said. George could hardly stop looking at her and tried to close the front door behind her, take her tasselled wrap and hold the champagne bottle as well. Inevitably he tripped over the wellies that were left just inside the door, somewhat spoiling the Noel Coward sophistication. Straightening again he ushered her into the living/dining room where the table was laid for two with flowers and a candle in the centre. Paul Potts was singing Classic FM songs on the CD player.

"Champagne, my love?" asked George, brandishing the well travelled bottle. "I have only just opened it". The bottle was half empty and there was no sign of his glass. Helen realised he had drunk it from the bottle like the lads drink beer. She hoped he wasn`t completely pie-eyed yet.

"Where is M.Y." Helen whispered.

"Somewhere up there" he replied, pointing upwards. Helen picked up her bag again, and placed it obviously at the foot of the stairs.

They had nearly finished the last of the champagne. It was nice, with a subtle rose flavour. In walked Mary Yvonne. "The boys are in bed. Do you want to read to them?"

She didn`t look at Helen, who had adjusted the dress she was almost wearing to its best effect. George wasn`t sure what to reply.

"You go ahead Georgie. I can talk to your housekeeper whilst you say goodnight to Luke and Robin"

"Psccht" said Marie Yvonne and left the room. Helen assumed this meant something meaningful in French, and then called after George

"Take my bag upstairs with you, Georgie, it will save me later."

The doorbell rang and Mary Yvonne went to answer it this time.

Helen relaxed and enjoyed Paul singing `O sole mio`, to which it was now impossible not to substitute `Just one Cornetto`.

George returned and brought into the room a chilled bottle of Chardonnay which he opened and poured for each of them.

"When shall I begin cooking?" asked Helen, hoping that she wouldn`t have to do anything in the kitchen, as she was dressed more for a premiere in the West End.

"The meal is almost ready. Take a seat at the table." He held out a chair for her. As Helen sat, there was a snuffling from under the table, and a black labrador appeared for the first time. "This is Rockbeare. He is old now and doesn`t get around like he used to, but the boys love him."

"Rockbeare?" queried Helen.

"Village he came from as a pup."

"Heavens, this skirt is too short. Rockbeare, no! His nose is wet and it`s getting to places it shouldn`t be near." cried Helen.

Rockbeare was banished to the back of the house. George and Mary Yvonne brought in dish after dish of Indian food, all smelling delicious. Helen knew Indian food well, both from England and Qatar. George lit the candle as Helen said to Mary Yvonne,

"You are going to join us, aren`t you?"

"Non, I will eat in my room."

"Thanks Mary Yvonne," George said as she quickly left.

Having taken some lemon rice and a little from each of the small dishes, Helen tasted the close similarity between the meal and the many she had enjoyed from one of the local Indian takeaways.

Wickedly she asked "Did you both cook all of this? I didn`t hear the smoke alarm go off"

George said, "The only dish I cooked was this one - the Tandoori Monkey!"

"How do you think it`s going?" Helen asked.

"Very well. She`s certainly got the message. She`s in her room now and will leave us alone. More wine? It goes well with the spicy food."

They moved to the sofa after coffee. At this point the coffee had cleared Helen`s head sufficiently to make her realise that the dress she had worn for the staged effect on Mary Yvonne, was now attracting George like a giant moth to a gas lantern. The natural instincts of Rockbeare were likely to fade into obscurity against the natural instincts of a six foot four inch sixteen stone farmer, who had spent his formative years introducing prize bullocks to willing cows in the fields of East Devon. At this moment he was leaning on the back of the sofa, with her sitting below him. He had put down his coffee and his large rough hands on her shoulders. She couldn`t turn her head much and had to stay seated because she had a full coffee cup in her hands. From his position she reckoned he could see about eighty per cent of each breast and between her cleavage to her waist and right down to her thigh. As the rest of her legs and feet were openly visible as well, she felt almost naked.

As he kissed her neck, Helen`s new decisive gene kicked in,

`I don`t want this now.' Seeing Carole`s blatant approaches to Erik had made her realise she wanted to save her body for Erik and any nakedness for his painting. She quickly drank her coffee and stood up.

"George. I am so pleased the trick seems to have worked, and thanks for the delightful wine and meal. I do hope that Mary Yvonne will be easier to handle in future."

"It may be the wine talking again, but I would much rather handle you. But of course, only if you want it."

"I am not sure what I want really. Let`s be friends and spend time together until I know where I am going," she added.

"Stay longer. I enjoyed kissing you" said George.

"We both know where that was leading, and I have to get back because Erik is helping out as a last minute babysitter."

"At least let me walk you home."

"Yes please. Don`t worry about my bag. Just give me my wrap to keep my shoulders warm." At Kirkhaven's front door, Helen kissed him properly, both because she felt he had earned it, and because she wanted to.

Lucy played well enough to win her tennis match on Saturday. She had a blip in the middle, probably nerves in front of fifty people watching, and wanting to do well in front of both Erik and Coralie. Six-four was enough to win her a small cup and a voucher for twenty five pounds of tennis equipment from an Exeter sports shop. There was also a medal to keep when she handed back the cup next year.

Helen again borrowed the book from the library and read up to the page she had reached before, all on the quiet Sunday when Erik took Callum, and his friend Harry, Lucy and Saskia and a packed cool box sailing along the coast. They sailed amongst a dozen holiday families in yachts and small motor craft, who were fishing and enjoying a warm weekend.

It was on one of Helen`s own holiday days that she found the courage to pursue her heart and confront Erik. Both children had left after lunch to go in separate directions; Callum to cycle to Lyme Regis and meet a friend from school, and Lucy to a party and sleepover. Erik parked the old porsche in its favourite space, and headed straight for the gate in the hedge and up into the Tower.

Helen followed having checked her artificially created `casual appearance` for a second time! As Erik went up the final step into the top room, Helen began the climb from below.........

TWENTY

THEN

"Greg. Come here for a minute. You really must not go around calling Mrs Gibson `Thunderthighs`! It`s not her fault that middle age has made her body that size" said Sally.

"She shouldn`t wear shorts to take games then" replied Greg. "A small tent would be better."

"It takes courage to take games when you are a big person."

"OK. But she should be teaching something like `Throwing the Hammer, instead of Badminton!"

"Mum. Can I have a few friends round for a party next weekend?"

"I suppose you expect me to make myself scarce for the evening?" said Sally.

"Yeah. Get Erik to take you somewhere nice."

"Why Erik?"

"Oh, come on Mum. Erik fancies you. I can see it from a mile away. Live dangerously. Dad won`t know."

"There is a thing called loyalty, and love leads to loyalty" replied Sally. Greg went off on his Lynx scooter.

Sally had deluded herself that Erik was keen on Maggie but, deep inside, knew that Greg was right. Perhaps he had come back partly for his painting, partly for his boat, partly for some relief from the tennis circuit, but maybe a little for her company as well. After all, he did say he had a deep respect and affection for her. Affection?

What does that really mean?. She looked it up in the dictionary: `fondness, feelings of love, emotionally disposed`.

`Don`t be daft` she said to herself, `he can have anyone on the planet. Why would he want a mother who is ten years older when he could have a fit athletic girl who still has everything firm and taut, and not so many fingerprints on her?`

Erik called by to say that he was going to be in the Tower painting and had two pasties in a bag for lunch. One was for Sally if she liked. A few minutes later, Sally put on a thin summer dress, and wrap around roman style sandals and followed him through the wood to the side gate.

"You should call the Tower `The Umpire`s Chair` she said as she stood on the top stair, looking into the room. It has the best view of the whole scene below."

"Bullseye" exclaimed Erik. "That`s it. I have been trying to think of a good name to put on the front gate." All afternoon there was a charged atmosphere in the new studio. Although Erik and Sally had already spent several hours together in the room, today was somehow different. They had sat opposite each other at dinner with the others in the pub. Sammy had only eyes for Maggie, and Caroline and Greg were also engrossed with each other. Unnoticed by their companions, Sally and Erik had several times passed whole minutes looking deeply into each others` eyes. This time it was a foot friendship that developed, with Erik gripping one of Sally`s ankles between his bare feet and caressing her lower calf with one toe.

Finally, Sally broke the silence inside the Tower and said, "Greg wants me to take you out for the evening on Saturday, whilst he has a teenage bash at home."

"I`m supposed to be leaving for India with Sammy on Saturday for a week at the Orphanage we support."

"I don`t think it would be good for your health if you went away so soon" said Sally.

"Whyever not?" said Erik. "It`s not that hot or humid at this time of year."

"Nothing like that. It`s just that I may hit you over the head to knock you unconscious and keep you here indefinitely. Erik put down his brush, and walked slowly over to her chair. "Don`t fall in love with me, Sally Shaunessy. I`m not good enough for you."

"I`m trying very hard not to." Sally remained sitting at her desk, and Erik could see that she had written very few words that afternoon on the A4 pad that rested on the desk flap. She stood up.

"Have you booked the flight to India?"

"Not yet. The plan is to go to London for the last of the events that Sammy has to attend for his Sponsor Company and then leave from Heathrow on Monday" said Erik.

"Stay, and let me arrange a nice evening for us on Saturday. Dinner and a show in Torquay or Plymouth perhaps." Sally tried to walk herself out of physical contact by roaming across and around the studio. The air was charged with electricity and desire. The spell was broken by a man`s voice from below. They had left the ladder down and could hear clearly.

"Mr Eriksson, are you there? Can you please let us in?"

Erik went down and unlocked the front gate to let the Council Building Surveyor make his final inspection of the re-furbished property. Whilst the Surveyor and his assistant ticked off items on their clipboards, Sally and Erik sat in silence on the sofa eating their pasties. Finally Erik said, "This pasty is really good. I bought it at Olivers."

Sally added, "Pasties are our most valuable commodity in the West Country. Do you know that there is a firm in

Exeter that has printed on the back doors of it's delivery vans, `No pasties are left in this vehicle overnight!`"

Samaraja was not spending many hours of the night in his rented room at the stables, and his plan for Erik to give him a conducted tour of the sights of East Devon had changed to giving himself a personally conducted tour of the delights of Maggie Soames! He was able to confirm to Erik over a late breakfast at Olivers, that, contrary to local rumour, the name of the frying pan manufacturer was not actually visible on either of Maggie`s cheeks.

"You are looking extremely weary this morning, my friend" said Erik.

"It must be all the riding I am doing up at the stables" Sammy replied, drinking from his glass of water. Oliver joined them. "How can I make a respectable living, with you always drinking water" he cried.

"Charge him for it" said Erik. "In Dubai the water is more expensive than Petrol."

"Well. This is England. If I go charging for water, all the old dears will go to Dirty Dorothy`s in the High Street."

A middle aged couple came into the cafe, and the woman pointed and said, in an eighty decibel whisper, "Look Ralph, it`s Sammy thing and Joseph Eriksson. Look. Over there!"

Ralph replied, "Well, bugger me."

"That can be arranged Sir," said Oliver. Please come and sit over here." Indicating a table far enough away from the two celebrities to give them some privacy. "Now, what would you like? Gob stoppers are on special offer this morning."

Greg roared up on his scooter, and came inside to join Erik and Sammy. They were taking Nasty out later together for a sail. There was a good swell outside the harbour, and the wind was blowing at Force 3 to 4. Just right for a lively sail to blow away the cobwebs, and the red wine from the night before.

"How long have you been riding that hair dryer?" Sammy asked Greg.

"About six months. It`s top of the hundred and seventy five cc range" said Greg.

"Get a car when you can. They don`t fall over and keep you warm in this freezing Northern climate."

"I have to be older and richer to do that" said Greg.

"I was driving the Orphanage minibus when I was fourteen," said Sammy.

"Not legally though - even in India" said Erik. "The drivers in India are something else. I nearly met my Maker three times on the same day during an exhibition match visit once in Dehli."

"Can I come with you next week?" asked Greg. "I want to work in the Charity world overseas when I finish school or University. It would be great to see the kids and all the things you two have done there. Erik has told me all about the Orphanage."

"What do you think Erik? Is it fair to let this beast loose amongst our beautiful Indian girls?" asked Sammy.

"I thought you were signing your name all over Caroline this summer" said Erik.

"She can wait a week" replied Greg.

"Will your Mum go along with this?" asked Sammy.

'Yes, but we will have to borrow to pay the airfare."

"Right. I have an application form in the car for a Visa for India. Get the photo today and whizz it off to Birmingham, not the London office. They are good, and will have it back to you in a few days. I`ll pick up your fare if you promise to raise some money when you get back for something new you find the Orphanage needs when you are there. OK?"

Sammy was taking charge of this trip.

"OK. Very OK" said Greg.

"We go on Tuesday now. In case the Visa doesn`t get back until the Monday post" said Sammy. "I`ll get the Visa form."

"Do it now, and go back and check with Mum" said Erik. "We`ll prepare Nasty, and wait until you get back."

Greg followed Sammy to the car, and took the form home on his scooter.

Greg`s party had been circulated as a `sleepover` for all who lived too far away to walk home, or whose parents were not prepared to drive a taxi for their son or daughter at two in the morning. As Kirkhaven house was fairly isolated this meant that everyone stayed. Greg`s friends, mainly from school, arrived in ones and twos carrying dishes and boxes of a variety of foods and drink.

Sally left as two girls arrived, making her feel overdressed. She had a sleeveless red dress that plunged at the back and not quite so far at the front, with a flared, very feminine skirt that finished above the knee. Everyone said she still had good legs, so why keep them hidden?

Erik collected her in his white car and saw he wore a white open necked shirt and black simulated leather slacks with slip-on black shoes. She envied the film stars who could climb into and step out of low cars gracefully, as she fell into the Porsche revealing a lot more leg to the audience than she had planned.

The audience, as well as Erik, comprised two seventeen year old boys and a Father who chivalrously held open the door to gain the best view of the display.

`A Midsummers Night Dream` at the Northcott Theatre in Exeter was a treat for Erik who had begun to read and enjoy Shakespeare`s Comedies. It was the third production that Sally had seen; the first being whilst she was at school when the play was part of the GCE curriculum. They enjoyed a light dinner at the Theatre restaurant, and the play was a lively production with many original and amusing features including a regency theme for the costumes.

Arriving home at just after eleven pm, they realised that the house was out of bounds for Sally, unless she tried to sleep to music by Iron Maiden! Erik drove the car into the parking space underneath the Umpire`s Chair. They walked up the wide metal staircase hand in hand, and Sally waited until the top ladder was unlocked and pulled down, still feeling light headed from the play, the wine at dinner, and the balmy stillness of the late evening. The room above was still warm from the daytime sun, and the lights of the town in the middle distance twinkled, obscuring the lesser stars and leaving the moon alone like a slice of lemon cast out of an empty glass of gin and tonic. Erik closed the ladder trap door.

Sally took off her shoulder wrap and the tassles folded around her fingers, as she stood mesmerized by the moon. She had worn the wrap for most of the evening. It had given her confidence as she had opted to wear no bra under her backless dress, with its thin shoulder straps. The quality of the cut fitted her shape perfectly, and the material was just thick enough to give her extra security.

Erik stepped behind her and bent and kissed her on the curve where her neck joined her shoulder. Her arms broke out in goose pimples, as she became acutely aware of her near nakedness in close proximity to this desirable man and his raw male fragrance.

"You have an amazing shape. One to match your irresistible personality. Can I paint you one day soon?"

"OK. But…..wait a minute, with or without clothes?"

"With for the world to see, and later without, for you and me alone to treasure."

"You can do the first whenever you like. My body is not firm enough to be exposed on canvas."

"Erik took his right arm from around her waist, and pushed his hand under her arm and through the top of her dress. His hand folded over her breast. She gasped! Her legs almost gave way, but he held her up with the other arm around her waist.

"This part seems quite firm enough" he said nonchalantly.

She continued looking out of the wide window at the crescent moon, not sure how to react. Erik bent down, and took the thin shoulder strap of the dress in his teeth, and pulled it off her right shoulder, exposing the breast completely. His left hand, reached her left shoulder, and this movement summoned her defences. She spun around and pressed herself against his chest. She lifted her head and kissed Erik full on the mouth long and hard. Sally had decided in the heat of the moment that, in these situations, you either declined the approach, or you took the initiative and enjoyed it to the full. When they eventually broke apart, she took a half breath and jumped at him again and kissed him even harder. She was intoxicated, not by the wine they had finished hours ago, but by this strong, kind, handsome man, by the moon, by his pass at her, but most of all, by the confidence he gave her, making her feel young and desirable again. He picked her up, enfolding her in his tennis player's forearms and carried her to the bed in the corner.

They awoke together at four thirty in the morning and made coffee. Sally wrapped the duvet around herself, and partly around Erik, as they sat side by side on the sofa trying to avoid the rogue spring, and looked out at the azure light in the west caused by the rising sun in the east. She climbed onto his lap and curled herself into his shoulder. He kissed her very gently and they made slow, exquisite love again on the duvet on the sofa. Awaking again at seven am in the bright light of the curtainless window, they said very little to each other, just basking in the glow and the haze of love. They made their way together through the small wood back to Kirkhaven House and let themselves in. There was not a sound, but after they had taken a few paces along the hall-way, it was obvious that a suicide bomber had visited during the night. Eight or nine bodies in various states of dress and totally unconscious were strewn across the furniture and the carpets. Plates of half eaten food were on table and floor, and empty bottles of beer, and some of spirits were scattered liberally around. A neat row of six wine bottles, all empty stood on the window ledge. Erik and Sally cleared a space on the kitchen table and drank tea, sitting opposite each other. The coffee had all disappeared.

"I am not going down to India this time. Would you be happy if Sammy took Greg on the trip?"

"Yes. He has already asked me. Why the change of heart for you?" asked Sally.

"More the realisation of the heart" said Erik. "I want to spend the week with you, before I go off to train for the next tournament."

"What will we do here alone?"

"Each other. Seven days just hibernating, and doing each other" said Erik.

"We won`t keep it secret from the village."

"I`ll hide in the `Chair`. You tell them I`ve gone too" suggested Erik.

"I`ll bring you food everyday."

"We`ll live on the fruits of love."

TWENTY ONE

THEN

"When did you last do this" Erik asked, as they sat on the sofa in perfect solitude. Greg and Sammy had gone to India with Oman Air via Muscat to spend two days with Chris en route. Sally had no pre-term meetings at a school because no offer of supply teaching had yet come through for the next term.

"Do you mean when did I last make love? I thought that was a question never asked by a gentleman. Couldn`t you tell? A long time ago," answered Sally, her head on his shoulder. Sensing this was not a subject to pursue further, Erik asked if he could paint her, starting tomorrow. He wanted her to wear the same dress as she had on for the visit to the theatre, and to carry a single flower. She picked a white antirrhinum on a short stem to hold and to stand out strongly against the red dress. Erik took a reel of twelve photographs of her with heels and without, holding her wrap in some, and two with her hair pinned back. She posed with growing confidence for the variety of angles he needed.

"Why do you want to paint me? There must be dozens of beautiful girls who would be over the moon to be your model"

"Simple. I have fallen in love with you" he replied. Sally looked at him, but said nothing. She bit her lip.

"You told me not to fall in love with you," she finally said.

"Yes, and I told you why."

"You are plenty good enough for me. Equal and better" Sally added, "But I am a bad long term bet."

"I understand. Could you perhaps be in love with two people at the same time?"

Again she did not answer.

Erik went on, "In case you can`t, I need a painting that has taken time to recreate every part and facet of you, one that expresses your very being. One that I can treasure and take around with me to view whenever I am alone." He used his thumb to smear away the single tear from her cheek. "I`m going to need some part of you to always be near me in the future."

The poor weather kept them inside for the next two days.

After collecting his developed photos of her, Erik worked long hours on the painting. He decided on the position he wanted her to sit, and Sally spent much of the day adopting and re-adopting a specific pose, whilst writing her life diary on her lap. She took a break to make their meals during the day and evening. They made intense love at night, closest to the perfect union that either of them had previously achieved with a loving partner.

The sunshine returned two days before Greg and Sammy were due to come back to England. Greg had phoned once to say how overwhelmed he was with the children and the efforts being made at the Indian orphanage to educate and care for them. He loved being there.

Erik and Sally came down to the House for breakfast on a bright, sunny morning.

"Sally, I want to paint you today down by the river. I

know a secluded spot where the blue/grey of the river flow will be enhanced by four or five shades of the green grass and bushes, and, with you in the foreground, it could make a special picture."

They parked the car and walked across two fields, and away from the footpaths to the place that Erik had earmarked. Without hesitation, and without any shyness now in his presence, Sally took off all her clothes and placed them in a neat pile next to his easel. She put down a small blanket amongst the six inch long deep green grass and lay on it. Erik made her move a few feet closer to the river, still in the grass, and then turn over, and rest on her elbows with her legs bent at the knees, ankles crossed, and feet pointing to the sky. In her hands she held an ear of corn and was to study it as she lay. He took several photos to assist with later work when back in the Studio, with a promise that these would be developed by a small company in Southampton that produced photographs for artists, and prided itself on the security of the negatives. I will need these later because you will be ten shades more tanned after two days of this. Posing on demand, Sally read her book and occasionally added another layer of sunscreen.

The experience was unique for Sally. She felt totally free, uncluttered by clothes, part of nature, free of cares and very much in love. They drank too much chilled white wine and ate strawberries and plums, all from the cool box they had thrown together in the morning. The sunshine persisted with a light breeze blowing down the winding river. By the middle of the second day a man in a kayak paddled unexpectedly around the river bend, and headed towards them. Sally looked up from her book and grabbed the blanket from under her.

"Do you know him?" asked Erik.

"No. I don`t think he`s a local" she said.

"Then go back as you were" he said. "He`ll only see part

of you. Give him a treat. He`ll be much more embarrassed than you, and it will make his holiday."

The white wine inside Sally`s head said "What the hell!" And she resumed her position, lifting higher on her elbows to expose more of the full breasts that Erik had helped her to rediscover. She waved to the canoeist, who lost the rhythm of his paddling, steering too close to the far bank. In a fluster, he reversed a few feet, and half way back, before moving off again at speed. They both laughed and laughed, until Erik left the palette on the ground and lay down beside her. He turned her over and into the grass, taking a discarded black feather, probably from a male blackbird. He pulled both her arms above her head, and told her to keep them there. Then he began running the edge of the feather along her smooth skin, starting with the inside of her upper arms. Sally closed her eyes, imagining that this must have been how the Gods had lived in Greek mythology.

"I have a qualification in an `ology`" she whispered aloud, in her rising state of ecstasy. "Yes, in `bonkology`."

"You certainly have" said Erik. "A Master`s Degree."

"It must be a Mistress`s` Degree." She realised she must be quite tiddly, as well as sexually aroused. They made passionate love on the river bank, without a thought that the kayak man may return for a second look.

Greg came home with Sammy in a car hired at Heathrow Airport, looking tanned, and full of his adventure. He poured out all the details, the history of some of the children, and his desire to raise money to buy them a generator. There were so many power cuts, sometimes fourteen hours a day, that the children often spent their evenings in the dark, and couldn`t do their homework. Sammy went off to find Maggie, and they all agreed to meet up at Oliver's the next morning. Greg went off to bed, the time having been four and a half hours ahead in India. He was tired from that, and the long journey.

When they arrived at the cafe, Sammy was already there, with Maggie, and talking to an audience of holidaymakers, who had either recognised him, or been told who he was by Oliver.

"Do you choose your Doubles partners, or are they allocated by sponsors or tennis federations?" asked one man.

"We choose by mutual arrangement. There are dedicated Double players who don`t rate their Singles, and Singles players who never play Doubles against us. I wouldn`t have chosen to play with this blond playboy arriving now, but he couldn`t find anyone else." said Sammy.

Erik laughed and added "I had to play with him, or he wouldn`t win any money for his Orphanage and the kids would starve!"

"Who will you both choose next year?" asked a girl who already had a paper ready for their autographs.

"It won`t be Erik in the Men's if I can avoid it said Sammy.

There is a young Russian girl who, believe it or not, is called Olga Legova. I thought her name linked with Erik here, would liven up the press again for him. They have been quiet since he had that run-in with the Snooty Beauty."

"Is that Olga's real name?" asked Oliver.

"You`d think her manager would have changed it. We don`t really know her yet. It may be her passport to fame" replied Sammy.

"Why don`t you want to play with Joel anymore?" asked the young boy looking concerned.

"He`s too fat. Enjoys the good life too much. He`ll probably eat three of Oliver`s cakes this morning. Look at him, holding his tummy in to try to convince you he is slim. Erik, if you suck your gut in one more time, your belly button will fall out of your backside" said Sammy,

"Don't take any notice of him" said Sally. "They are always making jokey remarks about each other. I can tell you his tummy looks pretty trim when he hasn't got his shirt on."

"Oh, really?" said Oliver, as Sally turned scarlet, and Maggie looked knowingly across the table,

"And how was your little soiree the other night, sorry evening?" he added pointedly.

Erik replied to save Sally. "It was great. I love Shakespeare and his comedies."

"I prefer Longfellow" said Oliver, with a gleam in his eye.

"You would," said Maggie. "Longfellow used to be appreciated more before the war. I studied English at A level, and they used to call him the poet 'loved by Edwardians'"

"Oh dear. Now I feel like an old man" said Oliver depressed.

"And where are we going to find one at this time of the morning?" Danny had appeared from the kitchen to more laughter.

"Get back to the cooker, where you belong" shouted Oliver.

Danny headed back singing, 'Home, home on the range........'

"Mum, Dad said he may have a surprise for you at the end of the month", said Greg.

"What sort of a surprise?" asked Sally.

"He didn't say any more about it. He is permanently based in Muscat now, and getting on well. He has opened a new Police Training College, and is in charge of all 'Areas of Confrontation'".

Chris phoned that same evening for his weekly chat with Sally.

"Greg said you have a surprise for me?" asked Sally.

"Yes. I was keeping it secret until I was sure I could get away. I can come home for about a week - six days I think."

"That's wonderful, darling. When can you get here?"

He thought he could get the flight in two week's time, and went on to say that he was missing her badly. The Sultan was very pleased with his new police force and their training to deal with the people in a firm but understanding way. Chris had been offered a house in a residential complex.

Sally was now spending her nights back at home. Erik had stayed in the Umpire's Chair, before packing to fly to the USA with Sammy, a couple of days later, for the next batch of tournaments in the hard court season. Sally lay awake wondering if it really was possible to love two people equally, as Erik had suggested. Whilst Greg was at school, she sat in the Tower looking westward out of the window, recalling the amazing heights of passion she and Erik had shared that month. The first painting of her, with the red dress and white flower stood on the easel in the centre of the room. It was finished, and it was spectacular. On a square forty by forty centimetre canvas he had created a likeness of Sally that made her eyes widen in the recognition of the face she saw every day in her mirror. Yet she knew he had never painted a portrait before. It was said that love above all inspires the greatest art, and she was reassured of Erik's love by the intangible emotion in the painting.

Chris emerged from Terminal 4 at Heathrow looking fit and happy. He threw his kitbag on the floor and hugged Sally and Greg.

They stopped for his favourite fish and chips on the way home.

"They can't make chips in Muscat, though the Hammour fish is good" he said. Greg said" Erik is sad to have missed you, but has given me strict instructions to take you out for the day on Nasty."

Chris` eyes lit up at the prospect of being on the water again, after the sea at the Commando Training Centre had seeped into his bloodstream during his time there, years before. They spent a happy, active day, in a strong breeze, sailing Nasty along the coast to Golden Cap and back, then along to Exmouth. They moored her and took the water taxi into the harbour for lunch at one of the old haunts of the Lympstone Marines. Over lunch, Chris recalled, for Greg`s benefit, some of his many stories of combat and also humorous incidents in the exercises he had been involved with.

Chris took the helm all the way back to the Seaton Haven.

"You know the one thing left in life that I would change is to be able to love you physically in the way I used to. I would really give up a lot to be able to re-gain that one thing." Chris said as he and Sally sat quietly enjoying the October evening on the seat in the garden. He had rarely spoken of this before, although Sally knew that it had been a big contributory factor in his earlier depression.

"True love is not only physical. Not even mainly physical" she replied, "Especially to most women."

"It`s the main topic of downtime conversation in the Corps. Even with the Omanis. We joke with each other about what happens in our different cultures. Usually with a lot of male exaggeration."

"It doesn`t matter to me, as long as you love me in every other way," she said, recalling her celibacy during the years after Bosnia.

"Do you really mean that? I`m beginning to believe it could be possible after reading a couple of books recently."

"Yes darling, of course" Sally glanced at the nearby green tower that had played such a silent role in her love life, providing the perfect venue for her recent cameo of physical enjoyment.

"You know I would never stop you breaking free to pursue a more complete love life with someone else, don`t you?" Chris said.

245

She squeezed his hand.

"I would need to check him out to see whether he was worthy of the best girl in the West Country" he continued.

Sally filled up with love for this man, whom she had loved for almost twenty years and shared all the challenges of living together, pregnancy, his injuries and rehabilitation, the ups and downs of finance, and daily chores.

That night they lay side by side in bed, under a thin duvet, each engrossed in their separate thoughts, each thinking the other was asleep. Chris had read two books recently that he had been given by a social worker some years before, each dealing with a woman`s aspect of love and listing in order of importance the love priorities in the average female mind. He had begun to realise that his impotence need not be a barrier to a complete love life for a partner. Sally was in a dilemma. She was brimming over with love, so much that she felt as though she glowed all over. Her mind and heart vibrated in harmony with love for Chris, who had come to terms with the most terrible disability and privations, to lift himself back to his prime. He was genuinely more concerned for her wellbeing than his own, by suggesting that she may be happier and more fulfilled linked to another man. She now felt quite guilty having thrown herself into Erik`s arms and enjoyed a deep and passionate love affair behind Chris` back. She lay for a while exploring the likelihood that Chris knew that she may have succumbed to Erik`s disarming masculinity. Then she went back to wondering whether it was possible to love two men so much at the same time. It certainly was, because she did! Yes, she did. So it is possible.

Cooking breakfast early the next morning, Sally saw that, whilst this was her great good fortune, the practicalities of loving, nurturing and caring for a love you were living with, would not easily sit with short bursts of wild passion with another who soon may want more permanence in a relationship. Chris added another ingredient to this mental casserole a few minutes later.

"I have been offered a lovely three bedroomed house in a compound on the outskirts of Muscat. The Interior Minister has told me that the Sultans` Council all want me to stay because they think that I both do a good job and also set a good example to people with disability. He said, "Bring out your wife and children.""

"If we can set Greg up with lodging to finish his A levels here in term time, and to join us in vacations, will you come and live in Oman with me?" Sally looked at him, her mind whirling around the prospect, and settling on the one topic; how will she be able to see Erik?

"It will be great for you" added Chris, "Permanently warm, with air conditioning when it`s too hot. You can continue writing there as you could here. You won`t need to teach any more because we will no longer have to rent a house in the UK, although there are jobs for English teachers in the schools there. Friends can come and stay in our spare bedrooms. There is a swimming pool in the clubhouse in the complex. You will be able to keep that lovely golden tan during the whole year." He had sold the whole idea to her, except the Erik connection. Greg, she was sure would be fine in the UK, alone for part of the school year. Covering her own situation she added, "Greg will miss his contact with Erik. They get on so well together."

"Erik can come and stay at the same time as Greg is with us" added Chris, "And he will be around here painting and sailing and golfing when Greg is still at school in Lyme."

"Let me go for a walk and think it all out" said Sally.

She went down to talk to Oliver. He took time out from the cafe, even though it was busy, and they walked together down Seaton seafront, to the Chine cafe, and sat beside the sea with a coffee.

Sally confided more of the details of her love life than Oliver had already guessed. At the end he said, with the wisdom of experience,

"Go to Oman. Have a great life. Treasure the memory of this summer. If you try to repeat it the journey is only downhill. Your future is the return to true love with Chris. We will miss you."

Sally hugged Oliver, kissed him on his cheek, and thanked him for his help. She drove to Maggie, who was mucking out a stable and smelling as strong as the pile of straw sitting outside.

"What shall I do Mags?" she asked after confiding in her.

"I remember what you had at the beginning with Chris. It was everything you wanted. He hasn`t changed, and loves you as much as he ever did. Erik was a lovely `takeaway meal` and you know that the takeaway never is as good when you go back to it the next day." Maggie went on to tell her that Sammy was returning to carry her off and marry her. "We are going to have a dozen cappuccinos – coffee coloured kids, and live either here or on a beach somewhere."

Sally was thrilled for her friend, whom she never imagined settling down.

`Dear Erik,

I so much want to say this to your face, but there will not be a chance for several weeks, due to our respective schedules.

I have decided that our love is too intense for us not to be permanently together. I love you more than it is possible to express in words that would justify its true meaning. However, I love Chris too, and that has never changed from the moment we met and married.

Chris has asked me to go and live with him in Oman, and today I have decided to do it. There will always be a welcome there for you, maybe at the same time as Greg visits during the school holidays.

Our loving will always be a golden chapter in my memory, and I thank you for every moment in our paradise. I hope your

beautiful paintings will leave a memory for you. Greg will keep
me posted with your whereabouts and successes. Please continue
your friendship with him.

I hope you will understand that a phone call would be more
than half spent with me in tears.

My love from Sally.`

Erik read this in Miami, told Sammy, and barely spoke to anyone else for two days. He lost seven out of the next nine matches, and failed to qualify for the top eight round robin tournament that finished the season in November.

Sally and Chris arranged for Greg to stay in the house of his personal tutor for the next six months until he had finished his A levels. Chris went back to Oman. Sally stored all their furniture, and shipped a crate of belongings to Muscat. After saying goodbye to all her friends, she went up into the Umpire`s Chair for the last time. She spent almost two hours in the room laughing and crying alternately as she thought of the magical moments, and regretting her decision, because it would be so good to have them all again.

Then she thought of her first wonderful choice of partner, and how much he meant to her, the constancy of their love, and the legacy of this for Greg.

Sally had decided to leave the keys with George and Phil Mercer. Phil would come along and clean the room from time to time. Maggie was driving her to Heathrow, and Greg was coming along to say farewell until half term, when he would come to Muscat for a week.

The last thing she did was leave a note on the easel in the centre of the room, which still held her portrait.

`Precious memories never die. I will always love you.`

A week later, Phil came to clean and tidy the Tower room.

He saw the note, and decided to preserve their secret,

in the same way he had decided to quietly care for Erik`s ketch, 'Nasty.'

Erik returned in November. He stayed on Nasty, which was late to be taken out of the water, and played golf with Greg, who won easily on both occasions. They agreed to keep closely in touch, and Greg told him of his ambition to go straight into overseas Charity work, and perhaps to university later. Erik was there for half the week, before he felt emotionally strong enough to visit the Tower. He took down the note and sat on the sofa, holding it in his hand. Then he folded it and put it in his wallet. Standing and looking at Sally`s portrait, steeled him to realise that he could not see her again, and must use only this image to re-live his memories.

He carefully wrapped the portrait in protective cardboard, tying it with string, and replaced it on the easel with the part finished canvas of Sally beside the river. For the rest of the day and until four in the morning, he worked on the painting of his `perfect mate`. He signed it and left it to dry, lay down on the sofa and fell into a deep sleep. At ten am he took three photos of the painting in the clear morning light, and put the painting amongst a dozen others, standing against the far wall in the barn. He picked up the first portrait, locked up and drove down to the harbour. An hour later, having arranged for the Mercers to winter the boat again, and having given Phil some money to look after the Tower. Erik drove away towards London in his trusty Porsche. That evening, in Monaco, he hung the portrait of his first real love on a wall opposite his favourite chair in his house overlooking the Mediterranean.

PART THREE

TWENTY-TWO

NOW

The village festival was a grand fete with all the usual games, produce stalls, Morris dancers and the Lyme Regis Silver Band. The proceeds this year were to be donated equally between the Church of England Primary School and a new Childrens` Hospice planned for East Devon. The Rev Penelope (Poppy) was busy sitting on the Committee, organising the stalls, encouraging the stall holders and trying to make tempting confections in her Chocolatiere kitchen.

Today, she was pleased to see her friend Oliver, and his partner Malcolm in the boutique cafe. He had been running the Stables on the Colyton road for some years for a woman, who had married and gone to live in Bangalore in India. Poppy had been visiting him in his house beside the stables, for the last three years, since his riding accident and later confinement to a wheel chair.

This was the first time he had managed to come to the cafe and christen the new wheelchair ramp.

"I am run off my feet this week, Oliver" said Poppy.

"Good thing. May slim you down enough to get into your cassock for Sunday" answered Oliver.

"Rude man! I wish you could be of some help. Maybe I

could fix your chariot in the kitchen and let you make the chocolates."

"Sorry Ducky. I can only do wheelchair basketball these days.

"What about Malcolm then?" asked Poppy.

"He`s probably got horse shit on his hands after working in the Yard this morning. Not that anyone would notice the change in the chocolate flavour. And you always know when he is cooking because the smoke alarm goes off."

Poppy and Malcolm agreed that he was a nasty rude man, who should be banned from chocolate tasting for a year. Malcolm said, "He will have to behave himself next week because Maggie Lakshmanan is coming to visit and will give him the sack if the books are wrong."

"The books are all up to date and audited as usual," said Oliver.

"The problem lies with the outside staff who are lazy."

"We work very hard, ten hours a day, hard physical graft. Keeping the books is hardly rocket surgery, is it?" said Malcolm.

"Science, dear. Rocket science."

"Whatever. I need a good cup of tea and a muffin!"

"You won`t get it in this dump" said Oliver.

"Behave yourself, or I`ll park you on the M5. Rachel, please can we have a pot of Earl Grey for two and that cherry muffin."

"Sorry, Malcolm, the cherry one is reserved for Erik."

"Eric who?" asked Oliver. "Is this Bronwen`s new lover?"

"No. Swedish Erik, *My* Fantasy lover!"

"Erik? Erik? Joel Eriksson? Is he down here again?"

Rachel nodded. Oliver went on, "Oh, that is great news. Where can I find him? We were close friends. It must be twenty years ago when I had my Michelin rated restaurant."

"Michelin rated! I heard it was a bed of gossip and naughty jokes" said Poppy.

"Just jealous rivals say things like that. No, seriously, I must see Erik whilst he is down here. We were good friends and I have missed him."

Malcolm was looking rather pensive.

"No, you fool. Not like that. Erik is as straight as the front of Rachel`s counter. A good platonic friend" said Oliver.

Helen had followed Erik up into the top room of the Umpire`s Chair. They stood together enjoying the stunning view.

After a minute or two, she summoned up all her courage, pushed away her natural English reserve and said, "Would you like to kiss me, Erik? I would kiss you, but you are so tall I can`t reach."

Erik turned towards her "You are very lovely, and I would very much like to kiss you, but it would quickly lead to an emotional commitment that I cannot honestly make, and I am not going to lead you astray."

"I like you so much that although I have never done it before, I will willingly sit for you to paint me as one of your naked women."

"Actually, Helen, I don`t paint naked women. Well, only one. And that was a long time ago for a very special reason. I paint females. They are naked because they never wear clothes anyway. In the animal world the male is usually the striking one. He wears bright colours to attract the female. Painters paint and film makers film, and photographers snap the male. The female is often an `also ran`. I try to capture their femininity, their passive nature, their lovely eyes, their silent strength. I also paint boats and ships, the moon and some trees. All female. Look at my paintings – no women!"

"You led me to believe that you mainly painted women, and now I am embarrassed that I thought you might think of me in that way," said Helen.

"Don`t feel bad. Sometimes the animal in me peers at you, and thinks you would look good in the shower. The trouble is that my heart is controlled by a pacemaker, an invisible twenty year old pacemaker, that limits how excited I can get. It keeps the pulse rate down when beautiful women like you are near."

She looked at him, half flattered, and half intrigued.

"There is only one star in my sky, and I fell in love with her here in Devon. There had been many girls and women before, during my teens and twenties, but never like this. I found real love, just this once, with someone who couldn`t return the passion for very long. The memory is still as crystal fresh today as it was then before the millenium. It probably always will be."

He kissed her on the top of her head. "Come on he said, I`ll show you some of my work, and tell you the story behind each."

They went down to the Barn, and looked at Erik`s females, one by one. Helen noticed the small group in the corner that Phil had replaced in their original spot. "What about those?" she said.

"Not for you to waste time on. Sometimes an artist has failures, or paintings he prefers not to make public."

That afternoon she read more of the book from the library. `Our love was exquisite. It seemed too precious to touch, or sometimes to move a centimetre in case it dissolved into silver dust` she read.

It was a romantic book of the type she most liked. It took her out of her own reality into a land of dreams and the kind of experience she craved every time she saw Erik.

When Erik listened to the voicemail message from Oliver, he immediately rang him back. Oliver told him on hearing of Erik`s recent visits, that he had been living nearby all the time. He explained that he had sold the cafe and had taken over the stables when Maggie had gone to make babies in Bangalore with Sammy.

He and Maggie were joint owners now. Oliver went on to describe the accident. He had been riding his favourite horse on a narrow lane which had warning signs to drivers on it. A large four by four came at him around a bend at about forty miles an hour. The car badly injured his horse which was later put down by a sympathetic vet, and they nearly had to put Oliver down as well. Oliver had lost much of the use of his lower body. Since the accident, his relationship with Malcolm had become permanent, and Malcolm both worked in the Stables as well as making use of the insurance payout to fit the house with aids to help Oliver`s condition.

"I am so fortunate to have met Malcolm, and the Rev Poppy. They have been terrific." Oliver and Erik agreed to meet at the Chocolatiere cafe the next morning.

`He looked unreal, with blond hair curled onto his collar, and such strong arms that would soon be pulling me close and safe`

Helen read on:

`His first painting was my portrait sitting in the red dress I had worn on the evening we first made love. The likeness was uncanny. He had never before painted a human face. Then came our precious intimate painting. I lay in the grass beside the river, every care having long before floated downstream to be lost in the sea. To make me feel less self conscious, he painted without his shirt, and I imagined he was a Viking prince come to carry me back to the Baltic.`

Helen sat bolt upright. This is Erik! She is writing about Erik, I am sure. Sally Shaunessy must have been his `Once in a lifetime lover.`

She checked the date of the first impression of the book. The year 2000. Fifteen years ago. I am sure he said twenty. Perhaps it was nearly twenty, and it took two or three years before the book was published. This just has to be Sally and Erik.

She read on, promising to ask Erik the name of his love. Sally knew she had broken his heart when she left, but she knew he was selfless enough to fully understand. She thought he would soon love again, but Helen knew better. He may never love again because it could never match his love for Sally.

Sally had finished the final chapter with:

`This has been the biggest challenge in my life. Love and Loyalty versus Love and Passion. I knew both, was most fortunate to know both, but I followed the former, keeping my dreams in a golden locket above my heart.`

Erik had gone down to Viti Levu so she would have to wait to ask the question. How amazing if this was his own story. One thing Helen could do whilst waiting was to go into the barn and look again at his paintings. Earlier she had recognised a boat in one of his paintings. It had been on the estuary mud for a long time and she had noticed it when she drove by, every time the tide had been out. Also she found the painting of her little chirpy chaffinch that she saw everyday the weather was dry enough to sit on the garden seat. The Barn was dusty and needed a good clean. She resolved to do it for him so that the dust and dirt would not damage his paintings. Unsuspecting of the secret hidden there; one that Peter had already discovered before his abortive night raid, Helen took the cardboard pieces away from the group of four canvasses stacked in the corner. The first was a picture of an old round-ended caravan. `Female?` she wondered. The next was an unfinished fox with two cubs - `Must be a vixen`. The third was finished and caused her to catch her breath. It was a completed painting of a naked woman enjoying the sunshine and privacy of the greens and yellows of the open country fields and the gentle flow of a river. Signed by Erik, this was definitely his Sally, his great love. She looked longingly at the lucky woman. Without looking at the fourth canvas, Helen quickly and carefully put the protecting cardboard and paintings around Sally, feeling that she had trespassed on a precious secret. She left the barn and returned to the house, no longer needing to ask Erik the name of his love.

Erik had left a message on Helen`s mobile to ask her to send Callum down to the harbour and join Erik on a mackerel fishing trip. Callum quickly changed into old, warm clothes, and cycled down the hill to Viti Levu. They pulled alongside the ramp at the Mercer`s yard, where, waiting for them, were Oliver and Malcolm both dressed for the sea adventure like lifeboatmen.

"Oliver, this is my friend and boat partner, Callum. We have equal shares in this fine craft, Viti Levu" said Erik.

With Phil`s help they lifted Oliver`s chair into the well of the yacht and secured it with ropes tied to the rails. It was a very happy evening. Malcolm had brought a six pack of lager, and included Callum when they discovered lemonade in the cabin to make shandy.

There was constant banter which amused Callum, and Erik realised how much he had missed the times in Outrageous Oliver`s Cafe. They only caught four mackerel which they sent home with Oliver and Malcolm for them to cook fresh later that evening.

Helen had stayed with Lucy during her evening tennis session with Coralie, and had brought her home in time for all the family, together with Erik to have a late dinner together. There being no mackerel, Erik had bought a large bass from a beach angler, and was cooking it in the kitchen when Helen returned. Lucy told him how she was regularly beating Paul when they played a set at the end of the tennis lesson.

"Are you enjoying playing?" Erik was very conscious of the many girls who, in the previous twenty years had been over coached and forced to play by ambitious parents, and who burnt out, or went off the rails in their late teens.

"Yes, most of the time." Lucy was still in the blatantly honest age, and Erik knew she had not yet learnt to water down her replies to what she thought the questioner wanted to hear.

"That`s good. Keep it going. Listen to everything Coralie tells you. She is a good teacher."

"She still loves you. Paul and I notice she mentions you every time we go" said Lucy, Erik had also brought a bottle of wine which he opened after Lucy and Callum had said goodnight.

"I now know where you are coming from!" said Helen.

Erik looked blankly at her.

"I have read all the book"

"What book?" asked Erik.

"Sally`s book."

Again Erik looked blank and a little startled.

"You know, her life story, her `life diary` as she calls it."

"I know nothing about this" he said.

Suddenly Helen was in a dilemma. Was she revealing a secret of Sally`s? No. The book was in print. It had been for fifteen years.

"You found Sally`s diary?" he asked. He saw that there must be something in this because he had never revealed Sally`s name to Helen, nor to anyone else since he had returned.

"Not her diary, her lovely book. It made me cry more than any other I have read in years."

"I know nothing of a book written about or by Sally. Are you sure it is Sally Shaunessy?" asked Erik again.

Helen fetched the library book and gave it to him. He held it like he would have held a hand grenade, almost as though it may explode.

"I have finished it. You read it now" said Helen.

"I am not sure I can. May I keep it for a few days?"

"As long as you like, but there may be a library fine if we don`t renew it."

Erik left to go back to the boat, still holding Sally`s book as though it were a kitten that may scratch. He placed it on a ledge in Viti Levu`s cabin, where he could see it whilst he summoned the courage to open its cover. This was an unexpected element in a chapter he was desperately trying to lock away in the past.

The phone call came from Rachel at Poppys the next morning.

"I have two friends with me who want to buy you one of my priceless cups of black coffee" she told Erik.

He rowed to the harbour wall and jumped into the car.

Poppy said to Maggie who had arrived the previous evening whilst Oliver was out fishing,

"Do you often watch Erik and Sammy play?"

"Not now. But I did. Now they only play exhibition Doubles and the occasional Senior Tournament."

She was sitting next to Oliver who added:

"I never watched him play in the flesh, so to speak. Only on TV. Although I always fancied Queens for a day out."

"Yes, dear," said Malcolm, "Queens would be like a magnet to you."

The usual laughter had begun.

"You are becoming a real wit" said Rachel to Malcolm.

"He is a `Shining Wit`" said Oliver. "At least according to Dr Spooner." It took a moment for them all to work out what Oliver had said, and Poppy roared with laughter all the way back to the kitchen.

Erik had not seen Maggie since she and the children had flown to Bangkok to watch an exhibition match in aid of `Daddy`s Charity`. They greeted each other warmly and remarked on how good it was to be all together with Oliver again. Maggie had left the children, all four, including the twins, with Shamilla, who was both friend and housemaid in their big house on the estate near Bangalore. Maggie had already spent a week in Muscat with Sally and Chris. She told Erik that she had a special message and some information for him, and asked if they could meet and have a serious talk later in the day. He invited her to the boat whenever she was free. Oliver chipped in:

"You better wear five pairs of knickers if you are going on his boat. You remember what happened last time!"

Oliver, Erik and Maggie, laughed at the memory, while Rachel speculated in her mind about all sorts of sexual possibilities.

Maggie hailed Erik from the harbour driveway in the early evening and he rowed across to collect her. They ate cheese omelettes cooked in the infamous frying pan.

"Sally asked me to give you a big hug, but not to sleep with you" said Maggie, "She is harbouring a long standing concern that she has somehow damaged you emotionally from ever settling down like Sammy and I have."

"You know the whole story, I suppose" said Erik.

Maggie nodded.

"Did you know she had written a book with bits in it about us?"

"Haven`t you read it? The whole key to its popularity is about you two and her terrible dilemma" said Maggie.

"I have only just heard about it" he replied, taking Helen`s copy down from the ledge beside him. "Greg has never mentioned it in his e mails."

"He probably was acutely embarrassed to know that his mother had been romping naked amongst the daffodils with a randy Viking."

262

"What on earth has she written?" asked Erik.

"All the lurid details of your amazing virility and capacity to lift a girl into the clouds, never to come down again. Read the book for God`s sake. Half of it is about you!"

"I suppose I had better" said Erik.

"Now, look. If you have spent all this time pining after her, you must have built up a huge reservoir of testosterone. How about you and me having a quickie for old times sake, and you can show me what a brilliant lover you were.... are...?"

"Maggie, you are still an amazing looking and desirable woman."

"Goodie, this sounds promising...." she interrupted.

"If I had known you when I was eighteen, I would have screwed you into every mattress in Sweden."

"Brilliant! Wow! Go on" she said.

"But you are married to my best mate, and I am in love with the memory of Sally, so it wouldn`t be any good. Anyway, I don`t do `quickies`."

"OK. Just thought I`d ask" she said. "That book has been quite a success. The publishers are still trying to get her to write another."

"It`s strange that Greg hasn`t told me. I was with him only a few weeks ago" said Erik.

Greg had finished his A levels getting a B and two Cs. He was offered a place at Nottingham University but preferred to work for a charity abroad. After a spell in their London office, he went to work in Pakistan, and then Haiti with Save the Children Fund. Now he was running the Field Operations of Sammy`s Foundation and based in South India at the original Orphanage. He loved the work, rehabilitating people who have been displaced by wars or natural disaster, or who were just very poor, with little prospect of improvement without some help, funded by the wealthier side of society.

"There is another thing he hasn`t told you" said Maggie.

"What is that?" asked Erik.

"If you had written to them you would have heard that Chris and Sally adopted a baby, a little girl called Padmini. Greg helped them to find her. That was good because she is now his little sister. They always wanted to have a second child, but Sally wanted to tell you herself. She said last week that she had started to write to you two or three times but couldn`t finish the letter. Padmini is ten now, and she plays tennis."

"That`s great, Maggie. I`m very pleased for them. It must have helped Sally with settling there. Tell me about their house" said Erik.

Maggie described the compound in Muscat where they had a spare bedroom in the same house as they had moved into originally. The compound was owned by the Exxon Oil Company, and Chris is one of only four people on this Estate, who are working in Oman, that are not employed by the Company. The house is lovely and they have a small garden. Padmini has a cat, and much of their spare time is spent in the pool at the Clubhouse, or attending functions on site. Sally has started to play golf and has said that one day, she wants to play a round with Erik and Greg.

"But I reckon she has been playing around quite enough with you already" said Maggie with a grin. "It was so hot outside in the daytime in Oman that the heat even melted the glue in my shoes and they fell apart."

It was dark when they stood up to leave. Erik gave Maggie a bear hug and Maggie kissed him so hard he thought he was having a `tonsilectomy`. He promised to read Sally`s book and try to write to her soon.

Phil and Cathy had launched their website and already had several bookings for the Umpire`s Chair. They had moved the bulk of Erik`s paintings back down to the Barn and set up his easel in the middle of the Barn Studio. Erik himself had taken the four canvasses that he didn`t display and put them back in the corner, where Helen had found them. After Cathy and her sister had cleaned the rooms and changed all the bedding, Cathy and Phil came down to see Erik in the Barn.

"We`d like some framed photos of you and Sammy to put on the walls of the Chair and use some photos on the website. Using your name will sell the weeks that are not yet booked up, though bookings are good so far" said Cathy.

"I`ll get my Manager to send down a selection" said Erik. "Use whichever ones you want."

"The lady coming in this afternoon says she knows you and asked if you were around this week" said Cathy.

"What is her name?" asked Erik.

"Can`t remember. It`s at home on the computer. Coming with her son she is, late afternoon. We`ve left the usual scones and cream as their welcome, and a few things in the fridge."

Erik waited until mid-morning on Sunday before climbing the metal stairs above the Avis hire car parked below the Chair. He pulled the toggle that operated the unusual doorbell. A blackbird appeared from a wooden panel near the withdrawn top ladder inside and whistled. He heard two people inside the room laugh and call out, "Wait a minute while we open this thing" in what sounded like an Australian accent. The wooden stair dropped down and a woman walked slowly down the steps.

"Joel. it`s been a long time" she said.

"Lindsay! My island girl. My South Seas Lindsay." They threw their arms around each other.

"What a surprise. How did you find me? Or is this just a crazy co-incidence?" said Erik.

"I cheated. I called Sammy and asked where you were because I was coming to Europe."

Erik spotted another face at the top of the stairs. Lindsay said, "This is my son Cameron."

"Hi Cameron, come down" said Erik.

"No. You come up" said Lindsay. They both went up to join the boy. "It`s still a mess. We got here late because of the traffic and I lost the way too."

They sat down and Lindsay continued, "I wanted to see you again, and, well, I wanted to see how you were, and I also needed your advice on a project." She was finding it difficult to find the right words. Erik sensed that, in Cameron`s presence, it may be unfair to ask too many questions about the intervening years. He waited for her to tell him what she wanted and made a tentative plan for them to speak privately later. Lindsay did not go back on to the tennis circuit. This is why they had not met up since parting at Auckland airport after their Island experience.

They arranged for Lindsay to come down to Kirkhaven House when she was ready and for Cameron to meet Callum. Helen was pleased to meet Lindsay and wanted her to spend some time during her stay to relate the experiences she had shared on the island in the Solomons. Cameron went off with Callum to explore Lyme Regis. Cameron borrowed Lucy`s bike and didn`t seem to mind that it was pink and too small.

"It`s hard to believe that he is fifteen already" said Lindsay, sitting on the top of the cabin of Erik`s boat peeling an orange. They talked through the twenty-one years since they had parted company. Lindsay knew a lot about Erik`s successes in tennis, having watched many of his matches on New Zealand television. She learnt a little about his love life that afternoon. No marriage and no little Joels running around the tennis courts of Sweden or Monaco. He mentioned nothing of Sally.

Lindsay had trained as a P.E. and Maths teacher and worked in a school for children of secondary age in Otago.

She lived with an engineer for four years and they produced Cameron. They split when he was nearly two and she moved away to Auckland with the baby. She had been a single mum for over twelve years, and became head of P.E. in her school four years ago. Her parents had died within six months of each other recently, and had left her a large enough legacy to make her think of change. Her adventurous streak had not reared its head prominently since hers and Erik`s venture into island life.

Lindsay had always had an ambition to run her own sports training establishment and, after comfortably handling the job as Head of P.E. and Games, her confidence had pushed this ambition to the forefront. Following an offer on the internet she had come to Spain last month to look at a Sports Hall and facilities that was being sold by a school due to the economic crisis in the country. The price was low as it was for all property for sale in Spain and much of Southern Europe. Lindsay was a little scared to embark on such a scheme alone, so far from her familiar surroundings in quiet New Zealand, with different laws and a different language and Cameron still at school. She had sufficient money to do it, but only just.

"I wondered if you may be looking to invest some of your winnings and vast sponsorship proceeds in a small venture with your wife" she said quietly.

"Did you say wife?" Erik shouted.

"Yep. Still married we are. Neither of us has been a bigamist if you are telling me true stories, although we probably both have a pile of legitimate grounds for divorce. I have laughed about this for a long time" Lindsay said.

"It probably means you are entitled to half of everything I own" said Erik hesitantly.

"Oh yeah. I can see that standing up in a court in the Solomons, can`t you?" she laughed. "Don`t be daft. We had a great few months and an experience I will never forget.

We may still be there if it wasn`t for the bloody mosquitos!"

"Yes. Lots of good memories" agreed Erik.

"I have never been done underwater since then."

"Did we do that? Goodness, I hope you didn`t tell your parents."

"They thought I was completely mad and told me so in no uncertain terms when I returned" said Lindsay.

"There is a Chocolatiere-cum-cafe in the village. Meet me there tomorrow morning at eleven and bring anything you have on the Spanish idea. We can talk when I have thought this through a little" said Erik as he helped her into the wooden skiff.

Erik went back to the Barn Studio and began painting a fledgling gull that he had seen on the wall of the harbour earlier in the morning. He found it much easier now to take a series of photos with his mobile and have instant prints than it had been when he began painting and had to wait days for developed photos. He laid the mobile on his easel next to the bases of the new canvas and centred his mind on Lindsay`s proposition. A sports facility and business near Marbella, near Gibraltar, with villa nearby would be less frenetic than using Monaco to get away from the cold Swedish and damp English winters. His brain ticked off the pluses and minuses.

Against were: Business commitment

He had only a cursory command of Spanish

The precarious Spanish economy

In favour were: A serious interest and good use of his time

Opportunity to pass on his skills in tennis

He had the money to invest

His investments now yielded little interest

He could help Lucy and perhaps Padmini to pursue their

talent in tennis, if they came to stay. Between the coverage he made of the Grand Slams, it would take his mind of Sally.

By the evening his painting was half completed and he had made up his mind.

Erik arrived at Poppy`s just before eleven am to find the regular quartet in full voice. Bringing over his black coffee Poppy said "We have all decided that, if we can`t have your body, then we should each have one of your paintings in our houses!"

"Helen is the only one of you who has seen my art" replied Erik

"And why mine? There are dozens of artists in the West Country, some are really good."

"Everyone should have a special painting to look at every day" said Rachel. "Even Abba, your compatriots, sang about it. Puzzled expressions all round as Rachel burst into song, `Monet, Monet, Monet. You need Monet in a rich man`s world.`

"Oh Good God. She`s been tasting the chocolate liqueurs I made last night" said Poppy.

Lindsay arrived and greeted Erik with a kiss. Bronwen said, "Hello. Another member of the Erik Fan Club."

Erik introduced her to the three she had not yet met. They sat together in the corner with Erik apologising by saying that he and Lindsay had business to discuss.

"Cameron has gone to play golf on his own, with some clubs he has borrowed from the Club Secretary" said Lindsay. "He will be back to meet Callum later from school."

Helen added "They got on well yesterday."

"OK, Miss Entrepreneur, I am interested. What details have you got?" Lindsay showed him the downloaded details and photos of the Sports Hall and its surrounding astroturf hockey pitch and one tennis court. She had already commissioned a survey and found a lawyer in Marbella town to act for her in a conveyancing capacity if she needed it.

"I just want a person with a small interest to share the load and listen when I have a problem" she said, hoping that low-key suggestion may spark his involvement.

"Right" said Erik "I am in!" How about fifty per cent of the purchase price and of a new business? We could start an Academy and house teenagers nearby on a term-at-a-time boarding arrangement. Personally I would like it to be a Tennis Academy but what do you think?"

"I think that would be great. I love coaching tennis best and there must be lots of kids with monied parents who would enjoy mixing tennis training with school work. Half day school, half day tennis. Maybe you could come down and do some coaching with the boys?"

"You know, I really like this whole idea. It could develop into something very satisfying" said Erik. "Can we see it soon?"

"Now, now, tomorrow, as soon as possible" said an excited Lindsay. She got up and kissed him on his unshaven cheek.

The quartet let out an united "Ooohh", and all six laughed.

"Erik then said, "She is my wife after all." Stunned silence greeted this as Helen nodded.

"It`s true" she said "They had a floral wedding on a South Seas island."

Lindsay was giggling in the corner, not expecting Erik to be telling anyone about their long relationship.

"Just don`t tell the `News of the World` please" she added. She produced a dog-eared photo from her bag of the wedding with both of them garlanded in flowers. The women gathered around.

"I have never seen this" said Erik.

"Auntie took them and sent them to me later. There are some more. I will show you some day" said Lindsay.

Helen was in the Spar shop looking for biscuits in the very place she had launched the wagon wheels that hit the bullseye in the centre of Mary Yvonne`s forehead, when she literally bumped into George.

"They should make these alleyways wider" she said.

"Why? I prefer bumping into you" said George.

"Have you been very busy since our lovely evening out?"

"Yes I have and Mary Yvonne has moved out - gone."

"Gone? Why?"

"Her plans were somewhat compromised when you came by."

"I am so sorry. How are you coping with the boys?"

He explained that his mother had postponed her holiday to come and stay until he could find another nanny.

"I still have some time in reserve if you are ever free" he added.

"On Saturday the boys and I are driving down to Flambards Theme Park at the other end of Cornwall. Would you and yours like to join us?"

"It sounds like fun. I`ll ask them. I am sure Lucy will come even if Callum has plans" said Helen.

`My dear Sally` wrote Erik after agonising over the prospect of putting any thing in an e mail.

`Maggie told me that I must write to you and that it would help us to move on. Greg had not told me that he had managed to arrange for you and Chris to have your Padmini. What joy she must be giving when you so much wanted another child. Chris has done so well that I am not at all surprised to hear he is a permanent member of the Sultan`s staff now. Please wish him well for me.

You will be surprised that I am to go into business - a new tennis academy in Spain, in partnership with a friend of twenty five years. We shall teach tennis and perhaps some other sports

271

to teenagers who will stay as boarders and pursue their school lessons as well.

Tell me how the world goes with you. I wonder every day when I look at your portrait, which now travels in the pouch at the top of my travel bag.

With love,

Erik.

"Will the boys think it strange if they see me holding your hand?" asked Helen as she sat on the wooden bench eating an orange lolly. George was sitting next to her, and the four children were spending a large amount of George`s money trying each of the rides in turn at Flambards. They had made an early start to drive the hundred and seventy miles to Helston and had already had lunch. Lucy was mothering George`s two lads and the boys were given first choice in the range of activities. George would have described himself as a `not very confident optimist` and had thought Helen had her eye on another relationship in preference to one with him. Women, however were difficult to read and he was quite buoyant that she still seemed to enjoy his company. It brought out a side of his character which she had not seen before. He had been accompanying the children on some of the scariest rides and made Callum feel good as just the two of them queued for the hairiest one.

He and Helen talked and talked in the car on the way home as all the children except Callum slept in the back. Two days later he came past Kirkhaven House, when she had returned from the Bank, and they walked along the cliff path towards Rousden and Lyme Regis. There was a Kissing Gate along the pathway so he kissed her after they had passed through it.

"I always thought for years that was what a `Kissing Gate` was for" he said.

On the way back when they had nearly exhausted each others` life stories, Helen kissed him at the same gate. Helen had even told him about her infatuation with Erik and how she had nearly made a fool of herself by becoming one of his fictitious naked females. George had replied that she shouldn`t lose the inclination because he was thinking of taking up painting tomorrow!

The subject of her infatuation had left the previous day with Lindsay and Cameron. As Helen and George walked Erik and Lindsay were closing a deal with the school governors near Marbella to buy a sports hall and surrounding facilities. The surveyor had met them on site and verbally given it all a clean bill of health. Cameron had an adventurous inclination and was not at all fazed by the prospect of living in Spain and learning a new language. That evening they sat in a restaurant garden and watched the moon low on the horizon over the sea. The chef was cooking a huge paella in a pan over an outside brick oven. The glow from the burning wood competed with a few chinese lanterns and the bright moonlight.

They had been planning the Tennis Academy and the thought of teaching and coaching was growing on Erik. He would keep his contract running with Swedish Television to commentate and summarise the world`s major tournaments and make the usual sorties to his `bolt hole` in Devon. He and Cameron would learn Spanish together while Lindsay ran the Academy. Her tennis and maths teaching would be the mainstay of the business and her maths would be useful in the money management. There was accommodation, advertising and staff members to arrange and employ. Erik hoped to persuade Helen and Sally to let Lucy and Padmini enrol with the Academy, in due course, to test their tennis potential and so he could keep a link with the two women.

Helen and George took Deirdre and husband Bill out for a pub dinner to celebrate the publication of Deirdre`s book. A publishing company in Newton Abbot had arranged to print one thousand copies of `Spontaneous Soups` written by Helen Walker with recipes from Deirdre Burgess. Deirdre was now the star of Jubilee Road in Seaton and loving every minute of it.

"I never thought I could write a book" she said, her face glowing after two large vodkas and lime. She didn`t know that the initial funding had come from Erik and she had forgotten the pages of introductory words that Helen had written before each recipe. Rachel and Poppy came to join them after the meal for a toast. They had agreed to sell the book from a display in the boutique cafe.

It was a Thursday morning in November when the Chocolatiere Quartet heard that Bronwen was confirmed as pregnant and were all as pleased as she was. Oliver had been left in the corner by Malcolm whilst he went shopping.

"Must have been that power cut we had in the evening last month" he said "When we all had to go to bed early."

The Brigadier strode in looking tired and sat down, ordering in a loud voice from his table. He hadn`t seen Oliver, whom he usually avoided. "Good morning, Brigadier" said Oliver.

"Huh" replied the Brigadier.

"Be nice to each other" said Poppy.

"That person is depraved. Lives with another man" he said, not quite so loud.

"You must have lived with other men in your Service days" said Poppy.

"Yes. But not like that" he snorted

Rachel changed the subject, playing peacemaker.

"Where did you serve? Was it during the war?"

"No. I`m not quite that old. He relished the centre stage. I passed out of Sandhurst and almost immediately saw action in Suez in the mid fifties. Then a spell in Germany with promotion before they sent me to Malaya. Promoted me again after a few skirmishes in the jungle. Then Colonel and Brigadier with the King`s African Rifles in East Africa."

"Really" said Poppy attentively "I had thought the King`s African Rifles was a black regiment."

"White Officers with black privates" answered the Brigadier.

"Oh! I say" said Oliver. "How exotic!"

END

This has been Book 1 of 'The Erik Trilogy'

Follow Erik's time in Spain at
The Trocadero Tennis Academy in Part 2 -

'The Marbella String Quartet'

The proceeds from all these books will be donated to Stuart's two charities:-

Star Action (Reg. Charity No. 1111137)
www.staraction.org

The Quiet Mind Centre (Reg. Charity No. 1029636)
www.quiet-mind.org

About the Author

Stuart Neil lives in East Devon. He played tennis at Junior Wimbledon and was a Scotland Hockey International. For many years he has led Emergency Medical Teams for European Charities working in crisis zones in Asia and Africa.

He has finally given in to the temptation to write and the novella *'The Tennis Racket'* leads into his 'Erik Trilogy':-

'Second String to a Tennis Racket.'
'The Marbella String Quartet.'
'The Court Jester'

Three romantic ventures into the world of Tennis and Ladies Golf.

Each of these books or the 'Erik Box Set' may be purchased through the Amazon website.

Printed in Great Britain
by Amazon